Catherine stood st... ...ale beneath her shining ... ...m, when Robert discove...

She knew. Some... ...ady Mathilde. *If you had wanted a comfortable wife,* said the small voice in his mind, *you would not have chosen this one.* The abbess said it as well, when she first spoke of Catherine. But he had been besotted at the sight of her and thought it a fine thing that she had a mind of her own. . . .

"It is only a matter of time," she continued. "Winter has just begun." Catherine's eyes darkened to a deep, bitter green, the color of a leaf in the last days before the frost. The last color before the killing cold. "I have seen her," she said. "William, I have seen her in the forest."

"Catherine—"

"She is no servant, William. No common woman. And she carries a child."

"How long ago did you see her?"

"Near the time of solstice. She is far gone with child, William. Whoever she is, she shouldn't be kept so far from comfort. Whatever you are planning, keep that first in your mind."

His wife had not ceased to astonish him. She had done as much as accuse him of bringing a pregnant mistress to take her place, then in the next breath upbraided him for failing to care for the woman.

His mind clamored with answers. Defenses. Fears. He set his hand upon the pommel stone of his sword and looked straight into his wife's eyes.

"You have left me no choice, Catherine. There is but a single way out of this trouble." He unsheathed his sword and raised it, hilt uppermost, blade pointed down to the black earth between them.

Her eyes widened.

"I shall have to trust you," he said.

A TWILIGHT CLEAR

Linda Cook

ZEBRA BOOKS
Kensington Publishing Corp.
http://www.kensingtonbooks.com

For
Leida van Vliet Poesiat
1914–2000

One

November, 1164
Northwest of Nottingham

An hour before nightfall, in the valley beyond the river, Lundale's fields glowed angry red beneath the cold sky. The smoke of the stubble fires drifted high in the still air; only a faint scent of its passing reached the ridge where William de Macon had stopped to look across the river to his wife's lands.

He had reached the turning of the road, found the place where a narrow track would lead him east along the edge of the great forest, on his way to shelter.

"There is trouble?" asked a low, near voice.

William glanced at the shrouded litter beside him, and gestured to his outriders to halt. "No," he said. "No trouble." In the distance, small figures showed dark in Lundale's radiant fields, keeping watch between the village and the swath of crimson fire that covered the late harvest lands. Beyond it all, Lundale's small keep caught the light of the lowering sun; at its foundations, pale smoke rose in undisturbed languor from the hearth fire of the old Saxon hall.

There were women among the folk who walked beside the fields. Catherine was not among them. Even at this distance, William would have recognized that quick grace, that swift glide that was hers alone. In Normandy, recovering from his wounds, he had seen small birds dart in such a way past the torn canopy of the tent.

"Your wife's people are doing this, burning the fields?"

William drew a short breath and turned from the sight of Lundale. He had forgotten, in the brief moment past, the task at hand. He nodded to the shadow beside him. "They are."

" All that land, at once?"

Behind him, saddle horses and pack animals had become restive in the cold autumn dusk. Darkening clouds, heavy and unmoving upon the horizon, covered the sun's slow descent. "The wind is down," William said. "There was little danger."

"You are not angry, then?"

William shook his head. "My lady wife knows when to wait, and when to act. She never takes a bad risk."

Low laughter answered his words. "Then she knows a threat when she sees it."

William turned in his saddle. Behind him, the silent column of riders had formed into a close line. In their well-trained ranks, not a single glimmer of steel caught the falling sunlight to betray their presence; forty able soldiers, well paid to forget what they would see this winter, waited in silence. William had taken care in choosing them, and had paid them well; he could afford no possibility of mishap in this journey, nor in the months to follow.

He leaned down and spoke to his companion. "I leave nothing to chance, my lady. Believe me, you will be as safe—and as solitary—as you wish to be. Each one of these men has sworn on his sword to protect you."

"And your wife? If she discovers me, will she not send me away?"

He pitched his voice lower still. "She will not see you, or know of you. I have promised this already, at Winchester. No one here will betray you."

William glanced once again at the crimson fields he dared not approach, then beckoned three foot-soldiers back from the edge of the forest, where they had withdrawn beyond hearing. Two took the reins of the broad-backed ponies bearing the litter; the third took his place beside the wool-swathed frame, one hand upon a bearing pole, the other upon the hilt of his sword.

"Forgive me," William said to the darkness within the woolen hangings. "We have but an hour of daylight left, and must reach shelter without lighting torches."

A gloved and jeweled hand drew back the curtain once again. "Then set a faster pace. I will not come to harm."

William shook his head. "We will go slowly, as before. And when we reach shelter, your women will be there; all will be ready for you."

The lady Mathilde, youngest daughter of the Baron Pandulf, smiled into the waning light. "Your kindness, my lord William, will bring its rewards." Then the woolen panel fell back into its place, and the face that had fascinated the king's midsummer court was hidden once again from sight.

William raised his arm and led the party east, along the high ground of the ridge above Lundale. As he rode, the lowering sun shone past him, casting a long shadow into the great forest beyond.

Lundale

Catherine of Lundale, wife of William de Macon, held her small daughter up to be kissed. "Is she not beautiful, cousin?"

A tickle and a giggle later, Robert drew back and considered the features of his youngest kin. "She will do. Your Alflega has her mother's face, and her father's golden pate."

"She does." Catherine lowered the child back to her lap, and settled closer to the fire. "Her hair will be darker than his, I think."

Robert's black gaze remained upon the child. "I wonder that you can remember the color of your husband's hair, cousin. When did you last see him?"

Catherine's hand stilled upon her daughter's cheek. "William has been fighting abroad, in King Henry's service. You know that."

"Of course."

"William was last here when I gave birth."

"And left within hours, they say."

Catherine felt the child Alflega grow heavy with sleep upon her knee. "He had come back to England, with dispatches from the king. He rode hard from London to be here for that single day. It was all the time he had." Catherine drew her daughter closer and began to smooth her yellow curls.

It had been in the springtime, scarce eight months ago, that William had come through the half-frozen roads to be with her. She had awakened, two days after her ordeal, with a memory of her husband's newly scarred face close beside her own, looking down upon the swaddled child in her arms.

Hadwen and the others had told her of William's brief, hurried appearance; without their account of that day, Catherine might have dismissed the memory as a dream, marred only by the odd, disturbing matter of the scar that crossed his cheek. In Catherine's true dreams, William would come back to her without injury, with his face untouched by war. There would be no mark upon him from a French arrow that had come so near to ending his life.

The silence grew longer; in the firelight, Robert's face was a grim, shadowed sight.

Catherine sighed. "William had no choice. He won this land by fighting Henry Plantagenet's wars, and he cannot stop now. William risked much, I think, to come to me when he did, to see this child born."

"Your husband takes many risks. Henry Plantagenet has grown to depend upon William at his side when the fighting grows hot." Robert glanced at the kitchen maids gathered at the far end of the hearth pit; his voice descended to a quiet growl. "Do you not find it odd, cousin, that the wife of the king's trusted warrior has no place of honor in the king's court, among the queen's ladies?"

Catherine beckoned to Hadwen, and placed her drowsy daughter in the woman's outstretched arms. She turned to Robert. "Come," she said. "Before you leave, I would hear what troubles you."

He nodded, and rose from the hearth. "There is a thing I will tell you," he said, "It is not for the ears of others."

From the far wall, there was a groan of protest as old John heaved himself from his place among the garrison men.

Robert frowned. "Your husband's watchdog is stirring," he muttered. "Keep him away."

Catherine laughed. "He won't leave the hall. It's the baby he follows about."

John's narrowed gaze passed from Catherine to Robert, then settled upon Alflega, bundled in Hadwen's arms. "Move back from the fire," he called to the maid. "She won't sleep with the heat on her face."

"Go polish your sword, old man. You know nothing of babies."

"I know you're a clumsy wench, like to stumble on your own kirtle. Move back, I say."

Their next words were drowned in laughter; taunts rose from both sides of the fire pit.

"Your daughter sleeps through the din?"

"She has heard it every night since her birth."
Catherine shook her head. " We stay in the old hall,
my people and I, and William's men live with John
in the keep. John would keep Alflega's cradle with
him in the guardhouse, given half the chance."

Together they passed between the ancient door
posts, out into the night. Beyond the stockade, the
thinning smoke of the stubble fires rose to obscure
the night skies. Only the moon, risen early in its
fullness, illuminated their way. They stopped beyond the rough walls and watched the embers flare
and darken as the night breeze moved across the
fields. Of the forty souls who had watched the
flames that day, only three had remained to see the
last of the embers die.

Catherine led her cousin to the edge of the
fields, far from the watchmen. "Tell me quickly,"
she said. "William is safe? He has not sickened from
his wounds?"

"No, he's strong, they say. Not as pretty as before,
but well enough." Robert kicked into a heap of
smoldering roots, sending a small shower of glow-
ing chaff across the dark earth. "What have you
heard, up here, of the king's doings?"

"That he fought rebels in Normandy and Anjou.
And that there may soon be peace."

"The king blows hot and cold," said Robert. "He
has lost control of Thomas Becket, and some say
that the priest will soon flee the country. And there
is trouble in the borders. Soon, perhaps as soon as
springtime, the king will take an army into Wales."

Catherine drew a long, painful breath. "Must William fight that war as well?" In the moonlight, Robert's dark gaze was fixed upon her. "Tell me now," she said. "Has he already gone to begin a new war?"

"Not yet." Her cousin stepped back and looked up at the moon. "The king has been back in England for a month now. Some say that he will pass the winter in the south, readying the army, watching his barons."

"Then William may come home."

"And if he does . . ."

There was coldness, a threat in her cousin's voice. Catherine stepped back from the field. "When he does, he will be most welcome. He is a good husband to me."

"If he does come home," Robert said, "he must take you to the king's Christmas court. You wed him, Catherine, to get your lands back. Our grandfather's treason, and your father's strike against the Plantagenets, are far in the past; and it is time you took your place among the king's favored people."

"William has the king's favor. Henry Plantagenet trusts him. You said—"

"—But can we trust William?"

Of a sudden, the night seemed colder. Robert's words brought to mind the dark imaginings that had surfaced once before, at harvest time, in an eerie, troubled dream. For her husband's sake, she must hide those fears from her black-tempered cousin. Catherine drew two steady breaths, then spoke. "I do. I trust him. Why should I not?"

Robert walked on, scuffing sparks and dust from the path. "You have been wed for two years, and given the man a child. He is lord here; you returned to Lundale not as its lady, but as William de Macon's wife. And he has done nothing to bring you into the king's favor."

"I live here, Robert. I wanted this. William gave me gold to repair the keep and the village. The tenants have begun to return; soon more will be back to work the fields again. I brought in a good harvest this year . . ."

"And you bore your husband a child. Yes, I see that there was little chance for you to look beyond this place and further your cause. But now, the king is back in England and in these dangerous times you cannot remain a stranger to Henry Plantagenet. Not when your lands and our name hold treason in their history."

One of the watchers in the fields turned toward the sound of Robert's angry words. Catherine waved him away, and placed a hand upon her cousin's arm. "The rebellion was years ago, when we were children. For now, we have the protection of William's name and the king's good faith in him. We are safer now than our fathers could have imagined, back then in the bad times."

"And if William dies next spring, in the borders? Will Henry Plantagenet allow Catherine of Lundale, daughter of the man who came so close to killing him, to remain on these lands? I believe, cousin, that you would be back under the abbess's care within a fortnight of William's death. You and the child as well. And the next man to receive these lands from the king might not be willing to wed a traitor's daughter and bring her back here." Robert stooped to pick up a half-burned brand and flung it into the field.

Before Catherine's eyes, the earth flared red, then subsided, as if it breathed a warning.

"Remember what you said to me when you sent word that you had accepted William de Macon as your husband? It was the last chance for any of our family to come back into royal favor, to have our lands back. Make sure, cousin, that your marriage brings you all it should."

With difficulty, Catherine kept her fears from her voice. "Robert, my husband has treated me with kindness and with honor. Promise me you will never speak against him. Your warnings must be only for me." She drew a careful breath. "Your brothers. My uncle. Though they are in exile, they must not be tempted to harm William when he crosses back to Normandy, as he must do, one day. Do not turn them against him."

"And you, cousin? What will you promise?"

She looked into his moon-shadowed eyes. "I will remember your words, Robert. When William returns, I will ask him to help us—all of us—to regain the Plantagenet's favor. At the Christmas court, if possible. On another occasion, if need be. And I will ask William to bring you with us, if the king agrees to have me at court."

Robert's voice softened. "My own lands will not come back to me," he said. "There are so few of us left, and only those who left this place will prosper. You have a chance to carry on. Make sure your husband helps your cause."

"My cause is his cause. When William returns—"

Robert covered her hand with his own. "Listen to me, and be strong. I will do as I promised, and keep my words for you alone. But know this—I came here, Catherine, to tell you that your husband returned many weeks ago. I saw him last month in Winchester in the king's retinue. Yet in these weeks he has sent no word to you, nor to old John in the garrison. Are you sure, Catherine, that he is content with this marriage? That he is content with the girl child you gave him? Or has he decided, having claimed your lands, that he will look higher, for a wife whose family has no blemish?"

"He—William is a man of honor—"

"With no lands save yours. Did he tell you, Catherine, that his own father lost everything in a rebellion against Louis Capet? That to save themselves the pack of them had fled to Normandy to serve Henry Plantagenet? Did he tell you that he has good reason to understand the plight of a rebel's child?"

"Yes. He told me all of it. Soon after we were wed."

Robert sighed. "I don't say he will abandon you, Catherine. But take care that you look after your own fate. And your child's."

Two

They reached the manor house in the last moments of dusk to find the scouts and Mathilde's women waiting on the road, just out of sight of the stockade walls. As ordered, they had turned back at the first sign of trouble.

William sent a party of ten men into the stockade to discover and rout the source of the campfires within. He waited outside, sword drawn and watchful, with his remaining men in a protective circle about the lady Mathilde and her two women.

Three of the scouts returned at a sedate trot, carrying brands snatched from those fires.

"Well?"

"They're not travelers, sir. Nor runaway serfs. It's five men sent up here from Lundale to make repairs to the roof, and to the stockade wall. They don't want trouble . . ."

The second scout moved forward. "They're dead afraid of raiders, and don't care who we are, as long as we let them go. They say they'll walk back to Lundale this night."

William sighed. "And by daybreak my wife would

be here with any Lundale man fit to raise a pitch fork against us."

Mathilde and her women began to whisper among themselves. The taller one, Ghislaine, pushed past the men-at-arms and seized William's arm. "My lady is tired and cold. She needs shelter. Do what you must, and do it quickly."

William had managed, in the slow ten miles they had traveled this day, to keep his impatience hidden, and to give a soft answer to each demand from his improbable charges. As he had sworn to do. As he must continue to do.

He had imagined, in those final ten miles, that it would be a simple matter to see the women settled by nightfall, have the guards encamped outside, and set the sentries to watch. Then, when the moon was at its height, he would ride back down the forest road, find the river's broad fording place, and cross the cold waters to Lundale. Catherine would be abed by then, the child at her side. She would rise, when she heard her sentries open the gates. Her soft, dark hair would be unbound, flowing down the back of her deep crimson kirtle, laced imperfectly in her haste. . . .

The whispering of Mathilde's women grew louder. William turned back to the first scout. "What have you told the men you found in there?"

"As you ordered, sir. We told them nothing, save that they must stay where they are, close to their campfire. And that if they did so, we would not harm them."

"Wait here, then. I'll take them behind the

house, where they will not see the door. When I send for you, bring the lady and her women past the gates, and into the house. When they're inside, close the door and take the litter from its frame. I remember a byre close against the wall—"

"Yes. They have two packhorses in it."

"Leave the beasts where they are. When the lady Mathilde and her women are in the house, close the door. Hide the frame and the litter behind the byre, then pile our saddle packs high before it."

William spurred forward and rode through the gates of his wife's dower house, taken by Henry Plantagenet from Catherine's rebel father, and forbidden to her these years past by order of an angry king. Had she told her vassals, when she sent them to repair the stockade, that they were helping their lady on the way to treason?

The five Lundale men, standing in a close huddle under the eyes of William's scouts, were unarmed. The youngest of them, a rangy, unbearded youth, reached down and drew a blazing brand from the flames.

William ignored the puny gesture; he dismounted and began to warm his hands at the campfire. "Why are you here?"

There was a long silence. William frowned; he had taken pains to learn the common tongue, and would not be denied speech with men such as these. In slow, deliberate words he repeated the question.

"My lady sent us."

"Why?"

The youth looked him straight in the eyes. "We know the lands belong to the king. We weren't taking deer. We were here to mend the rafters and the stockade wall. My lady doesn't want the house to fall. Says one day her lord will get the land back."

He had the boy repeat his words slowly until he understood. William knew his wife wanted the land back, if only to keep her people from running afoul of the king's law. Last year, Catherine had brought him here to see the deserted manor, a house and stockade on the dower lands of Catherine's mother. When the Lundale rebellion had failed, the king had taken all the lands once held by the family; two years ago he had given William a part of them, but kept the forest for himself.

"We're no thieves," said the youth.

William shook his head. "I believe you. Have you finished?"

"The roof is done."

He had expected to find the place deserted. The forest people, former Lundale villagers who hadn't dared return to their homes, had left the small fortress empty, for fear of Henry Plantagenet. He knew it would be sound enough to repair for the winter, and remote enough to keep Mathilde from discovery. There was no other place he knew where she would be as safe.

William looked across the stockade ground, then addressed the oldest of the men. "Have you used the well? Is the water clean?"

The old fellow nodded, but did not speak.

"He means yes," said the young one with the

torch in his fist. "We drank from it these three days past."

There were bedrolls placed around the fire. William gestured to them. "Why are you here, outside the house? Is it unsound?"

The young man glanced at his elders, then shrugged. "The lady said we were not to use it. Mend the roof and the wall, she said, then come home."

William looked more closely at the youth who spoke for them all, but did not remember his face.

"Your lady is Catherine of Lundale?"

"Aye."

He might be one of the forest people Catherine had tried to coax back to the village.

William pointed to the burning branch in the young peasant's hand. "Bring that and come with me. You and the others will show me what needs to be done to the walls." William turned back to his men-at-arms and spoke in his own Norman tongue.

He would keep these Lundale men with him, on the other side of the hall, until the women were within the house. In that time, he intended to learn from Catherine's people something more than the state of the stockade walls.

The Lundale men had done decent work on the rafters below the manor's broad roof, and had felled enough timber to replace twelve rotten palings in the stockade wall. If they thought it strange that forty Norman soldiers had appeared at nightfall to occupy the manor, they kept their questions to themselves. And once settled about the campfire for the night, they made no attempt to go near the barred door of the manor house.

Soon there were more campfires within the stockade as the men-at-arms warmed themselves against the late autumn night. William half-slept near the five Lundale men, waking often to be sure that they attempted no trickery.

At dawn, William joined the sentries outside the gate.

"There was no trouble," said the first watchman, "but at dawn the peasants at the campfire came out to talk. The oldest one says they want to go back to Lundale."

William nodded. "When they put the last timber into place, give them a penny each and send them back down to Lundale. Tell them to winter there, and not to come back here until the garrison leaves, in springtime. And when they're gone down the road, go to the door and tell the lady."

"Sir?"

"Tell her when these folk have gone. She will stay out of sight until the place is clear of Lundale people. Remember to tell her when it is safe."

"But—"

William turned back to the sentry. "Yes?"

"Sir, will you not be here to speak with her?" There was a note of panic in the hard warrior's voice.

"Do not fear to talk to the women. They won't bite," said William, "unless you cross the tall one with the yellow hair. And try not to stare at the lady."

"But when will you return, sir?"

"Tomorrow, and most days after that. I'll be living across the river, with my wife." He smiled at the sentry's confusion. "The lady Mathilde knows where I'll be. She will send you to find me if she needs to." He placed a hand on the man's shoulder. "Unload the wagon and tell me what supplies you need tomorrow. You are sworn—you are all sworn—to protect the lady and her women this winter, and to see that they have privacy and all they need for comfort." He glanced again at the stockade wall. "The people of Lundale, these folk working on the wall and the others in the valley, will know nothing of the lady. Nor will my wife. You are part of King Henry's army, wintering here and training for the war in Wales. That is all anyone needs to know."

The sentry's face flushed crimson with unspoken questions.

From the far side of the stockade came the sounds of spades attacking the frost-crusted earth, digging out the rotten uprights within the wall. "Watch the road. No one must come within sight of this place. No one but me."

William stepped back and watched the first party of scouts ride out to patrol the road. Only then, in the shadows of the byre, William led out his own palfrey and placed a worn pouch over the saddlebow.

It must have been the early morning chill that set his hands to trembling as he touched the dark leather that held his gifts. Now that his wife and child were near, the prizes he had carried from the wars in Normandy seemed small and tainted by their provenance. How would the lady of Lundale regard him, a husband back from the king's service with only trinkets, scars, and a party of hungry men-at-arms?

His men would take a small part of Lundale's new harvest, yet live apart from the valley, using supplies brought from Nottingham, offering no help to the small, aging garrison in Lundale's keep. How would he compel Catherine—his swift, impulsive, stranger-wife—to stay away from this manor, the house she loved enough to repair even though she no longer had a right to it? And how would he explain why he had brought so many of the king's own guards to winter here?

On this cold morning, the careless scheme he had accepted in Winchester seemed nothing more than madness. Within the hour, he would stand before Catherine and watch her face as he told the tale he had rehearsed for a week, up half the length of England, as he brought King Henry's impossible secrets home to Lundale.

He looked down into the water trough and frowned at the scarred, bearded image that rippled upon the surface. Would the sight of him frighten the child? His wife had not shrunk from the mark upon his face, that last time . . .

The trembling had gone into his injured knee; he took a single step towards the hall before turning back to climb into the saddle. If he held back now, afraid to face the wife he had sworn to deceive, he would pass yet another troubled night wondering, as he had all these months past, whether the mother of his child would look kindly upon her husband's return.

He rode past the sentries with a brief gesture of farewell, and rode out towards the crossroad, where he would turn north along the track to Lundale. The shadows of the great oak forest had shortened with the rising of the sun, and William imagined that the thin warmth of the new day had already begun to warm his face.

He pushed back the hood of his cloak and let the young sunlight reach the scar on his cheek. When he reached Lundale's fields, some folk among Catherine's people might recognize him. In the first weeks of their marriage, there had been only a few people rebuilding their huts in the village; there had been many more souls at work last night burning the stubble.

He touched the deep, numb line that ran from his cheekbone halfway to his mouth. Exhausted by childbirth, Catherine had hardly noticed the scar on the brief night of his last stay at Lundale. Today, would she be repelled by the old wound? There had been a time, in the single fortnight he had spent with her in their first summer, when he had imagined he had seen a beginning of passion in her eyes. Now, with his marred face and damaged knee and his forty soldiers in the forest house, there might be exasperation rather than longing in her gaze.

A shriek rang out on the road ahead, and the

voices of his scouts rose in anger. A second shriek—
a harpy's shrill cry—set William's horse sidling away
from the track. He wheeled his mount back to the
road, and spurred it forward.

At the crossroads, hurtling into sight of the
larger road, William's mount swerved inches from
the cluster of scouts, and bolted past the solitary
rider who faced them. William circled back and
stopped a few feet behind the rider.

It was not possible that—

It was Catherine.

"How many more will you call to block my road?
Send them all," William's wife cried, "and I will add
their names to yours and my husband will punish
you all." The rich scarlet of her cloak rippled as she
raised her arm and pointed down the road that led
to Lundale. "There is a garrison in the keep, and
they are readying themselves to ride to Nottingham. Down this road. They may be approaching as
I speak. Leave now and you'll live to see tomorrow."

One of the scouts had thought to draw his sword.
The man began to back his mount away from
Catherine's ire. "Whoever you send, they will not
pass us. No one goes down the track to the forest
house. Man or woman, we will turn them back. We
have our orders—"

"This is my road, and five of my people are beyond you, at the forest house. If you have harmed
them in any way, you will wish you had not. Send
them to me—all five of them—and be on your way
out of the forest. You have no right to be here. If
anyone does, it's the king, and I know he hasn't

brought you. Get out. By noon. If you do not, I will send—"

"Your husband."

She lowered her arm and turned, very slowly, toward the sound of his voice. For a brief moment, she looked as if she might slip from the saddle to the road, and he raised his reins, ready to spur forward to catch her. She steadied herself with a hand upon the saddle frame, and continued to stare at him.

"William?"

He passed his hand across his jaw. He should have shaved before riding out to seek her. And cut his hair back to look as it had on their wedding day. He should have—

Catherine waited, her eyes large with surprise. Or fright.

He attempted to smile, but thought better of it as the scar tugged at the corner of his mouth. Where were the words he had devised during the long ride north?

"Catherine. I have come home."

Behind her, the nearest scout sheathed his sword.

She glanced back at the line of horsemen. "Harm this man and King Henry will feed your livers to his hounds." She paused, and raised her voice higher still. "The king will send an army to hunt you down and give you traitors' deaths. Keep the damned forest house for now. My husband will deal with you soon enough."

"Catherine—"

She turned back to him, tears glittering beneath her eyes. "Not today. They are too many, and you haven't even seen Alflega—"

"—these are my men."

The men understood William's brief gesture, and turned their horses to ride back into the forest. Then he was alone with Catherine, and only the width of the track lay between them. The words he had prepared still would not come to him. "Catherine," he said again.

"There are five Lundale men up this road, at the manor stockade. Tell your men not to harm them."

"Your men are safe, and on their way here."

Her gaze did not waver. "You have seen them?"

"Yes. Last night."

She made a small sound of surprise.

William looked up to the greying sky and cursed himself for a fool. There had been no need to tell Catherine he had spent the night nearby. "There will be no trouble for them."

He drew a short breath. Where were the words?

"Then I thank you." Catherine pushed the hood of her cloak back and stared at him in silence. She did not ask him why his men had blocked her road, nor how he had come to see her tenants. Nor did she make a move to approach him.

"Catherine—"

She set the reins upon her saddlebow and raised her chin. "Yes, William?"

Her eyes were larger than he remembered, a darker green. There were shadows now, where there had been naught but beauty. Was it possible that her hair was darker, as dark now as a raven's wing? And how, in this moment of anger, had she become more beautiful than she had been?

These were not words she would be pleased to answer. Later, there would be time for the careful phrases he had devised and forgotten.

"Who is Alflega?" he said.

She drew a long breath. "She is your daughter, William. Alflega is the name of your daughter." Her voice was flat. Calm. Did she imagine, staring into his scarred face, that he had gone simple from his injuries?

He had not realized, until that moment, that he had been afraid to ask if the child had lived. It had been such a small thing, and had cried so long into that first night. "Then the baby is well?"

Catherine smiled, and her voice softened to a lover's timbre. "She is well. Beautiful when she smiles. She has your look, William."

"You hadn't yet given her a name, the day I left."

The smile faded. "She was but a few hours old when you went back to the king."

William heard no rancor in his wife's voice as she recalled the day. "I had thought to name her after my grandmother," he said.

"Then you should have stayed for her christening."

"I had to go back. There were dispatches waiting, to be entrusted to me."

"I know."

Her tears—so nearly shed when she had thought he would fight the men upon the road—had dis-

appeared. William had imagined, as he had traveled north, that Catherine would be angry that his
soldiers had taken the manor house, or tearful
about his scars, or eager to show the child, impatient for him tell her of the wars. And curious to
hear of the king's court. Her quiet, watchful demeanor was worse than his darkest imaginings.

"What was her name?" Catherine said

"Name?"

"Your grandmother's name."

"Ah. It was Rosewitha."

Catherine closed her eyes and muttered to herself. "Alflega is better," she said at last.

Her heart had sensed his presence before she had
heard his voice, or seen past the stubble and scar that
now marked the lines of his face. From the moment
he had hurtled into sight, one more armed rider
among so many, her racing pulses had stilled, finding
unnatural calm in the midst of danger.

And when he had spoken—when that honey-dark
voice had sounded behind her—and she had known
him at last, and feared that he would draw his sword
upon the four burly men they faced, still there was
calm in her soul as she sought by words and threats
to keep the interlopers from attacking him.

All was well, now. Beneath her puny forewarn-
ings she had known, somehow, that they would be
safe. For William had returned.

His voice had reached her in that same way
months ago, as she had labored to bring forth their

child into the soft spring night. He had appeared beside her, and spoken her name, and her heart had ceased to pain her. His hand had taken hers, and in that moment, fear had moved a great distance from her soul, and she had drawn strength into her weary body.

This day, as she had watched the four strange soldiers turn and ride away at William's silent gesture, she should have asked how he had compelled them to leave. Instead, she heard herself speak to William of names, and reproach him for his long absence. Catherine felt her face flush crimson in shame that she had greeted him so; fierce Hadwen, upbraiding her husband for spending the day beside the ale tub with his cronies, was never so spiteful.

She heard William say that he had wanted to name their child for his grandmother. Rosewitha. In that moment, she would have agreed to call the child Jezebel, if it pleased him. But instead she had been stubborn. "Alflega is better," she had said.

And William had shrugged, and smiled back at her. "Alflega," he repeated. "Hard for a child to say."

"She knows her name. Speak it, and she will look to you and smile."

William's own smile broadened, then vanished as his hand went to the scar beside his mouth. "I doubt she'll smile at the sight of my face. Not since an archer made his mark upon it."

"Does it still pain you?"

"No. Not any longer."

Catherine felt the tears return. There was pain—

her own, as she imagined the terrible moment when the arrow had reached him.

His wife was frowning, staring at the mark upon his face.

The pain of it had gone, but the sting of recollection had not. The dull, tight tug of that scar would be ever with him, reminding him that his life, and the lives of those he held dear, could be taken or saved by his smallest hesitation. By the tremor of an archer's wrist.

"When did it happen?"

Her voice. He had prayed, that dark day of the archer, that he would hear Catherine's voice again.

"William?"

"Ah. Last year." In that last day of fighting outside the walls of Chinon, the fates had allowed him to live, but left the track of an arrow's flight upon his face.

"I remember now. It was there on your face when you returned—when the baby was coming."

"Yes, it happened before then." The cold pressure of the scar upon his face had forced him, when he had smiled at the sight of his tiny daughter, and when he had kissed Catherine's trembling hand, to remember that he would not live forever. That he must make sure of his new lands so that his wife, and now his child, would live on at Lundale if he should fall.

He glanced over his shoulder at the road north to Lundale. "Will you ride with me, Catherine?

Your men at the forest house will follow later. I promise you, they are safe."

They traveled in silence, careful of the deep ruts left after the autumn rains. Near the final downward slope to the river, the runnels converged into a small brook that ran with the road down to the river that skirted Lundale's fields. The mud-slick road widened into a broad fording place, and rose beyond, on the north side of the river, to Lundale's dark, rich fields.

William halted above the fording place. In the distance, three men labored at the edge of the village; a solitary horseman tarried beyond them. None of them had looked up to notice riders watching across the river. William frowned. "You were alone on the road, in trouble. Why didn't you have an escort? Where is John?"

"I chose to ride ahead." Catherine looked past him. "John's coming now."

The rider had moved a few paces past the edge of the village. Upon the roof of the keep, a single watchman stood unmoving. From the old timber gates in the palisade wall, three women bearing panniers walked toward the village.

He might as well have left the defense of his family to the nunnery down the road. "If that is, in fact, old John slouching to follow you, he must be replaced. If those had been raiders you met at the crossroads, you would be dead by now, your cattle would be on the road north, and the hall would be in flames. And the child—God knows—" The scar upon his cheek had begun to throb hot. There was pain now. In plenty.

She moved closer, and placed her gloved hand upon his arm. "William, look again. The men you left to protect us should be in the keep. The women know to take the baby there if John raises the alarm. See—the men are close enough to run from the fields to the keep, and the cattle are safe enough in the pasture if—"

"And my wife, who was riding alone along the forest track, would still be dead at the hands of raiders. John has not done well. I'll find someone else—someone younger—before I leave."

"Don't send him away."

He stared at his frowning wife. Last year, when he had brought ten men-at-arms to Lundale to defend the settlement, she had predicted that they would do nothing but eat the crops and frighten the tenants away. Now she was defending the oldest and worst-tempered of them.

William pointed to the approaching rider; the man was hurrying now, urging his mount into an ungainly trot. "Look at him, Catherine. He's useless. And I remember that you disliked him."

"Don't send him away. The baby loves him. He's the only one who can quiet her when she's fretful." She removed her hand from his wrist and narrowed her eyes. "Who are the men who stopped me? They must be yours, but you sent them away, into the forest."

He straightened in the saddle and met her careful gaze. "They are the king's men—here for the winter. You need do nothing for them but sell them some grain to keep them. They will hunt—"

"Where—"

"In the forest, of course. They are the king's men—"

"Where will they live?"

The dark moment had come. William drew a long breath. "At the manor. They will stay the winter at the manor—"

Catherine's small gasp sent ice into his veins. "At the manor," William said again. "On your mother's old dower lands. The king will be grateful to have them sheltered and housed for the winter."

At the edge of his sight, William watched John's careful progress. Would the damned sluggard never reach them and distract Catherine from her questions?

"How many?"

He wished she would raise her voice, and show what she was thinking. Catherine's chilly calm had endured longer than he could bear.

"Forty." He pitched his voice to say the next words as if they were of little importance. "Forty of them. And a woman or two."

She turned in her saddle to look back at the road, as if she expected to see a small army swarming across the fording place. "William—"

He held up his hand. "There is gold in my saddlepack. Enough to feed them this winter, if need be."

"Gold from the king?"

There was a quiet caution he had never before

heard in her voice. "Yes, of course. From the king," he said.

Catherine expelled a small breath. "Good," she said.

William watched the fear leave his wife's features, and understood. "What did you imagine, Catherine? That I would keep an army for someone other than King Henry?"

She looked into his eyes. "I am the daughter of a failed rebel, husband. I was raised to ask just that sort of question."

And because his wife was the daughter of a man who had died trying to kill Henry Plantagenet, William would never tell her what he must attempt to do this winter. No matter what the cost, he would not drag her into this matter. He would not tempt her with the truth.

William shifted in the saddle. "And if I swear to you that I'm the king's loyal man, will you leave these questions and ride home with me?" He picked up the reins, then hesitated. "Tell me—will my face frighten our daughter?"

She smiled then, and nudged her mount closer. "Not if you learn her name, and use it."

A distant cry reached them from the path between the fields; John had come close enough to recognize his lord. William raised an arm in salutation, and turned back to Catherine.

"Remind me again," he said.

"Alflega," said Catherine. "She will smile if you call her Alflega."

Three

William rode ahead, guiding his mount past the stand of leafless trees that marked the fording place where the road traversed the river.

Catherine loosed the reins and let her horse follow as it would; she could not look away from the gaunt-visaged stranger who was her husband. She had lived with him little more than twenty days in the space of their marriage; the memories she had kept green for the two seasons past did not resemble, beyond eyes and voice, the scarred and weary man now riding before her.

The differences went beyond the stubborn scars that marred him, not faded with time. There was something unfamiliar in the way his tall frame moved with the gait of his mount; he held the reins with as much care as a king's standard bearer might do, and did not turn, as Catherine remembered he used to do, to rest his hand on the saddle's high cantle as he spoke to her.

A quail flew up from the ground, sending William's horse sidling into a dead elm wrapped in holly; in that instant, Catherine saw her husband's small shudder of pain. William's cloak, pulled back as it brushed past the barbed leaves, revealed that his knee was wrapped in many layers of woolen padding.

She rode forward. "You are hurt."

"The leg is mending." He smiled then, as if to distract her. "I was lucky. My arm is as good as ever, and I can ride."

The holly had not yet relinquished its hold; the cloak came farther back, revealing the leather scabbard at William's side. Deeply scored and stained, the leather sheath did not resemble the fine gear William had used when Catherine had first seen him, scarce two years ago. The saddle, too, was marred and darkened with more than simple use.

He reached down to free his cloak. "It looks worse than it was," William said. "I survived, as did my mount."

"This horse?" Catherine leaned forward and frowned. The beast's dark flank was smooth beside the mended stirrup.

"No, the big roan gelding. I left him in Hereford at the abbey there, and bought this fellow with the king's gold."

"It happened in Hereford?"

"West of there." William lifted the reins and set his heel to that unmarred flank, as if to show that his leg was not useless.

Catherine trotted forward to catch his words. "You were fighting the Welsh?"

"Not fighting. Riding east from Hay. It was a lad—a short, half-grown lad—who came at me from the bushes. Got my leg, then went for my horse. I gave him the flat of my sword to run him off, and then when he was gone I saw how much knifework he had managed to do. The marshal sent two men after him, thinking he was an assassin who had mistaken me for the king."

Her throat closed in dread. "And caught him," she managed to say.

He shrugged. "No, the boy escaped. It was wild country near the marches beyond Hereford, where a man can move faster than a horse."

They had reached the fording place, and would soon cross to where John awaited them. "Wait," she said. "Tell me—"

He pulled the cloak forward to cover his leg. "Another question?"

How long had he traveled with the pain of that wound? The Welsh border was far from Lundale. Many days of hard riding. "No," she said. "I'll wait until we reach the hall."

William raised his hand in greeting to John, then turned back to her. "I remember," he said, " that you don't keep a question unasked for the space of an hour. Ask it now, before we reach the others."

She looked across the river and knew that there would not be another moment of privacy for them. Not before night came. "You said the young assassin thought you were the king. William, is that what you do for Henry Plantagenet—to ride out into danger in his place?"

He looked down to hide his consternation; these words had alarmed him beyond all else.

Catherine moved closer. "There are those who

say that you look much like the king, and that Henry Plantagenet has come to rely upon you, to trust you beyond others to act for him. Is it because he expects you to put yourself in danger when he cannot risk himself?"

When William raised his head, his features were once again composed in that familiar, half-mocking expression Catherine remembered from their first days together. "I have the king's color in my hair," he said, "and some folk may mistake us, one for the other, at a fair distance. But any decent assassin would see the difference before he struck."

"A clear difference?"

"Plain enough." He was smiling now as he urged his mount into the fording place. "The king hasn't half my good features," William said. "Or so they tell me." He reached up to touch the cold-darkened scar upon his cheek. "That archer brought me some good luck with his arrow shot last winter; there's no chance an assassin would mistake me for Henry Plantagenet, now that my face is marked."

His smile was steady, as if he had spoken of small matters. Yet his hand continued to trace the evidence of his close brush with death.

Catherine rode beside her husband across the broad river. "The scar should fade," she said. " but you will bring bad luck upon yourself if you jest about it."

"Then I place my luck in your keeping, if you will have it."

His voice was as soft and low as she had heard it on the night of her child's birth. Even here, in the new morning with the autumn sunlight breaking through the clouds, the sound of his words conjured memories of that rainy spring night.

There had been few nights in any season for them, in the months of their marriage; she had counted those nights, over and over again, in her solitary bed. And there would be very few nights to add to that number, if she lost William to Henry Plantagenet's wars.

She would lose him sooner if he became careless with his injuries. "You should never have traveled this far with your leg wounded," she said.

William shrugged. "I couldn't wait."

"Why not? Wouldn't the king let you rest for a time before invading the forest house with his guard? Or is this some new war in the making?"

"Catherine, don't be foolish. It was time to ride north, and I did. I came to no harm."

William's palfrey shied as a clutch of dried leaves floated past his legs. He calmed the beast and guided it toward the far bank. The sun came from behind the clouds, shining upon the swift-flowing water.

At the edge of Lundale's fields, John waved his arms in a broad greeting.

William waved back, then reached back towards Catherine. "Come, wife. Foolish or not, I made the journey and I didn't fall in the river just now, and I'm home for the winter. Are you not pleased to see me, Catherine?"

She placed her hand in his outstretched palm. "William, I am pleased. So very well pleased . . ."

Catherine looked away and blinked back the sudden, hot tears.

William's hand tightened about her fingers.

She focused her gaze upon the frost-silvered leaves floating upon the water.

"No more questions from my lady wife?"

Catherine brushed her cheek and turned back to him. "Just one. How is it that you were in the Marches last month, dealing with Welsh assassins? I thought you were with the king's army in Normandy."

"If questions were arrows, Catherine, you would have an empty case by now. Do you never stop shooting while you make new ones?"

"I have had these six months past, William, to fashion a hundred questions. Will you not tell me why you were in Wales?"

His smile disappeared. "It's a long story, too green to be told now."

William's voice had turned cold, and he was gazing back across the river as if he wished himself anywhere but in her company. If not for the steady warmth of his hand about her own, Catherine would have thought he already regretted his return.

She forced herself to smile. "No matter. It will be months—a winter full of months—before you are fit to go to war for the king again. Take your time, husband, and tell me in springtime, when the fields are green again." She hesitated. "God willing, you won't go back south before then."

"I'll stay the winter, if you'll have me." He smiled

again, and released her hand. "Don't worry, Catherine. I didn't come close to dying."

William turned back to look across the fields and bellowed his greeting to John.

Catherine held back and watched her husband ride on. Tomorrow, when he had dressed his wounds and slept the night in their own bed, she would get the truth from him.

This homecoming would go better than the first one. Last year, when they had been wed but a month, William had pounded home along the south road to Lundale and burst into sight in noisy high spirits with the small band of men he had recruited to form a garrison. Catherine's tenants, so recently tempted out of the forest to return to their fields, had dropped their spades and fled back to the safety of the wildwood.

In the following ten days, Catherine had sent the few souls who remained to seek out their fellows and tell them that there was no danger. They were to explain that their new lord and the ten men-at-arms, though given to blood-stopping whoops as they trained in weapons, meant no harm to Lundale's tenants. A garrison in Lundale's high keep would see the approach of raiders and protect the village. Prosperity in the Lundale's shallow river valley would once again be possible.

Then William had left to rejoin the king's army in Normandy, leaving old John and nine other men-at-arms to protect Lundale, and Catherine had begun to miss the husband she hardly knew.

When spring came, more folk had come out of the forest to repair their abandoned huts in the village. They had begun to clear fields that had last seen a plow in King Stephen's time, before war had brought death to Lundale's old lord and destruction to his settlement. And when the nearest land had been plowed and sheep brought up from the south to forage upon the farthest bracken-choked fields, and Catherine had been abed in childbirth, William had appeared for a single day, and disappeared again before she had awakened from an exhausted sleep. At the time, she would have given every last one of her tenants back to the greenwood, if she could have kept William at her side. A woman in childbed, Hadwen had told her, was often given to such foolishness.

Somewhere in his travels, William had learned something of the common tongue; he surprised Catherine by halting at the gates of Lundale's palisade and attempting to speak to the folk who had gathered there.

Catherine listened to her husband's awkward phrases, so unlike his well-turned Norman speech, and began to catch the sense of what he was trying to say to the villagers. Those nearest to William frowned as they strained to catch his meaning; farther back in the small crowd, there was some whispering and a hint of laughter. A child giggled;

his mother caught him to her skirts and hissed a warning.

William paused as if he expected an answer, then smiled and repeated his words in a louder voice, moving his arms in broad sweeping movements meant to encompass all of Lundale's astonished people. He seemed to be saying something about the king, and prosperity.

Catherine caught Hadwen's eye and made a small, desperate gesture of her own. Hadwen leaned forward and whispered into the ear of the smith, who muttered to the woman beside him. Soon after, they began to nod, and smiled back at their lord.

William turned back to Catherine with a smile of his own. "Do you see? They won't run away this time, now that I can speak them fair."

"Well done, husband," Catherine said.

"They're fair amazed, they are," said John, "and like to stay around, just to hear you speak again." Catherine caught John's grizzled wink and turned back to beckon William through the gates. As he passed, William set his hand upon the bindings about his knee, as if to keep it from jostling against the post.

Catherine slipped from the saddle and placed a hand upon William's leg. "Can you dismount?"

"I spoke the truth, Catherine. It's healed." He eased himself to the ground, and took a small leather bag from the saddlebows. "Is there someone who looks after the garrison's horses?"

Above John's grey beard, his face colored in confusion. "They care for their own mounts. And there's a young lad who helps out, when he's not too busy . . ."

"No matter." William looked about him, as if searching for a familiar face. In words he must have practiced on the many days of his journey, he directed Hadwen's young son to stable his horse. "This winter," he said to John, "you will train two lads to look after the beasts and clean the byre. With so few men in the garrison, we need them watching the roads and training in weapons rather than working in the stable."

Catherine caught his arm. "It's not his fault, William. There aren't enough tenants, even now, to clear all the fields we had before. Most of the lads—even the youngest ones—did some work on the land this summer. I asked John to have the men-at-arms work in the byre."

William's face darkened. "Forgive me," he said. "I left you with a babe in your arms, without enough folk to keep the settlement going. This winter, I will go into the forest myself and find some of the people who still fear to come back to the village."

This hour, in the sunlit yard with Lundale's curious folk still within sight, was not the time to remind William that the timid souls still living in the forest had long memories, and a decade-old reason to distrust Henry Plantagenet's men. "Tonight," said Catherine, "we must talk."

He looked down and smoothed the frown from her brow. "Tomorrow, you may talk all day, and tell

me what you would have me do about the land.
Tonight," he said, "may be for other matters."

Her blood raced hot at his words; Catherine felt
the heat of it rise to her face. Around her, the
voices of her people in the bailey yard receded into
muffled insignificance.

With slow grace, his hand moved to rest upon
her shoulder. "If you are willing," he added.

John turned about to see why they tarried. "In
here," he called to William. "The baby is in here,
with the women." At the doorway of Lundale's old
hall, John pushed ahead and cleared a hasty swath
through the women who gossiped at their looms
along the length of the fire pit. The nearest two,
young maids who had come out of the forest into
the household at harvest time, rose in alarm at the
sight of a new Norman face.

John muttered to himself as he waded through
the confusion of spindles and wool the women had
dropped as they rose to their feet. He dismissed
their alarm with an impatient gesture, then beckoned to William. "Come see our little Alflega," he
said. "Come and see the prettiest babe in all Christendom."

William covered Catherine's hand with his own
as they made their own way through the snarl of
benches, looms, and skeins. "Old John speaks as if
he owns this place," he murmured.

"He does, in a way," Catherine said.

William took a last step forward to the shallow
dais at the head of the hearth pit and sank to his

knees, careless of the harm he might do to his injured leg. "Jesu—"

Catherine moved to his side. "Your knee . . ."

William did not hear her words. He touched the cradle, then again to set it rocking gently upon the floor planks. "Sweet Jesu," he said. "Do you see how she sleeps?"

John drew the baby's coverlet back from her chin and growled a quiet greeting. "Wake up, little lass. Your father's come home to see you. Do you have a smile for him?"

Catherine held back and allowed John to hover over the babe. She had long since given up suggesting to this aged sergeant of Lundale's garrison that his duties lay far from Alflega's cradle.

William glanced up at Catherine, silent amusement in his gaze.

"There—look at her now," said John. "See how she lifts her hand and waves it about? She's a strong one, this little babe. She wasn't nearly two month old when she started doing that thing with her arm. And look there, when she smiles. There's a tooth somewhere in there, or I'm a blind drunken bard."

Alflega smiled at the sound of John's voice, and answered him with her own burbling chatter.

Catherine placed a hand on William's shoulder. "You may touch her," she said. "Don't be afraid to pick her up."

John raised his head. "Give the lass some time to get to know her father. Leave her in the cradle or she'll cry."

"She won't cry," said Catherine. "And if she does,

there's no harm done. It has been many long months since William held her—since the night she was born."

John shook his head in dismay. "Don't make her cry. She has a full voice, does my little Alflega."

William offered his hand for the baby's inspection, and held it still as the baby frowned and reached for it. And smiled.

Catherine breathed a prayer of thanksgiving that Alflega had not awakened hungry, to greet her sire with the ear-stabbing cries to which Lundale had become accustomed.

The child began to inspect each finger with solemn care. "Look, Catherine. She's not afraid," said William. He smiled then, broader than before. And he seemed to take no notice that his scar pulled the smile askew. He raised his hand and laughed as his daughter pulled it back to her. "See, Catherine? Your daughter has a mighty grip."

Hadwen appeared at her side and tugged at her sleeve. "Come away," she whispered. "Leave them and come away."

Alflega's careful study of her sire's thumb had distracted both William and John. Hadwen could have dropped a cauldron at their side and they would never have noticed her. Catherine retreated from the cradle and drew Hadwen aside. "What is it?"

"Osbert and the others are back from the manor. They're in the byre and won't come out. They need to speak to you." Hadwen inclined her grey head towards William and John. "Don't tell them. Just come."

In that moment, William raised his head and reached for her hand. "Thank you," he said. "She is beautiful."

It was a time she had seen in her dreams, these lonely months past. It took all her resolve to slip her fingers from his warm palm and step away. "I must go . . ."

He extended his hand once again. "Come, Catherine. Stay with us now. Can it not wait?"

She shook her head. "I'm sorry, William. It's a small matter in the kitchen. I'll be back."

A brief sadness crossed his features. William nodded, and turned back to the cradle.

Four

". . . And then the big one—the leader of them—comes into the stockade and sends the others away and tries to speak to us. But he's a Norman and can't talk so well. So he gathers us up, this big one who can't talk, and takes us around back of the old manor hall, away from the campfire, to the blind side. So I figure he's going to kill us."

"That's right. With his sword. He had his sword drawn, my lady."

Young Radulf stood straight and raised his arm to brandish a half-burnt branch above his head. "But I kept hold of this. It was still burning, and the Norman let us use the light of it as we went around to the blind side of the hall."

"—and made us show him the work we had done, and what was to be done."

" And then he didn't kill us."

"But if he had tried," said Radulf, "I would have struck him down with this brand, and we would have run out through the rotten place in the wall, and through the forest, back to you."

"And his soldiers would have cut us down before we cleared the forest," said Radulf's father. "There were so many of them. We were lucky they let us go this morning. Pray they won't come after us, my lady. It's best we leave before they do—"

Radulf shook his head. "And give up the hut we built, now that winter is coming?" He placed the burnt end of the branch on the ground, and rested his folded arm upon the top, as he must have seen the garrison men do after training with longswords.

With effort, Catherine managed not to smile at Radulf's new-found bravado. "That will not be necessary," she began. "You will be safe here. I know who—"

"I say we stay and fight them, if it comes to that. We got the better of the big one—"

"—He let us go, Radulf."

"He saw I wouldn't just stand there and be cut down. If he had tried, he'd be one blind Norman today, he would."

Catherine placed a hand on her brow and tried not to imagine what would have happened if Radulf had carried through his plan. "Enough," she said. "Now listen—"

"Don't you worry, my lady," said Radulf. "We'll not leave you undefended, with only that old woman John and his lazy garrison to keep you from harm. I'll be watching from the forest, and if they come down the road I'll—"

"Enough!"

Seven faces turned towards Catherine in the silence that followed her angry cry. Radulf's scarce-bearded jaw began to tremble.

"The big knight—the one who tried to speak to

you—is my husband. Your lord. He is a Norman, and doesn't speak the common tongue."

"He thinks he speaks it. Someone should tell him he sounds like a—"

"Silence." Radulf's father cuffed his son behind his ear.

Catherine raised her voice. "The soldiers at the manor—forty of them, not hundreds—are the king's men. Here for the winter."

"Why?"

"Put that down," said Catherine. And waited until Radulf had dropped his makeshift weapon. "My husband, your new lord William, has returned with those men-at-arms. We are obliged, as Henry Plantagenet's subjects, to house those forty soldiers this winter and we will do so. The king has given them leave to hunt in the forest for their meat, and we must send them whatever else they may need."

She paused, and looked at each of the men in turn. "There must be no killing of the king's deer while the soldiers are so near. I know you have been hunting and there was no harm done—before. Now you must stop going into the forest, and if we are lucky they will leave in the springtime and tell the king that we treated them well. If we are very lucky, William may be rewarded and we will all prosper from it. I will ask my husband to get the king's leave for you to hunt in the forest next summer."

"And after?"

Catherine smiled. "And after. If all goes well."

Radulf's father scratched his head. "It will be hard to feed them all."

"My husband has gold from the king, to buy what we don't have. Before the snow comes, I'll send you and some of the garrison men down to Nottingham for supplies. The king has sent more than enough coin to see us through."

"There are more than forty of those men," Radulf said. "Many more. And the women—you didn't count all the women."

"What foolishness is this," his father said. "We saw no women."

"I heard them," said Radulf. "Just before dawn, they were talking inside the house, and I heard them through the loose timbers."

"Spied on them, more like. Risked your foolish neck by looking in the hall."

"They're not worth the spying," huffed Radulf. "except for the one who—"

"Hush." At her back, Catherine heard William's black palfrey tug against his halter rope; the rough timber was groaning as he pulled against it.

Osbert touched her sleeve. "If we're to stay out of the forest, how will we take the solstice gift to the holy well?"

She had forgotten the coming solstice. "I'll see it done," she said. "I'll do it myself, if need be. Promise me, Osbert, that you'll let me manage it . . ."

The palfrey tugged again and whickered as he moved restlessly in the slatted sunlight that streamed between the wall planks. Catherine turned to see William's tall figure out in the yard, framed in the crooked doorway of the byre.

Catherine spoke quickly to Radulf and the others. "Remember all I have said, and do not spread rumors about your lord." She turned and walked back to the door.

William touched her cheek and looked beyond her, into the farthest dimness of the stable. "Won't they come forward and speak?"

Catherine shrugged. "They're still frightened of you."

"As I promised," he said, "your carpenters came to no harm. Do they understand they must not return to the forest?"

Catherine had guessed that was the message William had attempted to give them. "They understand," she said.

"Then come back into the hall. We must discuss this matter of the king's soldiers with John, and he won't budge from the cradle. Is he always thus?"

"Since the day she was born."

"And what does he do for you? I told him to keep you from harm."

"He does his best," said Catherine.

It was nightfall, and the last hour of Catherine's solitude in the square sleeping chamber behind the dais of the great hall.

There had been twenty-four days and twenty-three nights before this. Catherine had marked those first days with small stitches near the hem of the long linen cloth that lay folded within the single chest she had brought with her from the abbey.

Though wed to William for a year and a summer

and the harvest that followed, she had spent a scarce two fortnights as a married women with her husband at her side. And if she counted the days when she had been a true wife to William, sharing his bed and the comfort a man might offer his wife, there were a paltry dozen of those days. They had been together as man and true wife for twelve short summer nights.

Catherine smoothed the folds of heavy linen and drew a small skein of silken thread from the deepest corner of the chest. Wrapped within the rich green twist was the greatest treasure of all—a small needle, sharp and straight and untarnished. The fine sliver of steel, too precious to give to Hadwen for her mending, too narrow for the tough woolen thread she had spun for kirtle seams, was meant for fine linen. She had used it, day by day, to mark the nights William had spent in her bed.

There were other small treasures she had left behind on that day of haste when she had accepted William as her husband and wed him at the abbey door. Eight days later, after that sudden marriage, back upon the lands she had never expected to see again, Catherine had watched William ride away, and in the same hour had turned back to her task of restoring Lundale's filthy, disused hall to decent condition. Within the month, she had tempted a few of Lundale's vanished tenants to return to their fields, and had agreed to have ten men-at-arms repair and settle into the abandoned keep beside the ancient hall.

Eight green stitches, small as new leafless shoots

in a false spring, had marked those first days of her marriage to William.

Then after midsummer he had come riding along the forest road, a solitary rider splashing across the fording place, sending Lundale's skittish tenants fleeing in panic at the sight of him.

Catherine smiled as she remembered the day of his first return. The four women who had set up their looms in the hall had vanished at nightfall, leaving Catherine alone with her husband beneath the wide, soot-blackened rafters that had sheltered Lundale's lords and their people centuries before the Normans came.

William had brought out a leather flask from his saddlepack and poured brandywine into her drinking cup; then he had asked her, in that low voice he seemed to use for her alone, if it would please her, now that she was settled, to become his wife in truth. And in his eyes she had seen that William had asked an honest question; though he had the rights of a husband, there had been no demands sheathed within his words.

She had taken his hand and walked with him into the sleeping chamber, and had begun her fortnight as a truly wedded wife.

Now, Catherine folded the linen along its lines, and placed it back in the coffer. William was home again. The saints had been kind to her, and William had survived to come home.

"Are you asleep?"

It was Hadwen's voice beckoning her from the dense hangings at the entrance to the chamber.

Catherine drew the curtain aside and looked beyond Hadwen to the hearth. "He's there," said Hadwen. "What do you want us to do?"

William lay sleeping beside the cradle, his hand curled about the near rocker. His unshorn, golden hair shone dark in the firelight, and the scar upon his face, diminished in the kindly shadows of the hall, did not mar the peace of his countenance.

"I could call John and the others to carry him to bed," said Hadwen.

She looked again at his large hand upon the cradle base. "No," said Catherine. "Leave him there to sleep." And she brought her own fine crimson cloak to cover him, for the nights were growing longer and the fire would begin to die down before dawn.

Young Alflega slept on, snug beneath many layers of white woven wool. Upon the soft heap of coverlets at the baby's feet lay a folded square of dense green stuff, a soldier's blanket, much worn from use in a saddlepack.

Hadwen reached for the dark blanket. "She'll roast, beneath all this."

"Let it be," Catherine said. "She'll come to no harm, with William here."

She waited for a time in case he might awaken, and saw that her husband was deep in exhausted slumber. Catherine walked back alone to her solitary bed.

Five

William awakened at dawn beside his daughter's cradle, and watched the pale eastern light flow through the cracks and seams of Lundale's ancient walls. At his feet, the long hearth pit glowed warm; smoke curled from the embers past the blackened rafters, up into the narrow slit of night sky at the peak of the roof.

Twenty Lundale folk slept along the hearth, as their fathers had done long ages before the Normans had come to their lands. William frowned as he counted them. Had Catherine not said that the huts clustered outside the palisade gates had been repaired, ready for her tenants' use? Was there some threat or hint of danger that had brought Catherine's people into the hall to sleep?

An arm's length from the far side of the cradle, John snored on his pallet, too far from the keep to watch or even hear the men-at-arms he had sworn to oversee. Hadwen slept beyond him, across the curtained entrance to Lundale's only sleeping chamber; William knew without moving the hangings that Catherine would be there, within earshot of the baby.

The baby.

From the cradle, there was only silence.

William pushed himself up to peer into his child's face and saw that she slept peacefully, her round, perfect face rosy and warm. Little Rose. Rosewitha. The child should have been given a better name, one he could speak easily, one that would come to mind without hesitation. Rosewitha. Little Rose.

When she took the time to consider the matter, Catherine would agree that her daughter was in truth a little Rose, not a child to be burdened with the guttural name of—whatever. William's frown deepened. Before Catherine awoke, he would have to ask John to remind him how to speak that ungainly word his daughter must bear as her name. Once christened, might a child get a new name? A good sum of gold might persuade the abbey priest to change it.

He felt a cold wind rising to pierce the flaws in the near wall; as he brought the blanket up around his shoulders, William recognized Catherine's soft crimson mantle across his knees.

Too late to follow his wife into her bed, and too dirty from his journey to join her there, William folded Catherine's cloak and set it aside.

The bag with his gifts for Catherine—bartered, not taken in booty, he must remember to tell her— lay forgotten beside the saddlepack where he had rested his head for a moment, now many night hours ago. William thrust the small pouch into the saddlepack; later, there would be a good, quiet time to give it to Catherine, and tell her how he had come to find the treasures within.

He stretched his arms above his shoulders, and stopped, mid-yawn, to reflect that he would be here, with Catherine and the child, for all the cold months to come. He would pass Yuletide here, within the ancient, drafty place his wife so loved. William smiled; he would save the gifts to give her then.

With some difficulty William rose to his feet and rubbed the sore leg until the pain retreated; he picked up his saddle pack and made his way in silence past the sleeping forms of Catherine's people, and carried his burden into the bailey yard.

In the early dawn, William heard someone stirring within the grey stone keep. The narrow oaken door was ajar.

The clean, deep well around which Catherine's Norman grandfather had built his small fortress was but a few steps from the unbarred door. Beside it, set in a bed of sand, a brazier glowed hot with a new morning fire. Despite John's neglect, the men of the garrison had kept to the hours William had set them on their arrival last year, and were already out of their beds.

At William's bidding, his men drew water from the well to fill the great cauldron and set it upon the cooking brazier. As it warmed, William returned to the door frame and looked back at the old longhouse where his wife and child slept.

He had come home in good time to move Catherine and the baby into quarters here in the keep. John should have done so as soon as the harvest was in; he was a good man, but seemed too old now to organize the defense of the household. Even now, Catherine and little Rose should be sleeping up in the highest chamber of the tower, where they would be protected from raiders; John should have taken his place on the level below them, where he and three or four stout men could stop an assault from below.

As if beckoned by his lord's doubts, John appeared in the yard and came to join William in the keep; he found a staved tub upended against the wall and summoned two men to move it into place beside the brazier.

John waved a gnarled hand at the cauldron. "Bring more wood. The water here is colder than a witch's smile, and hell's own fires wouldn't boil it beneath an hour." He scowled and turned away to draw his morning ale from a crock upon the table.

William pulled his surcoat over his head, took his place near the brazier. John offered him a cup of ale. "The folk hereabouts may be odd," said John, "but they make decent drink for us."

William smiled to find that John's bad morning humor had survived the years, and displacement to these northern lands. It was one of the few things that had not changed since William's childhood days, so many years ago in Macon.

William looked out the door into the rising morning mist. "I like it here. There were worse places I could have settled."

John lowered his cup. "Well, they had a good

lady here to wed you. Your lady Catherine is a fair woman, and has good sense, when she stops to think before she acts."

What would that good sense have told her, if she had been given a month or two to consider his offer of marriage? With luck and an eye to the Plantagenet's whims, William hoped he would prosper, and never cause his wife to regret her hasty choice.

He turned his mind back to the present. "Why do Catherine and the child sleep in the old hall?"

John made a dismissive gesture. "She won't come here. The chamber up there is ready, and aside from the sentries passing through on their way up to the lookout place, it's never used. She likes the hall, and it's blasted hard to change her mind. About anything."

"She'll be here, both Catherine and the child, before Yuletide." William lowered his voice. "There are reasons, John, to be ready for trouble."

"Those men up at the manor fort?"

"They're part of it. I may have brought trouble home with me, John; there was no way to avoid it."

John sat back and considered William's words. "Ah," he said. "I can guess. Another one of the king's small problems?"

The cauldron began to hiss upon the brazier. William picked up a bucket and began to fill the bathing tub. "Something of the king's making. A problem. Not small." He dipped the bucket back into the steaming water. "Later," he said. "we'll ride out together and I'll tell you all. It's not for the ears

of the garrison. Only you and I, and the men up on
the forest ridge will know why they're here."

William hoisted the bucket and stopped to consider his next thought. "And maybe Catherine," he
said. "Maybe she should know."

John shrugged. "If it's something to do with the
king, best be cautious. That hothead cousin of your
wife's was here twice in the summer, and again yesterday, and may return before the snows come. He
doesn't speak fair of Henry Plantagenet. Remembers the rebellion here, and how the grandfather
died. Catherine listens to him. Maybe too much."

William emptied the bucket into the tub. His
real burdens—the burdens upon his mind and con-
science, felt suddenly heavier at those words. "This
cousin Robert—is he some kind of young rebel,
ready to follow in his forebears' tracks?"

"May be. He doesn't speak when I'm near, but he
has much to say to your lady wife. She will know
what he's thinking. You might ask her." John
drained his cup and set it down. "And then again,
you might not want to."

William began to unwind the bandage from his
leg. "And how does she answer you, when you
speak of the king?"

"She says nothing. Not surprising, after all the
trouble they had here when she was a little lass.
Still, she's happy enough to be back on the land—
most of the time."

William's heart stilled. "And when is she not
happy?"

"She's pretty quiet just after her fool cousin has

been here. Every time he comes to Lundale." John heaved a final bucket into the tub and stood back. "If I were you . . ."

Years ago, William had learned that it paid to listen to John when his voice took on that grim tone. "What?"

John cast his voice lower still. "If I were you I'd watch her cousin's comings and goings, and if he plagues Catherine with plans for vengeance against the king, have him killed before trouble comes."

William looked up. "No. Don't think of it again. You will do nothing without my leave. Do you understand? Catherine has little family of her own left living. If she loses this cousin by our doing, there will never be peace here."

John sighed. "If the fellow becomes a nuisance, there are ways to rid ourselves of him without alarming Catherine."

"No." William lowered himself into the warm water and began to knead his throbbing knee. "Do nothing about him. Don't consider it unless I ask you to. Swear it."

John muttered a string of oaths. "I don't want the madman giving Alflega ideas of treason."

"The child is a few months old. It may be a few years before she turns her mind to armed rebellion," said William.

John did not smile.

William closed his eyes. Catherine had spoken the truth when she had told him that John's world now revolved around the baby. "You realize," he said at last, "that if Catherine's cousin comes to harm, she will remember that you disliked him, and she may want to send you away."

"You'd not stand for that," said John.

"Catherine can be stubborn. Make no trouble with her cousin."

"Until you change your mind."

"Aye," said William. "Until then."

An hour later, as he was peering into a polished buckler and scraping the beard from his face, Catherine came to find him. At the sight of her darkened eyes and pale face, William set down the knife. "Is something wrong?"

She placed a hand across her forehead and caught her breath. "You," said Catherine.

A small thud told him that the boots he had caught up had slipped from his hands. In that moment, he imagined that she had seen into his mind. "Catherine, I didn't mean to bring you trouble—"

"Bring trouble?" She stared at him as if he made no sense. "I saw you were gone, and your saddlepack was not there. I thought you had gone away again."

He touched her shoulder, then took her in his arms as he had wanted to do all these lonely months past. "I would have told you, Catherine, if I had been called away. In truth, did you think I would go without speaking to you?"

She raised her face and stared at his half-shorn jaw. "You did last time. I awoke and you were gone.

I thought I had imagined you there, beside the bed as Alflega was born."

"Catherine, you slept all that next day. I spoke to you, and you wakened long enough to answer."

"I didn't remember."

William traced the corner of her mouth. "I thanked you for our child. And you answered me fair." He paused to catch the memory of it. "When I reached home," he said, "it was the last hour of daylight; I found you were already in great travail. I spoke to you many times through that night. And each time you sent me to the devil."

"I did not. I would never—"

"You did." He smiled at the memory. "Something to do with childbirth, and my part in the cause of it."

Catherine frowned. "I spoke aloud? I suppose I should beg your pardon."

"As I begged Hadwen's pardon, when it was all over and you were safely delivered."

Her eyes lightened at his words. "Oh yes. Hadwen told me you had cursed her for a clumsy trollop when the baby didn't come quickly. She showed me the silver coins you gave her as amends, once Alflega was born and safe in her cradle."

"Aye. She's a fierce soul, and set a high price for forgiveness."

Catherine reached up to touch the scar upon his cheek. "I remember seeing this," she said. "I felt a shadow pass before the fire, and I looked and saw you beside me, with that deep wound on your face."

"I frightened you."

"I feared you were a vision, come to tell me that you had fallen in battle. But then you took my hand and I felt the warmth—of a living man who had survived the blow."

He caught up her hand and kissed it. "And then your pain returned, and you sent me to the devil, whether man or ghost."

She crossed herself, and muttered a swift prayer. "I thank the saints that the devil wasn't listening."

"Curses don't count," said William, "when spoken by a wounded man. Or a woman in childbed."

Catherine's hand returned to trace the scar upon his face. "You rode so far, with such a wound, and heard nothing from me but curses." She looked down at his leg, and stepped back. "And now you are wounded again. I should have looked at that leg yesterday."

He smoothed the clean woolen legging that covered his newest scars. "It doesn't pain me."

Catherine glanced at his saddlepack beside the bathing barrel. "You said you would stay the winter."

"Aye," said William, "we will have the winter. As I rode north, I began to count the days we have had together. They aren't many, Catherine. A week at first—"

"No, only eight days that time."

"—and then a fortnight last summer."

"Twenty-two days in all," said Catherine. "Twenty-one nights. I counted them."

"I would have stayed, had it been my choice."

"I know." Once again, she touched the arrow's path across his face. "One day, the king will send you home for all time. I pray he will do it soon, while you yet live. You have grown enough scars in his wars."

In the past two years of turmoil, he had not dared to dream of coming home for all time, with his limbs intact, and his strength still with him.

Catherine shook her head, as if to dismiss an impossible dream. "We are lucky to have the winter, I think."

"Aye. It's more than I had hoped for." All the summer long, he had thought of Catherine at the end of each day, as he had thanked the fates that he had not met death in battle or ambush. Each time he found refuge or made camp at the end of day, he had welcomed the twilight hour when darkness would come to hide the squalor of war and leave his mind free to dream of the wife he had begun to know. Wondering how she fared, and whether the child had survived. . . .

"It's less than I had prayed for. Much less."

Catherine's words brought his mind back to the present. There was something in her expression that he had not seen before, a kind of sweet sadness. He touched her cheek and pitched his voice to give her heart. "My lady, I'm more a stranger than a husband to you. By springtime, you will know me well. I will hope, as the days pass, that you won't decide to send me to perdition, after all." He drew her back into his arms. "I will make myself so agreeable that you will forget how to curse."

Her eyes narrowed as she considered his words. "You could begin," she said, "by deciding whether you want your beard trimmed the same on both sides of your face." She reached for the small knife, and smiled up at him. "Do you trust me to continue?"

When offered the choice of riding out or staying back at the blazing hearth with Alflega's cradle at his side, John did not hesitate. "Your lady wife will show you all that she and her people have done in the village and about the fields." He looked up at the windy grey sky and shivered. "Hadwen may ask me to watch Alflega instead. It's not a day for my old, aching bones."

William placed a hand on John's shoulder. "Yes," he said. "Please watch over the child."

He walked back into the misted morning and looked up at the grey stone keep rising above the low fog. He had been wrong to leave John in charge of the garrison; he had been more than lucky that there had been no need for the men-at-arms to defend the settlement without a strong sergeant's hand in the planning.

John had aged much in the comfort of the past few seasons at Lundale. Catherine and her women had been generous with the old soldier, allowing him to sit beside the hearth with the child he loved. The king's gift of Lundale to William had given John a place to call home in all the cold winters to come. And Catherine, from what William had observed, had made it possible for John to accept that comfort in good grace.

He told her so as they rode out together into the morning mists.

"John does help," she said. "And he knows better than anyone how to keep Alflega from fretting when I'm not there. And he does go over to the keep once each day to speak to the men-at-arms."

"I'll need to find someone else before I go; whoever he may be, he'll have to answer to John in some way, to keep the peace. We will need them both, to protect the settlement when I can't be here."

Catherine looked at him with an odd expression in her gaze. "Have you ever imagined," she said, "that you might tell the king that you're finished with war?"

He laughed. "Ah, that would be a strange day."

"Will you wait, then, until you're as old as John, or until the king is too old to fight?"

"Henry Plantagenet will never be too old to fight. But one day, before I'm crippled from it, I'll give up fighting for the king."

Catherine pointed to his leg. "You're already on your way to such a state. Will you not consider staying home from the new war in Wales?"

He smiled at her through the mist. "I might be tempted."

"You must be tempted."

"Aye," he said. "I look forward to your efforts."

She smiled back. "I'll do my best."

The land had ceased to seethe from the stubble fires, but the lingering warmth of the dark earth in the cold of morning gave forth mist into the air.

The low ground fog brought to mind the seas that William had crossed from Normandy to England and back again each time King Henry had needed a message taken to Winchester.

Thinking of those sea voyages and swift runs across Kent and to the west, Catherine's words came back to him. Was there a reason why Henry Plantagenet had chosen a man of similar height and coloring to carry his messages in the royal flagship, riding the fine mounts Henry kept in royal stables along the English roads? In the winter to come, he would think on it, and take Catherine into his confidence on the matter.

On the other matter, the much more frightening task he had ahead, he might have to do without Catherine's wit to help him. It would be a hard thing to do. William frowned. It would be harder still to keep John from quarreling with Catherine's testy cousin.

"Sad thoughts, William?"

He shook his head. "I'll not waste the day with them."

William looked up and about them. The ground fog was deep and white and moved in the morning breeze. Catherine seemed to float upon the billowed whiteness as she rode at his side.

"Not the best day to see the fields," she said.

"I can see where you have had the land cleared. The open fields are larger, now. How did you do it, with so few men to work?"

"There were more who came out of the forest in summertime, and left when the harvest was in."

From the middle of the fields, William could see the forest surrounding Lundale on all sides except to the south. There, the broad-banked river curved beneath the ridge that marked the end of Lundale, and the beginning of Catherine's lost dower lands. William could see no sign of passage, no obvious track through the great trees, save where the road passed through at the fording place, and where it entered the forest once again to continue north. "Which part of the forest do they use, when your people run from Lundale?"

"They don't run from Lundale, William. They're not fugitives. We—my father—never forbade them to winter where they wished. Some feel safer in the forest, where raiders don't go." She cast a cautious glance at him. "The soldiers who have taken over the old forest house should know that the people in the greenwood are not law breakers."

William's heart sank. "There are some of your people wintering near the old house?"

Catherine shrugged. "They make their huts where they will. I don't search for them, or spy upon them. More of them will move back to the village if they come to believe that the king won't come back to fight here. The old ones," she said, "remember that many died on the day Henry Plantagenet came to fight my grandfather."

"So they won't like to see forty men-at-arms wintering at the forest house."

With a small, swift movement Catherine turned her mare about to face William. "Please send the king's men elsewhere. To a town. Nottingham always needs soldiers on market days, and the abbey might take a few to keep the road thieves away from travelers. Please send them where they won't frighten away my tenants."

"I can't. The king wants them here."

"—Because he doesn't know what a burden they will be to us. What will they do, up there at the edge of the forest? Why would the king want them wintering in such a place?"

"Catherine, there are reasons."

"Yes?"

"You'll know them later. In springtime. Before I take the men back to Shrewsbury, to join the king's army to go into Wales."

There was a long silence. "You don't trust me," said Catherine.

"If all goes well, you'll have your dower lands back from the king."

She would not be turned from her suspicions. "Tell me why they must stay there, in that unlikely place, for the winter. Tell me why. If you trust me."

If he had wanted an easy wife, a comfortable wife, he would not have wed himself to this swift, stubborn mind. She was right to press him so. Henry Plantagenet should have allowed her to take back her mother's dower lands two years ago, when she had wed a man in whom the king had placed his trust. How could he expect her to accept forty dangerous strangers living across the river from Lundale's fields? And how could she order her people away from the manor if she had no reason to give, nothing to tell them?

William drew a long breath. "Catherine, if you will swear never to speak of this to your people—not even to Hadwen, or to the folk who live nearest that old house—then I will tell you one of the reasons."

She sat straight in her saddle and watched him as he spoke. "I swear I won't speak of it, not even to Hadwen. Nor to John."

He hadn't the heart to tell her that John already knew all he was about to tell her. And that John had heard much more—so many things that Catherine must never know.

A distant sound, and a sudden prickling upon his neck sent William's hand to his sword.

Far across the fields of mist came a rider at dangerous speed.

"Behind me," William said. "Catherine, get behind me."

He drew his sword and held it aloft, half-doubting that the hurtling figure was mortal, skimming as it did so swift above the low fog, heedless of the rough ground beneath the hooves of its dark steed.

A flash of steel came into the rider's hand. Whether mortal or spirit, the dark figure had the means to do mortal harm. "Run, Catherine. Ride away." William moved forward to meet the rider; living man or angry ghost, it would not get past him to reach Catherine.

Six

"Get behind me," William said again.

Catherine turned and saw a solitary horseman riding above the banks of fog, moving towards her at a dangerous speed across the burnt earth.

She hauled her mount around and saw that William had drawn his sword and raised it high above his head.

The dark figure moved forward, low upon the black steed's neck, heedless of William's bellowed warning. At his side, the bright silver of a blade cut an unfaltering path above the low, smoke-laden mist.

Somewhere in the white distance behind Catherine, there was shouting from Lundale's palisade.

William glanced behind him. "Ride away, Catherine. Ride for the gates and close them behind you."

"No. Come with me. William, you're injured. You can't fight—"

The horseman rose in the saddle and cried out.

Catherine gasped. "William, it might be—"

"No time, Catherine— Run, damn you. Ride—"

The rider shouted once again across the narrowing distance between them.

It was Robert. Hot-headed Robert, riding too fast in the mist.

Bad-tempered Robert—with a sword in his hand. Robert had seen William's weapon, and must have thought the worst.

William moved his horse ahead, blocking her view of Robert, and spurred forward.

"Stop," she cried. "It's Robert! William, no!"

With an effort that sent clods of earth flying above the low mist, William wheeled his mount back to face her. "Who?"

Catherine kicked her mare and shot past William to stop Robert's unflagging charge. "Idiot," she screamed. "Go back."

Robert's mount swerved aside, then circled back upon her. A stream of curses and hoofbeats behind her told Catherine that William was once more on the attack.

Words would not stop either of them. Not now.

Once again Robert came in her direction, his eyes fixed upon William, murder in his face. At the last moment, as Robert hurtled past, she seized his surcoat with both her hands and set him off balance.

Empty saddled, Robert's mount trotted past William toward Lundale's gates.

A stinging pain shot up Catherine's arm. She gathered her reins but could not seem to hold them. She looked down and saw that one small finger was jutting out where it should not be. Puzzled, she willed it to go back.

It did not.

"William! . . ."

Her husband was a short distance away, his dark gaze focused upon Robert where he lay sprawled upon the ground. William's sword was leveled at Robert's throat.

The long blade wavered as William looked up and saw Catherine's face.

It was important, she knew, to speak clearly before the sick darkness closed in about her. "He's my cousin," she said.

She saw the sword fly far into the mist, flung aside as William shouted her name.

The gates of Lundale moved past her vision. She turned her face back to William's dark crimson surcoat and rested her head upon his shoulder. "My cousin Robert," she said. It was important to get the words right.

"I know," said William. "Your cousin Robert. Now don't move. I'm going to get us down now."

She raised her head and saw that Radulf and Osbert were dragging a sawhorse across the bailey yard. William muttered orders to them as they positioned the narrow frame near his stirrups.

"They cannot understand," Catherine said.

"Hush," said William. "Close your eyes."

"No," she insisted. "They cannot understand you. None of them do. Speak to me, and I'll speak to them."

He growled one more order, then sighed and looked down into her eyes. "Tell them to bring the bench closer, and be ready to catch you if I fall."

The yard spun about her as she looked down at Radulf's bright copper pate. "Stand still," she said.

Radulf frowned twice, once in each of his faces. "Tell the lord to let go and we'll bring you down safe."

Hadwen's two heads appeared between Radulf's faces. Catherine smiled in relief; Hadwen could speak Norman words. "Lord William," said Hadwen, "you have a bad leg. Let my lamb down and these lads will catch her."

"Her finger is broken," said William.

"Well, that won't make her any harder to carry," Hadwen said. "Now give up this nonsense about the bench and let the lads bring her down."

Slowly the ground drew nearer, yet William's arms did not relinquish their warm grasp of her waist. Then young Radulf appeared beside her, only one of him, and she came to rest upon his pungent, sweaty arms. Her own arm—the left one, with the chilly, sick tingling coursing through the wrist—remained in William's hold.

Hadwen stepped forward to support that arm, and a moment later William was beside her as well. "I can walk," Catherine said.

"Of course," said William. And lifted her against his chest.

Something was wrong.

William stopped walking. "Where does it hurt?"

Catherine raised her head and looked around the bailey yard. There were fewer people now, each of them with only one face. "Where is Robert?"

"He's coming," said William. And carried her through the doorway into the hall.

"How?" said Catherine. "His horse ran away."

They passed John as he dozed beside Alflega's cradle. "Let them both sleep," said William. "The baby is pretty rough with fingers."

He was trying to distract her. "Where is Robert? Is no one helping him? The garrison men should go—"

"He's walking," said William. He brought her into the sleeping chamber and set her down upon the bed. Hadwen appeared at his side and began to mutter in a low voice.

"Is he injured?"

William and Hadwen seemed to have more important matters to discuss. At last, William turned back to her and placed his hands on either side of her face. "What did you ask?"

She looked straight into his eyes. "My cousin Robert. Was he injured when he fell?"

"No."

She felt Hadwen's hands upon her arm. "Look at me," said William. "Your cousin is walking here. Should be here by sunset, at the rate he's moving."

"William! You must send someone to . . ."

With a small, sudden pressure, Hadwen pushed the errant finger back into its place. Catherine gasped and forced her head around to see Hadwen binding the fingers, straight once again, onto a narrow board. The pain was greater now, but the sickness was gone.

"Now lie down," said Hadwen.

"Not until you send for Robert. He fell."

"Lie down and sleep. I'll get him," said William.

"Not you. Anyone but you."

He waited until she had her head on the pillow, then pulled a coverlet over her. "No one but me," said William. "I'll go out and get him, and treat him as gently as he deserves."

Catherine groaned.

William touched her forehead and leaned down to whisper in her ear. "I'll treat him well because he's your cousin," he said. "Robert will have his second chance."

She pulled her good hand from beneath the coverlet and caught Hadwen's skirt. "Follow him, and keep him from killing Robert."

Hadwen raised her grey brows. "I'll send one of those useless layabouts from the garrison."

"No. You. You'll keep him from killing Robert."

"I could."

Catherine sank back into the bed. "Keep him from hurting Robert, and keep Robert from stabbing him if there's a quarrel. And tell me," she said, "every word they speak to each other. Every word."

"Every word," said Hadwen. And left her to sleep.

"Now don't you worry about the baby. John never lets her out of his sight until bedtime anyway. And your lord is right—Alflega likes to play with fingers," said Hadwen.

"Then sit down and tell me what happened out there."

Hadwen set her mouth in a line of exasperation. "Well, I did as you said, and put on my pattens and went out there to walk through the wet ashes and ruin my second-best leggings," she said. "Your horse had come back and Lord William was halfway across the field by the time I left, and I saw Robert coming this way, dragging two swords."

"Oh, no."

"His sword, and the one your lord left out there. So Lord William walks up to him and takes one of the swords and starts to walk beside Robert. I was too far away to catch what they were saying, but young Robert was not looking too feisty and he was carrying a load of mud on his backside." Hadwen paused. "I guess your Lord William thought Robert was poor game, in that condition, and didn't give him many nasty words."

"Thank the saints," Catherine said.

"Well, the saints had better spend some time at board with your Lord William this night, for Robert has bathed and borrowed dry clothes from John, and he's looking a little more like himself."

"Oh dear." Catherine looked at the doorway. The hangings were tightly drawn across the opening. "How late is it?"

"Almost nightfall. There's pottage and mutton for you. Robert hasn't eaten yet either."

"Will you help me? I'd better go out there before they sit down together."

Hadwen nodded. "Aye, if the saints don't have time to watch over them, you'll have to do it."

Catherine placed her bound hand upon the bed

and climbed out onto the floor, and stood balanced against the door frame as Hadwen slipped her shoes onto her feet. "Your kirtle didn't get muddy," said Hadwen. "Lord William caught you up before you fell out of the saddle." A sly smile appeared upon her face. "And it is your almost-best kirtle, isn't it—worn for your lord's homecoming? So you won't want to change it for another."

Hadwen opened the clothing chest and brought out a creamy linen coif to set upon Catherine's hair. "There," she said. "You look as you should."

Alflega was the first to see her emerge from the sleeping chamber. At the sound of her daughter's cackled greetings, Catherine held out her good arm to take her child from John.

John shrugged and pointed down the long board; his lap was empty.

Alflega was perched upon her father's knee, her small feet drumming against his shins. Across the board, Robert sat before a trencher piled high with roast mutton, his ale cup drawn near. Before him stretched an untidy row of crumbly spheres that Catherine recognized as bits of trencher bread, ruined to amuse Alflega.

She took her place at William's side and smiled across the table at Robert. "I remember," she said, "that you did the same for me when I was a child and you scarce older." Catherine pushed the nearest tiny ball into the others, sending them back across to Robert. Alflega crowed in delight, and waved her fists to demand another round.

Hadwen placed a round of trencher bread before Catherine, and brought a dish of mutton from the fireside. "Welcome back," said William. He persuaded Alflega not to throw herself into Catherine's lap, and offered the child his own bread to amuse her.

Catherine glanced at the faces of her men—the cousin she had known as a child, and the husband she had only begun to know. There was no sign of animosity between them, nor was there the kind of easy fellowship she hoped one day to see.

Robert raised his cup and smiled across the board, as if he had heard Catherine's thoughts. "Sorry, Catherine. Sorry to break your hand."

A small growl at Catherine's side was the only hint that her husband found Robert's words inadequate.

"I did it myself," she said. "I'm sure that if I had stayed away from the two of you, you would have been clever enough to realize that you shouldn't kill each other."

"Which of us was the idiot?"

"Why do you ask, Robert?" Would he not see her frown, and avoid this dangerous teasing?

William looked down at Alflega's restless feet, ignoring the question.

"When you rode out between us, you called someone an idiot."

"I don't remember. All I recall," said Catherine, "was that it was not difficult to topple you from your saddle. This business of fighting," she said, "might be easier than men will admit."

William reached for her right hand and raised it to his lips. "Don't try that particular move again.

I'd hate to see you hurt another finger." Alflega looked up at the sight of her mother's hand at William's mouth, and offered her own. Her father showed her the same courtesy, and won a dribbling smile from the child.

"I agree," said Robert. "Swear to us both that you'll not take up arms."

"If you both swear you'll keep peace between you."

There was a silent moment, then a quiet word of assent from both sides of the board. Catherine filled the moments after that with talk of small matters and praise for Alflega's wordless chatter. It was a beginning, she thought, that Robert and William would drink together at the same board. With luck, they would keep the peace they had sworn.

At the end of the board, John set down his cup and leaned forward. "What brings you back, Robert? I thought you were riding south, all the way to Winchester."

In the confusion of Robert's arrival and the setting of her broken hand, Catherine had not thought to ask him. She raised her head and saw that Robert's face had flushed dull red.

He bowed that darkened face in William's direction. "I'd not break peace between us by speaking of this, but Catherine should know that in the marketplace at Nottingham there was talk of you, William de Macon. Rumors that you had brought a small army north with you."

"I see."

Robert drank from his ale and continued. "I looked about this afternoon, but saw no sign of more men-at-arms. If the rumors are true, the men were not brought north to protect this small place; you must have an encampment somewhere not far from Nottingham."

"Why did you return?"

Robert set his cup down with a little more force than courtesy allowed. "To warn Catherine, of course. This family cannot survive a rebellion, or the smallest hint of treason."

"I knew," Catherine said. "William told me about the soldiers when he returned. He keeps them in the old manor this winter, for the king's sake. Robert, there is nothing wrong here."

William's hands remained still and loose about Alflega's small body. "For the sake of this family," he said, "do not speak of rebellion anywhere near this place. There are no rebels. There is no treason. If you hear such rumors, Robert, kill them. They grow from the speech of fools."

Robert's gaze did not stray from William's face. "I understand," he said at last. "If I should hear other rumors, I will return, and tell you what they are."

"You are always welcome, Robert. With or without such tidings."

He turned his gaze to Catherine. "Your hand is broken, yet you welcome me still?"

"Of course."

William beckoned John and set his child in the old man's arms. He turned back to Robert and raised his drinking cup. "Why should you leave? Do you have duties in Winchester?"

Robert's eyes narrowed. "No. I hoped to offer my

sword to King Henry. Our family—Catherine's and mine—have been too long outside the king's grace."

In silence, William drank the last of his ale. "The king left Winchester last month," he said at last. "Some say he will have a Christmas court at Marlborough. Others expect he will be in the borders, treating with allies for the coming war. The king himself changes his plans on the whim of a moment. Men who wish to find him, even those who know him well, have often crossed England twice or thrice, trying to catch up with him."

Robert reached for the ale jug and filled William's drinking cup. "You must know where to find him. He has given you forty of his fiercest men to keep for the winter."

"Is that what they say?"

Robert nodded. "They said forty. Dangerous ones, from the looks of them. And a baggage train of eleven carts. And some women."

William took up the cup. "If you stay here for the winter, I'll bring you with me when the war starts in the springtime. On one condition."

Robert slouched back from the table. "What?"

"This winter you stay here in Lundale to protect Catherine, and leave the king's men to themselves. Don't go near them. If you do, they may mistake you for a spy."

Robert leaned forward and looked into Catherine's eyes. "Will you not ask your husband, Catherine, to tell the king's men that, as your cousin, I have the right to go wherever I please on these lands?"

Catherine felt the new-forged peace failing before her eyes. "The manor lands—my mother's dower lands—are the king's property now, taken away from me when Grandfather rebelled. You have no rights—and I have no right—to go there."

William placed his hands upon the board. "Rights or no rights, I can promise you that if you stay clear of those soldiers and let them use the lands as they wish this winter, there is a good chance that the king will be pleased, and one day give you the land back. If there's trouble this winter, Henry Plantagenet will do something else." He looked from Robert to Catherine. "The king has troubles, this season, with his bishops. And an invasion of Wales to plan. Pray he doesn't give your dower lands to some new order of monks to live there and pray for him these next few years."

He turned to Catherine. "You have not eaten. Be at peace, and I'll cut your meat for you. Your cousin and I will now speak of small things. Peaceful things."

A moment later, when she had given up the effort to show interest in cold mutton, William rose and placed her bandaged hand upon his arm. Together they walked to the deep curtain hanging before the sleeping chamber. Behind them in the hall, Alflega slept in Hadwen's arms. And Robert watched them every step of the way, until the curtain swung closed.

Seven

Hadwen had dressed the bed in good linen from the abbey looms, and spread coverlets of wool upon it. Beneath the coverlet, wrapped in wide strips of close-woven fleece, were river stones, heated at the hearth and brought to the chamber a scarce hour ago.

"Leave them there," said William. "You'll be cold tonight."

Catherine's heart stopped. "Will you not be here?"

Her bandaged hand still rested upon his arm. He touched her arm, smoothing the sleeve of the kirtle back from her wrist. "I'll be here to warm you, but the hot stones will help. Broken bones chill your blood."

Catherine had noticed imperfections in the line of his powerful sword arm, and had seen that one gauntlet had been made for a less than perfect hand. "You would know," she said.

"Many times over." He thrust his hand into the light of the chamber's single taper. "John set this for me. Twice. He has a good eye for it."

Catherine shuddered. "I don't want to have that

particular pain ever again. The second time you must have known what was coming."

He led her to the bed. "Don't think on it, and it will never happen."

"Does that work?"

He waited until she was seated on the edge of the coverlets, then turned to rummage through his saddlepack. "For you, it may. For me, broken hands are part of war." He returned to her with a battered leather flask.

"I remember that," said Catherine. "Brandywine."

He took out the wooden plug and offered it to her. "You'll sleep better."

"I remember that too." She drank a shallow draught. "That night—later that night—I slept so deeply. . . ."

"I'll not forget it. Ever."

She offered back the flask. "Before that night, in all the first eight days we were here together, I had begun to think you didn't want me."

William smiled. "Then I'm a better liar than I thought. Would you have forgiven me if I had taken you that first night, when, only hours before, you had expected to live your life in the abbey?"

"Not the first night. But when eight days passed and you left me here with only a kiss good-bye, I thought you had decided to give me back."

"After you had scoured the forest for your old tenants, and beaten the spiders and mice from the hall? You must have thought me ungrateful."

"You must have thought me a terrible sight, after days of fighting the cobwebs."

He leaned forward and kissed her. Slowly. With a touch so gentle she might have imagined it. "I'll help you with the kirtle," he said.

She raised her good hand to pull the knot from her laces.

"I'll do that." He loosened each narrow strand in the web of her laces, then began to untie the smaller knots that held her sleeves to the robe. He traced the seam above her bandaged wrist. "This one will have to go by the knife," he said, and brought the taper near as he worked Hadwen's small stitches free from the cloth of her left sleeve.

He did not offer to remove her chemise. Instead, he drew back the coverlet and placed a bolster at her side, to bear the weight of the splint upon her wrist. And moved the softly wrapped hot stones about her feet. "Sleep now," he said.

"Leave the taper burning."

He shrugged. "As you wish."

He rose to his feet and pulled the tunic from his shoulders. By the light of the candle, Catherine could see no new scars crossing the deep muscles of his chest.

William lay down beside her, and pulled the covers over them both. He had not removed his chausses.

Between them, Catherine's injured hand throbbed upon the bolster.

"Now I regret my vow," said William.

She raised her head. "Which vow?"

With great care, he reached over her splint to touch her cheek. "Not the marriage vow," he said, "but the oath I made to keep peace with your lout of a cousin." William settled back and placed his hands beneath his head. "If your cousin hadn't come back, your hand wouldn't be broken and we would be together in every way. The whole night through."

Catherine felt the blood sing in her veins. "I'm not as I was," she said.

Beyond the bolster, she heard a soft snort. "True enough, with your hand broken, and tied into splints."

"No, it's more. After the baby—"

He sat up then. "Are you ill? Were you hurt in birthing the child?"

"No. I lost my milk when the fevers came last summer—"

"Then you were ill."

"No more than the others. Hadwen found a tenant's wife who didn't catch the fever, and brought her here to nurse Alflega. She's one of the women who set up their looms in the hall. She's clean, and has milk enough for two—"

"Good. Now tell me what's wrong with you."

"My body is ugly now."

He closed his eyes, and dropped back upon the mattress. "You had me frightened for a moment." He raised his hand placed it lightly upon her splints. "Aside from this, your body must be as it was. You look the same to me as you did when we wed."

"My belly is covered in purple scars. It's worse than your chest, William."

"Ah. Then it must be unsightly."

"It's not funny."

"Of course." He ceased his laughter, and reached once again to stroke her face. "I want you, Catherine. In Normandy, I thought of you each night, and imagined coming home to you, and holding you the night through." He sighed. "If not for your oaf of a cousin—"

"It's not Robert's fault."

William sighed again. "I shouldn't have drawn my sword. But if I had not, and if the rider had turned out to be the first in a band of raiders, it would have gone badly for us." He lay down again and crossed his legs. "We were both idiots. As you said."

"And I was foolish to ride between the two of you. But if you had harmed him, or he had hurt you, I—"

"You're weeping? Catherine, don't cry. Or I'll give your cousin the drubbing he deserves."

Her tears became laughter.

Above her, in the light of the taper, he was smiling that crooked way she remembered. "The brandywine is stronger than I thought," he said.

She smiled back. "William, if you want me, there should be a way—"

"Not tonight. It's too soon."

"You must want another child. A son."

"Must I?"

She hesitated. "I want another. Many others."

"This, from the woman who says she couldn't

survive the pain of a second broken bone. In truth, you are eager to go through childbirth again?"

"I don't remember the pain. Not really."

"I do," he said. "Catherine, we have the whole winter before us to make a child. We'll wait."

"Until my hand is whole again?" She moved it slightly and grimaced at the sensation. "That will be years from now."

"We'll see when you can move it without fainting. That would be a start."

"Then our nights," she said, "will be for talking. Tell me about the soldiers at the forest house."

"You have a sense," said William, "of when to attack. When your opponent is distracted, you make your move. Remind me to take you with me when I go off to war."

"And you have a sense of how to cloud your opponent's mind with distractions of your own. Will you not answer my questions, William? Tell me about the soldiers. Why will you keep them up there in the forest?"

"They aren't here because it would be dangerous for everyone. I had no choice, Catherine, when the king asked me to take them north for the winter."

"They were fighting for King Henry in the borders? Fighting the Welsh?"

"Some of them."

The ease had gone out of William's voice. As had the warmth. "Something happened," said Catherine. "Something happened in the borders, and you had to take them away."

She caught the sibilance of a whispered oath.

"Yes," he said at last. "Something happened. I wasn't there, and know little about it. And what I know, I am sworn to keep secret. For the sake of these people, and for Alflega's sake, do not ask me more. And keep your foolish cousin from prowling about and spreading rumors."

Catherine sank back into the warmth of the bed and considered all that William had said. Never before, even in their first days together, had he seemed such a stranger.

The silence grew between them. "Thank you," whispered Catherine, "for offering Robert a place with us this winter."

A brief sigh sounded beyond the bolster. "I did it for your sake, Catherine, but there was another reason. Robert's mind is already stirred with suspicions of me, and had he gone back to Nottingham he might have encouraged the rumors. I don't want him to leave here before springtime. It's better that I have him where I can keep him out of trouble."

"What would you have done if he hadn't agreed to stay?"

William yawned. "Well, I would have picked a man from the garrison and sent him to follow Robert as far as the far edge of the forest—"

"No. You wouldn't have—"

"—and told him to cross Robert's path before he reached Nottingham—"

"I cannot believe that you would—"

"—armed with a rumor that I have given the forest house into the keeping of Scots, every man of them a spy for an invading army. Robert would be back within the day, demanding to see you. And I would need only close the gates behind him."

It was impossible to tell, from William's sleep-laden voice, whether he was in earnest. "You can imagine doing that?"

"It's better than bloodshed." He yawned again and pulled the coverlet closer.

"Robert can be loyal," Catherine said.

Nothing but the low sound of William's breathing answered her words. She closed her eyes against the candle's light, and slept.

Eight

It was not an honest thing to do, but neither was it disloyal. And it was, in the very roots of all she remembered from the old days, a thing that must not be neglected.

Osbert had carved the small apple from wind-fallen oak, just as his father had taught him to. Just as he would one day teach his son Radulf. The lady saint who watched over the forest spring would be waiting for the carving, as she had done each winter, at the time of the longest night, since the forest had first come into the world.

In the old days, before Henry Plantagenet's many swords had cut down the settlement at Lundale, there would have been many people walking to the holy well, bearing this small, all-important gift to the lady. With some difficulty, Catherine had persuaded Osbert and the other old ones that in these strange times, with the village at the beginning of its second settlement and armed strangers in the manor house, only one person should bear the lady's gift across the river, up into the forest, and to the well.

Catherine walked from the village along the

near edge of the fields, the carved shape of an apple within the pouch tied into the belt at her waist. She paused along the way to look back and wave at Osbert, who watched her from the low doorway of his hut.

It was nothing more than luck, and the benediction of the lady, Osbert had said, that the day was mild. There was no snow to mark Catherine's progress to the forest. And William, who would have stopped her from going, had already gone up to the ridge to oversee the settlement of soldiers, as he had done each second day since he had returned from the wars.

Radulf had objected to Catherine's plan, and said that it was cowardly of his father and the others to let their own lady risk Lord William's displeasure by going into the forest. And would the lady of the holy well be pleased that the solitary pilgrim this winter was herself injured, carrying the offering, and casting it into the waters with a damaged hand?

Last night as these matters had unfolded, Catherine had put a stop to the argument by promising to carry the wooden offering in her good hand, and never to touch it with the other. And she countered Radulf's outrage at her own choice as bearer by threatening that she would tell Lord William if any others walked before her, or tried to walk with her. "What would the lady of the well think if Lord William found us there and spoke angry words over the water?" She had paused to let her words soften Osbert's stubborn resolve, then went on to say that of all people in Lundale, she was the only one who might, if found at the well, be able to deflect Lord William's anger. As she spoke those last words, Catherine had crossed two fingers of her good hand behind her skirts; it was a necessary lie, a small sin.

Though Osbert would not be able to see her after she reached the top of the slope beyond the river, Catherine would not cheat and bury the little wooden apple at the edge of the forest rather than take it all the way to the spring waters. Last year at this time, she had made the pilgrimage with the villagers and had asked the lady's help when it came time to bear the child she had carried beneath her heart. From that day, Catherine had ceased to fear the future, and she had gone to childbed with an eerie certainty that William would survive his war and return to see his child born.

And so it had happened. Alflega had appeared as she should, healthy and pink as a little rose, and somewhere in the middle of the night of her travail, Catherine had looked up to see William at her side. The mark upon his face, showing how close he had come to death, was yet another sign that the lady had heard Catherine's prayers to protect William and his child.

The priest from the abbey had come to Lundale at Yuletide, a fortnight after the procession to the well, and blessed them all. He had said nothing of the old tradition he had mocked in years past nor did he question Lundale's people about that year's procession. Osbert had told the priest, during the long years following the Plantagenet killings at Lundale, that if the folk at the abbey had not opposed the pilgrimage to the lady's well, Lundale might not have fallen into bad times.

The villagers and Catherine herself had taken the priest's silence as a sign he had come to agree with Osbert, and forgiven them all for their attention to a lady who existed outside his universe.

Catherine reached the riverbanks and looked west, to the fording place, to be sure that neither William nor his soldiers were there to observe her. She dared not cross the water at that broad, shallow place where the waters barely rose above the road. Instead, she descended the bank to the secret place where only a few souls knew to cross. The river was narrow, running deep and dangerous for most of its course. The water flowed swift and cold in this stretch of the river, but there was a place, a single line of large rocks close beneath the surface, where a man could ride his horse straight across without swimming. On foot, a man could walk across with the water well below his knees. There was a trick to staying on that line of stones, a trick that had saved Catherine's life, and Robert's, long ago when they were children and the Plantagenet had brought his soldiers to Lundale.

Catherine walked along the shore of the river until she saw the great, heavy oak that she sought on the far side of the water. Was it the right one? Had the right one fallen in all these years past, and had a wrong one grown enough to resemble the other? She stood opposite the oak, turned to look behind her and expelled a breath of relief. The other marker, a great white stone jutting out from the slope of the riverbank to form a mossy shelf, was there. Once she knew where to look, it was right where it should be.

She threw the hem of her cloak up over her shoulders and held the skirts of her kirtle and tunic about her knees, and waded into the water. Her sheepskin boots slickened in the water, but would keep her from cutting her feet on the rocks. It would be easier to explain sopping boots, if William noticed them, than it would be to convince him that she had cut her feet in the course of a day at Lundale.

Catherine gained confidence as she crossed the water, and imagined that she remembered the place of each bridging stone and how it felt. As she had been taught, she never looked down to see the water racing past the rocks that supported her. Sooner than she expected, the water shallowed and she stepped from the river.

Without pause, she gathered her skirts higher and made her way through the soft earth below the marking oak, and walked up the short, steep slope to the ridge.

Her feet were cold, but not yet numb. Though she intended all proper respect to the lady of the well, Catherine did not wish to tarry; she looked about her, remembering the landmarks that would lead her to the unmarked spring.

One day, the abbey priest had suggested that Catherine should build a chapel at the well, to remind her people that the lady of the water must be a saint known to the church. She had turned away the question with words of regret that she could not afford to build a chapel in this remote place, so far from Lundale's hall. When she had gold enough to make a chapel, she would build it where her people could use it every day.

Those were the words she had given the priest. The truth of it was something more: Osbert and the others had assured her that the lady of the well did not wish to have shelter made by the hand of man to mark the holy place. And that, Catherine understood, must be the end of the matter.

The great forest rose before her. Behind Catherine, the light of day shone from the open space about the river. Ahead, shadows crossed shadows beneath the leafless oaks. The unburdened boughs, darker than the earth itself, formed a tangled canopy, restless in the rising wind.

Catherine's feet were numb now; if she stumbled, she might fall upon her broken hand, and damage it despite the splints. With dawning irreverence, Catherine wished the lady of the waters had been a little more tolerant of mortal efforts to mark the location of the spring. Once again, Catherine thought back to luck she had enjoyed in the past year, and dismissed the small voice at the back of her mind that urged her to set the little offering beneath a likely tree and rush back to Lundale before her feet turned to ice.

She walked along the edge of the forest, secure in her recollection that the spring would be found within sight of the river's edge. The old forest house, the manor that had been the dowry lands of long-dead Lundale wives, was much farther south, deep within this forest, so far distant that sentries on watch at the gates would never see her. Nevertheless, Catherine stayed close to the river so she would know which way to retreat if she heard trouble approaching.

At last, the way along the border of the forest became easier as a deer passage widened into a path. And moments later, the dense forest to the south revealed another passage, and an ivy-swathed tree, much larger than the others. This was the place.

Catherine walked south towards the ivy tree, crushing deep rustling leaves of seasons past beneath her trembling feet. There, in a small clearing sheltered by massed oaks and holly bushes, overlooked by the tallest tree, was the lady's holy well.

The wind stopped as Catherine approached, and there was silence about her as she knelt upon the wide stone that bordered the spring. The moss had grown deep and soft upon the flat slab, as if made to welcome the knees of the lady's pilgrims.

Faithful to her promise, Catherine stretched an arm high to hold her injured hand away from her body, and with her good hand she opened the pouch at her waist and drew forth the carved offering from the village. With a short prayer and slow reverence, Catherine placed the wooden apple upon the waters of the spring, and watched as it bobbed on the surface, and floated free. Catherine thought that she saw a tint of red upon the carving, as if it had become a real apple, red and full in late summer. When she looked again, the carving had paled, and begun to disappear beneath the ledge of rock on the far side of the well.

The wind began once again to blow through the forest.

If she had not looked up at that moment, she might not have seen the drifting robes of a figure beyond the well, far away, in the deeper forest. Catherine bolted to her feet and looked again.

Was it the lady herself, come to take up the offering Catherine had left? And was she offended that only one pilgrim had brought the offering? If Osbert were here, or Hadwen. . . .

Catherine clutched her injured hand to her heart and stepped back. In the far distance, the lady moved on, her robes floating in the cold but mortal wind that reached Catherine's face. The woman was not moving towards the holy spring.

An instant later, Catherine was behind the great oak, holding her own cloak close against her body, her face turned to watch the progress of the likely mortal woman who was walking south and east, in the direction of the old manor, with ten very likely mortal men-at-arms at her heels.

She was flesh, not spirit. And she was walking slowly, turning her head from one side to the other, as if she did not need to travel far. As if the ten armed men behind her did not mind the slow pace, or her wandering lack of direction. The wind turned north, and gusted harder. The woman halted and gathered her green mantle closer about her.

In that moment, Catherine saw the reason for the lady's pace. She was heavy with child. She was with child, and she was walking toward the old forest house, in the company of the soldiers William had forbidden Catherine to approach.

They were too far away to hear Catherine's gasp. Still, she covered her mouth lest the north wind carry the sound to the soldiers, and did not move from her hiding place until the lady and the last of the soldiers had disappeared from sight.

She sank down to sit with her back to the ancient tree, and regarded her wet boots and benumbed feet with concern. If she slipped on the way back across the river and returned to Lundale wet and half-frozen, William would guess where she had been, and if he looked into her eyes, he would know that she had discovered the thing he would not tell her, the unspoken reason why he had taken a small army into the forest and forbidden her and her people to go there.

Catherine rose to her feet and began to walk back to the river edge of the forest.

The lady she had watched was no camp follower, no soldier's woman brought north to cook for the men-at-arms, to warm a soldier's bed. The cloth of her cloak had been wide—no peasant's cloak would have blown so broad in the wind. And the color of it was no dull thing boiled from herbs and roots; it was a clear, clean green. The color of springtime, to be drawn from a city weaver's store of dried flowers and herbs from foreign lands.

Even if the lady had worn the poor, rough cloak of a peasant woman, Catherine would have seen that she was a woman of consequence. She had walked at her own pace, and paused when she wished, and the soldiers had followed her every move in silence. They were in her service, it seemed, and owed her much respect.

The child, then—the child soon to be born of that woman—was no common soldier's get.

"William." Her voice sounded young and weak to her ears. "William, what trouble is this?" She repeated the question that she would not dare speak to her husband when she returned to Lundale. And how would she manage in his company to keep the question from her face, from her manner, and from the dreams she might speak as she slept beside him?

Save the single night he had spent in Lundale when she was in childbed, William had been absent from her for more than a year. And that single fortnight when they had lived as man and wife had receded into the past too swiftly in these seasons of war and uncertainty.

William must have found comfort with other women in those long seasons of war in Normandy. Any man would have done so, and William, for all the courtesy he had given her, was a stranger. A stranger who did not, by any reckoning of priest or poet, owe her the loyalty of his heart.

It would be a simple thing for a rich man to put

aside his wife. Kings had done it. Louis of France had done it. And those close to Henry Plantagenet would know how to go about it.

William was not rich. Before Lundale, he had possessed no lands of his own. Catherine frowned. There had been gold to buy food and pay carpenters that first summer of their marriage, and William had said that he had gold from King Henry to pay for the keep of the soldiers this winter. How much of it might he set aside to pay a priest to end his short marriage to Catherine, and wed the mysterious woman so carefully protected by forty men-at-arms in the forest?

If not for Alflega, dear tiny Alflega, it would have been best to go back to the abbey, and find again the blessed, dull peace she had known before William had come into her life. Lundale was stronger now, and would grow and prosper without her. But Alflega would have no place in the world without her mother's protection, in the household of a father who had found a new wife.

She reached the river and gathered her skirts above her knees. The crossing was easier this time, despite the heaviness of her benumbed feet. At the far side, Catherine stopped to drink from the river, and cool her oddly blazing face in the icy water.

All her life, she had been too swift to judge, too fast to act upon her thoughts. Robert often said so, and in the early years, her parents had said so.

Catherine scooped a second handful of stinging cold water and rubbed her face. She must not allow this day's events to shape the rest of her life.

She blinked the tears from her eyes and looked at the clouds racing overhead. She had seen a woman and soldiers in the forest. That was all. They might have been travelers who had lost the road.

Osbert was waiting at the edge of the village, concerned that she had tarried so long in her small pilgrimage. And then worried that she had not tarried long enough, and hadn't done the offering with sufficient reverence.

"I did it," said Catherine, "in proper fashion. With respect."

Radulf appeared at his father's side. "And what did you see, when you made the offering?"

"Why? What should I have seen?"

Osbert blinked. "The usual. A crow, or a rabbit. A deer. A fish in the river. What did you see, after you gave the lady her gift?"

Catherine considered his words, and realized, for the first time, that she had not seen another living thing in the forest. Aside from the lady and the soldiers.

Osbert and Radulf still waited for her answer. "I saw nothing before I reached the well," she began.

"Aye, sometimes we don't. When the lot of us go up there, the noise scares off the birds. But afterwards, what did you see?"

If she lied, and named any one of the creatures of the forest, would Osbert know? She hesitated, and forced herself to choose her words slowly. As she had never learned or needed to do before this day. "There was no forest creature," she said at last, "but before I left the holy spring waters, I had a thought . . ."

"A vision?"

"No, just a thought. Of Mary the mother, carrying her child."

Osbert nodded. "Yuletide is coming. The lady must have sent you thoughts of the holy birth."

Radulf frowned. "Are you sure you didn't see a wolf's track, or think of one? That's what you see, at times when men must think of defending their lands. Now that we have all those soldiers up there in the forest, that's what I would have looked for."

Catherine glanced at Radulf's hands. He had recovered that half-consumed staff of wood, and sharpened the burnt end. "No," she said. "I saw nothing of wolves or other such creatures. Just thoughts of Yuletide, as your father says, and of peace. There will be peace here, and no one must disturb it." She reached for Radulf's makeshift weapon and took it from him.

She walked towards the hall, using Radulf's staff to steady her footsteps. More than anything else, she needed to hold Alflega in her arms.

Nine

She was still carrying Radulf's sharpened staff when she reached the hall and found Hadwen upbraiding John for keeping Alflega too near the heat of the hearth.

Catherine placed the staff beside the sleeping chamber curtains and returned to the fire. "Come to Mother," she whispered. Alflega stretched forth her small arms and hurtled herself into Catherine's embrace.

"What have you done to your feet?" Hadwen rushed forward and began to draw the sodden sheepskin boots from Catherine's feet. "And your skirts are wet. What have you done to yourself?"

"I walked to the edge of the fields, and along the river. I stopped to drink, and stepped too far into the water."

"Catherine, you're as bad as you were at Alflega's age. You shouldn't have walked out alone, especially with that broken hand."

"I couldn't ride. Not with a bad hand."

"You could have waited for Robert."

"Where is he?"

The force of her words startled Alflega, who

ceased her happy babbling and looked up at her mother in surprise. Catherine soothed the child, and looked back at Hadwen. "Where is he?"

"At the abbey. Robert said he'll winter right here at Lundale, since your lord said he'd allow it, so he went back to the abbey to collect the packhorse he left there yesterday."

John looked up. "Your cousin would have been a lot less trouble if he had kept the packbeast in tow, and come back here looking like a decent traveler. He's too old, that one, to ride rough across the fields in such weather. And you, my lady, might have lost more than the use of your hand, if William and that young fool had fought."

"Our lady wouldn't have broken her hand if you had gone out with them, and stopped the fight yourself." Hadwen shooed John aside and placed Catherine's boots beside the fire.

"Your lady's injuries are her husband's fault— mine alone. If John wants to warm his old bones by the fire, let him do so."

Alflega turned to the sound of her father's voice, and answered him with a string of words of her own devising.

William walked through the doorway, down the side of the long fire pit to reach them. His stride was steady this day, as if his wounded leg had come closer to healing. And there was nothing, Catherine thought, in his gaze to hint that he was a man with secrets.

Catherine tucked her own bare cold feet beneath her skirts and managed to smile at William. "Where were you?"

His eyes were the same clear blue that had seemed yesterday to be honest. Nothing in his deep, gentle voice would support the dark imaginings she had faced this day in the forest.

"I went up to the manor and saw how the men are settling in," said William.

"You said there are women with the soldiers."

He stretched his hands over the fire to warm them. "A few. Three or four, I think."

"Then there are fewer than fifty, in all? Forty soldiers, and a few women?"

"Yes. About that." He glanced at her, a subtle wariness in his eyes. Yes, thought Catherine. There was something.

"Why?" he said.

"I'm wondering how to feed them this winter. You said they would hunt for their meat."

"Yes, they have already done well."

"And need grain. Do they have a cow?"

"No. They will need cheese and other foodstuff. I have already sent their packbeasts and a wagon down to Nottingham, to buy most of it there. Don't worry," he said. "You won't have to send much from here. And the king's gold will pay for what you do send."

"They will need bread. I could ask Radulf to take a packhorse up there every two or three days."

"No. Keep your people away."

"Then how are we to feed them?"

William turned from the fire and smiled at Alflega. "My hands are warm. May I hold her?"

Feet entwined and tucked far beneath her skirts, Catherine did not move from the bench. She lifted Alflega into William's arms.

"There's my little rose," said William. He walked a few steps to the end of the bench, then stopped to stare into the flames. "And where," he asked his small daughter, "are your mother's boots?"

Alflega giggled.

William sat down and set his child upon his knee. "Those heaps of sheepskin look a little like your mother's boots, but not as pretty. And not very dry."

Had William returned early, and watched her cross the river? Had the soldiers following the lady in the forest seen her, and told him that they had caught sight of a crimson cloak among the trees?

And why should she allow her husband, a stranger with secrets of his own, tell her where she should and should not walk? If he discovered her disobedience, did it matter? Catherine raised her chin and faced her husband's level gaze. "I took a walk today, while you were in the forest. All the way to the edge of fields, and down to the river. If I could ride a horse with my broken hand, I wouldn't have ruined those boots."

Her words had surprised him. William looked down at his daughter and steadied her on his other knee. "I'm sorry. I should have asked, before I rode away, whether you wanted me to take you out to see the fields. Tomorrow I'll carry you on my saddle. Anywhere you want."

"Then tell me which days you'll be here. I don't want to keep you from the forest house."

William brushed Alflega's head with kiss, and drew her closer, as if to distract the child from the strained tone of Catherine's voice. "We should talk of this tonight," he murmured.

The women at their looms had ceased to chatter; Hadwen and John had abandoned their quarrel about the proximity of the cradle to the hearth. Lundale waited for their lord and lady to ease the tension in the long hall.

Catherine rose and picked up her steaming boots. "It isn't important," she said. And walked into the sleeping chamber, dropping the curtain behind her as she passed.

She stood just beyond the hangings, listening to the silence in the hall. Then Alflega made a small sound, and William spoke to her, and Hadwen began once again to berate John. Soon, all were chattering as before. And Catherine, in the darkened chamber with the curtain blocking the warmth of the hearth, chided herself for speaking in anger.

There was not a soul in all of Lundale who could tell her what to do next. Hadwen would have an opinion, if Catherine dared tell her what she feared. John would understand, but he would take William's part in any dispute that might come between them.

The abbess Alflega, the kindly nun for whom the

baby was named, would be discreet, and would know how to proceed in this swiftly-worsening dilemma. If William wished to make amends, and offered again to ride with her, she would ask him to take her to the abbey.

From beyond the hangings, Alflega's voice rose in musical laughter. Catherine sighed and leaned against the door frame, half tempted to ask William to bring the child as well when they rode to the abbey. She would then have the choice of demanding that William leave her there with the baby until the strangers in the forest house had left—

Once again, Catherine forced her mind away from the possibility that William intended to set her aside. Once again, she repeated the words that had calmed her after the vision at the holy springs: the sight of ten distant figures in the forest might have no significance at all. They might never touch her life, or Alflega's. Or William's.

The curtain jerked open. Catherine cried out in surprise; her bandaged hand came up to steady her, and she reeled back at the sudden pain of contact.

"Catherine, are you ill?" William's arms were about her, half-lifting her from the rushes as he drew her across the chamber to the bed.

He sat down beside her and frowned at the sight of the splinted hand she held to her breast. "Show me," he said, and drew her hand towards him.

He began to unwrap the linen bindings that held her fingers to the splints.

"Don't!"

"Hush. Your fingers have swollen, and the bandages must be loosened."

"I'll ask Hadwen."

William looked up with an odd expression in his eyes. "Will you not trust me? I know what to do." He began to unwrap the bindings, and to speak of Alflega.

"She's a beautiful child," he said. "All these months past, I imagined what she must look like, and how she would regard me; she is so bright, Catherine—more affectionate to her old scarred father than I had dared to hope."

"Did you mean what you said?"

"Catherine, what is wrong with you? Of course I meant it. Do you doubt that I love the child? She is beautiful and happy and—"

"Not about the child. What you said about offering to take me wherever I want to go."

"Ah." He frowned at the sight of her bruised fingers, and covered them again with a gentle touch. "Yes, I meant it. I thought you knew me better," he said, "You should know that I mean what I say. I'll take you riding tomorrow, if you wish."

He began to wrap the bandages back into place. Catherine moved her damaged fingers beneath the cloth and murmured a word of thanks. William was right. It did feel better.

"I'd like to go back to the abbey, with gifts for the nuns."

"I'll take you tomorrow. John will choose five men from the garrison to go with us."

"Five men? It's only seven miles from here."

"We have ten garrison soldiers eating Lundale's food and wearing Lundale wool. They might as well protect you." He tied the ends of the bandage together and placed her hand between them on the coverlet. "Please don't go out of sight of the palisade walls without me."

"Then tell me what I should fear—trust me, rather than hint at trouble. Is there a new war coming? Is there something at the old forest house so dangerous that we must all fear intruders here at Lundale, over three miles away?"

William shook his head. "Do you believe I wouldn't tell you if there were a clear threat to you and your people? What I want from you is prudence, simple caution. There may be brigands on the road, or cattle thieves, or fugitives in the forest."

He stood up and strode to the curtained entrance. "Please, Catherine. I'll have the winter here, and after that I'll have go to fight in the Marches, and then there will likely be another journey to fight for the king in some distant place. It may be another year before I can get back here, even for a fortnight. Please, Catherine. Don't fill these months with doubt and distrust. And don't risk your life by wandering alone, down at the river where you can't be seen. Catherine, I would go mad if something happened to you. . . ."

"Listen to him, Catherine. Your husband is right."

Robert pushed through the curtains and looked from one face to another. "Hadwen tells me you are in here quarreling about a pair of wet boots. There are better reasons abroad for your quarrels."

"What do you mean?"

"The abbess is in a fury. Barely spoke to me when I went to bid her farewell, and to thank her for lending me the horse. Seems she was on her way to Nottingham with messages for the sheriff's couriers to take south, and she ran into a pack of foreign brigands with a priest in tow."

William rose to his feet. "Brigands with a priest? Had they taken him hostage?"

Robert shook his head. "Nothing that simple. They blocked the road, bold as pirates, and made the abbess's maid get off her mule and one of the ruffians made her take off her cloak."

William growled an oath. "They ravished her?"

"That's the strange part. The priest had come up close, near enough for the abbess to demand that he stop the brigands from ravishing the maid. But once the girl's cloak was off, and the brigand had taken her surcoat from her—"

William placed a hand on Catherine's shoulder. "What?"

"He spoke to the priest, who climbed back on his horse. The brigand threw the maid's cloak back into her arms, and mounted his horse and they rode away without a fare-thee-well."

"They took nothing?"

"Nothing. Not the abbess's money pouch, nor the maid's cloak, nor the girl's—"

"Yes," said William. "I understand."

"It's passing strange, this story. I spoke with the

lads who were riding with them, and they said that
there were six brigands, well-armed, riding fast
horses. Even the priest was well mounted. The lads
hadn't a chance to stop what happened; it was a
miracle, they said, that it ended as it did."

"And the maid," said Catherine. "What did she
say? Is it possible she knew them? Was there an
angry suitor among the men?"

"I don't know. The lads said she was weeping all
the way to Nottingham and halfway back."

"Of course. She must have been afraid."

"Aye. Afraid that they'd return. And maybe insulted that the brigands rode away at a gallop, once
they saw her chemise."

"Robert!"

He shrugged. "Don't worry, Catherine. I didn't
say that to the abbess." Robert paused; his mouth
formed into a thin, tight smile. "Is there a priest,
William, among the men in the forest house?"

"No." William's hand upon Catherine's shoulder
rested lightly, as if he hadn't heeded Robert's
words.

"William, in truth—are there foreign folk among
those men? Or any who might appear to be a
priest?"

"No." He moved his hand along her shoulder,
then with a brief caress he left her and walked past
Robert to the hall. At the doorway he paused as if
remembering a near-neglected matter. "Stay here,"
he said. "Don't even leave the hall until I return.
Robert, stay with her."

"Let me guess—"

"I'm going to the manor. I'll be back by sundown tomorrow."

"Then you think it might have been your men."

William buckled his swordbelt and found his cloak where it lay across the bed. "No, it wasn't them. Robert, tell the men in the garrison all you have said here. And tell them to double the sentries."

He walked from the chamber without a word of farewell.

Ten

William returned the next day before nightfall, ice caked upon his boots, the scar upon his mud-streaked face livid purple from the cold. In the moment she saw him ride through the palisade gate, Catherine feared that he had taken another blow to his leg, for he rode with his hand set upon his knee, as if the touch of the saddle against it pained him.

A smile, startling white beneath the mud, transformed his face as he saw her standing beside the byre. He climbed down from the saddle and wiped his face on the sleeve of his surcoat, then drew his hand from a gauntlet and touched her cheek.

She reached up and brought his face down to her lips, kissing the frost from the stubble on his chin, taking the chill from his mouth. Beneath her hand, the meshed rings of his iron helm were barbed with shards of ice.

"All is well," he whispered.

"You found them?"

He pushed the helm from his head. "No. We searched the roads all the way to Nottingham. No sign of trouble, no tales of brigands lately come. And no one in the town had complained of foreign ruffians in the streets." Again, the smile flashed white through the grime. "There were ruffians aplenty, but all were Nottingham-bred."

She touched his matted, sweat-darkened hair. "I'm sure you gave the home-grown rascals in the alehouses a fright they won't forget."

Ice-laden brows rose at her words. "There was no fighting. We only searched."

She tilted her head to admire the line on his temple where the mud ended and the imprint of chain mail began. "I don't think you needed a fight to send any Nottingham rascals into retreat."

Behind them, his men-at-arms were carrying their saddlepacks into the keep. Catherine reached up with her good hand and helped him pull the heavy cloak from his shoulders. "Forgive me. I have kept you from thawing by the fire."

"This is one time I believe I might frighten the child with my appearance." He glanced over his shoulder and turned back to plant a swift kiss on Catherine's lips. "I'll see to the garrison, and wash away some mud before I come to you."

And he disappeared into the grey tower for the last hour of daylight.

Alflega was fretful that night, for her beloved John had left her with Hadwen and had spent the day in the guardroom of the keep, directing the small band of garrison men as they readied their weapons and kept watch.

Radulf had caught the mood of the day and hadn't needed prodding to appear at dawn to feed and groom the garrison's horses. By noon, he had been at Catherine's side to ask for leave to cut a length of leather from the storehouse to replace a worn saddle cinch.

By afternoon, Radulf had set the byre to rights, with the saddletack of each mount piled nearby, ready for use on short notice. Catherine had brought the sharpened staff out of its place of concealment, and returned it to Radulf at the end of the day, with instructions to ask John to show him how a proper spear should be used.

Osbert and the other men of the village, hearing that ruffians, foreigners, and a brigand priest had outraged the abbess's maid, had by nightfall burnished the tale to grand dimensions: abbey treasures ripped from the walls, rapine, and blasphemy. The gates of the yard stood open, ready for the tenants to move their cattle inside should raiders appear; Osbert himself had spent the day watching over the fields at the sentries' side, his great horn ready to call the villagers into the palisade.

Catherine had spent the day with Alflega in her arms, moving from the hall to the keep and back again, pausing from time to time to wonder why she hadn't devised a tale of brigands months ago to inspire Radulf and the other lads to clean the byre.

William emerged from the keep at sunset, and looked into the byre to cast an approving glance at the newfound order within; he took up Radulf's crude weapon and suggested that if John could find an old spear, Radulf might keep it in his hut and bring it each day to practice in the yard.

"The lad has done well," William told her. "And the garrison men are working hard to be ready. John didn't do badly either."

Catherine nodded. "When you have dealt with the foreign brigands, and freed any hostage priests, please don't tell anyone here until the guardroom is cleaned and the byre walls repaired."

"Alflega will lose her slave if this hard work goes on much longer," said William. "And I don't know how many of these days John will tolerate before he returns to the hearthside. He'll be pleased when the searching is done, and the garrison back to normal."

William shrugged the leather hauberk from his shoulders, and pulled his mail shirt over his head. "I hadn't thought to wear armor again, not for the winter."

Catherine extended her arms to take the mail shirt from William. He hesitated, then took it himself to hang it upon the bed frame. "It's heavy," he said. He turned back, hesitating as his weight moved from one leg to the other.

"Is it worse? Did you ruin your leg again?"

He shook his head. "I was lucky today. No skirmishes, no sign of trouble."

"Then the bandits are gone?"

"If bandits they were—yes, they're gone. I set the king's men to patrol the forest road all day. They found no one, and saw no sign of camps in the forest. My guess is that the brigands were passing through these parts, and thought, on a whim, to abduct the abbess's maid. And changed their minds when they saw the abbess's cold eye."

William stretched his arms about his head and grimaced. "We might have used your abbess to good effect in Normandy."

"I certainly hope not."

"To negotiate. Or frighten the barons into loyalty."

Catherine frowned. "She's a good woman and cared for me when I was left an orphan."

"For that, I have thanked her. Twice."

"And may thank her again, if you take me to the abbey. I have silver—five pennies—from the cattle market at Nottingham. If you agree, William, I'd like to give them to Dame Alflega."

His eyes widened. "Dame Alflega? The abbess is called Alflega? You named our child for the abbess?"

"She is a good woman—"

"I know. And she kept you safe when you were orphaned. Still, the name has a bad sound to it. Like a crow's chatter."

"Not if you speak it softly."

"There's nothing soft about your abbess. Not now. Never was, I think. Not with that name to burden her. The baby should be called by a gentle name. Rosewitha—"

"No."

He stopped and stood silent, looking into her eyes. "Yes," he said. "I can see it. Dame Alflega gave you something of her character, along the way. Now that we are old wedded folk, I begin to see it." His mouth twitched, then yielded to a half-smile. "I'll take you to the abbey, when it's certain that the road is safe."

"And the silver? You agree we should give the pennies to her for the abbey?"

"Aye. And I'll add a gold piece of my own to the gift." He shifted from one leg to the other.

Catherine's smile faded. "Your leg is worse. Don't deny it. It was too soon to spend another day on horseback."

"Never mind."

"Hot water cured it before. Do you want a bath brought here?"

William rubbed his leg and began to look about the chamber. "It's almost sunset, and your people have worked hard this day. I won't ask them to carry water now."

"I'll get Radulf to build the fire and fill the tub in the keep."

"Will you join me?"

The man had an uncanny way of bringing sudden crimson to her face. "In the keep, with the garrison walking through the room? I think not. Radulf will bring the tub here, in the morning." Catherine picked up William's clean tunic and held it for him.

He took it from her arms. "About the keep—I want you to move there, to the upper chamber, you and Alflega."

"We decided—"

"Last year it didn't matter, and I let you have

your way. For this winter, until I know that the forest is clear of brigands and other threats, I want you and Alflega safe in the keep."

He looked about the sleeping chamber and shook his head. "It's a miracle this old hall still stands. An enemy would need only to break down the timbers of the palisade and throw a torch or two on the roof of the hall, and your shelter would be gone."

"It survived Henry Plantagenet's army."

William sighed. "I heard the tale of that day. The fighting happened around the keep, and in the fields. If there had been men in this hall, the attackers would have burnt it. It was your good luck that they didn't burn it anyway."

Catherine's blood grew cold. "There was little luck for us, that day. And the keep—that useless great pile of stone—did not keep my father from the Plantagenet's hired swords. Once inside it, there is no escape from the keep. You have to fight your way out, if you can. And if not—"

"Where were you?"

There was something in his steady, passionless tone that gave her the strength to answer. "We were far from the keep, Robert and I; we hid at the edge of the fields. Our fields were bigger then; the far ones are grown over, now."

"Go on."

"Father had seen that the Plantagenet's army was large, and might win the day. Robert's father, my father's brother, had died the day before in a skirmish near the Plantagenet's camp. King

Stephen—our rightful king, had he lived—had sent no troops north to help us. That is what my father said when he took Robert and me out beyond the fields and told us to stay among the sheep at the edge of the forest. The sheep were the last thing the army would look for, if the wrong side won. They would loot the hall and take the cattle first and only then ride across the fields to take the sheep. If we saw the fighting come in our direction, or if we saw them coming to get the sheep, we were to go into the forest and climb up into a tree."

"So you did."

"And stayed there, with Robert, for a day and a night. When the soldiers left, the villagers had run away. Only Osbert and Hadwen had returned, and left their families in the forest. They took us to the abbey, for they feared the soldiers would return and discover us. Hadwen thought we wouldn't survive in the forest. And she knew that she and Osbert wouldn't have enough to feed us."

"You have good reason to hate Henry Plantagenet."

Again, William's voice was quiet, without emotion. Catherine hesitated. Had she said too much?

Robert's words came back to her. Was there a reason, a dark reason beyond the hazards of the roads and the birth of his child, that kept William from taking her into the king's presence? Did William regret that he had wed the daughter of a minor baron who had perished in rebellion against the Plantagenet throne?

He waited in silence for her to speak.

"It was long ago," she said.

"You lost everything. You and Robert both."

Catherine's damaged hand began to tremble. "Robert was a child when it happened. Scarce older than I was. We didn't really know who it was that our fathers were fighting. Only the name—the Plantagenet. We went into the forest. And—we didn't watch."

She looked up and saw that William had not moved, nor changed his expression. "Do you believe me a traitor, living an ancient conspiracy to harm your King Henry?"

"No. I never thought that. Continue. Tell me what happened next. You and Robert went to the abbey, and the abbess took you in. She knew who you were?"

"Of course. Our fathers—Robert's and mine—had built the abbey, and given lands to support it. The abbey priest was ours as well."

"Ah. That's the reason there is no church here."

"No, there was one. A small wooden church, outside the palisade. It burned." Catherine forced the memories of that day back into the farthest corner of her mind. "The hall didn't burn," she said. "The church went, but the palisade remained and the hall. Old wood is hard as iron and won't catch fire easily."

"And when it does," said William, "it burns hot and fast. Tomorrow, Catherine, we will move the bed up into the keep. You and Alflega and I will sleep there, with the guardroom below and the sentries above."

"And leave Hadwen, and Osbert, and Radulf—"

"I have doubled the sentries. There will be warning if trouble comes. Osbert and the others will come into the keep if there's time, or get to the forest to hide, as they must have done before. You and Alflega are my kin; an army of brigands would know that and search for you, to take you hostage. You might be harmed."

"And Robert? What would become of him? Even in Nottingham, they know he's your kin by marriage."

"I want him with us in the garrison, sleeping in the guardroom."

"And if he wants to remain here in the hall?"

"He must come into the keep, like it or not. Or he may leave this place altogether. The choice is his."

A band of ruffians had insulted a girl on the road five miles south of here, and within the day William had demanded that she take her child and leave this fine, comfortable hall for the cold stone tower with its narrow, twisting stairs. To leave behind this sleeping chamber near the long, blazing hearth pit, and wake in a dark chamber with only wind-pierced arrowslits to admit the light of dawn.

Catherine sighed. "You always preferred the keep, and disliked this hall. William, are the brigands so many, or so dangerous—"

"Yes. There may be many, and they are most certainly dangerous. We are moving to the keep. Tomorrow."

"Then what of the women and the priest at the abbey? The strangers were there, not far from the gates."

"I have sent ten of the king's men to protect them."

"Then our Dame Alflega will have your soldiers—the ones you called too dangerous for any Lundale folk to approach—camped outside the abbey walls."

William sighed. "Yes. It had to be done. I couldn't leave the abbey undefended. But before they left, I warned the men to respect the abbess and never to cross her, if they could help it. Nothing they saw fighting in Normandy would prepare the men for that lady's disposition." He yawned and put his hands behind his head. "And I forbade them, on their honor, to move their tents away from the walls into the forest, where they would have only the wolves to frighten them."

He looked aside and saw that his words had not amused her. "Come, Catherine," he said. "These days are not as I had wished them. Every night in Normandy I thought of you before I slept, and I dreamed only of returning here. To you. Can we not agree, in the time that we have together?"

Yesterday, his words would have made her weep, for she would have thought he spoke of death. Now, there were other fears. Had he already thought to put her aside? She tried to take the fear from her voice. "What do you mean?"

"I have only the winter, Catherine, before I must go back to fight."

"But you will come back."

He touched her cheek. "I will come back. God willing, I will come back."

His was not the voice of a guilty lover. It was the

voice of a man who wished to calm his wife, to make her believe that death would not soon part them.

Catherine looked about the familiar chamber where she had been born. "When the king has finished his wars and you come back to me, will we return to the hall and live here as before?"

"Of course. As soon as the danger passes. We are agreed, then?"

"The Yuletide feasts must be here in the hall."

He sighed. "Every night, if you wish. But we will go back to sleep in the chamber at the keep. Every night."

"Every night," said Catherine. "until peace comes."

He took her into his arms and sank down upon the bed. "Don't be sad, Catherine. It won't be so uncomfortable, sleeping in the keep. The walls are sturdy, not so drafty as the hall."

"Stone is cold," said Catherine.

"I'll keep you warm. And I'll have the men bring out some of the hewn timber from the guardroom and put a bedframe together, and we'll leave this bed just where it is, ready for our return." He raised his head. "You laugh?"

"Have you not noticed that this bed is built from the floor? Even a great strong Norman knight couldn't budge it if he tried."

He nuzzled her neck until she shrieked in laughter. "You might have told me. I would have discovered the problem soon enough."

"Yes," she gasped. "But it would have been a way to delay you."

He bent his head once again to her neck.

"No, William! Everyone beyond the curtain will hear me. Please don't make me laugh again."

"In the keep," said William. "I'll make you laugh as often as I can. There won't be someone just beyond the curtain, up there. And when the sky is clear, we'll go up one turn of the stairs, right up to the roof of the keep and stand at the sentry post to see the stars."

"And the sentries will think it odd, to see us wandering about in the middle of the night."

"I will bribe them all."

"Or choose old ones, with bad eyesight."

"Yes," said William. "That would be the remedy."

"There will be Alflega in her cradle. We won't be able to put her just beyond the curtain for Hadwen to watch."

"The child sleeps."

"Most nights."

William frowned. "We'd better make the most of our last night in this chamber, then. If you're willing."

She nestled against him and drew the coverlet closer. "Blow out the taper, then."

"No," he said. "Before I do, I must see that purple belly that frets you so."

"You have seen it."

"Madam, I have not."

"The night Alflega was born, you did."

"That was different." He rolled aside and blew out the taper. "Now, Catherine, in the darkness, are you willing?"

It was not the marks of birth she wished to hide

from William. It was the look in her eyes that he must not see.

At the end of their summer fortnight together, she had begun to desire him with an intensity that was not seemly. In the darkness, he wouldn't see her face, and read upon it how far she had traveled toward unthinking desire. And now, after two seasons of solitude, her desires had grown too strong for the light.

"I am," she said.

"I'll be careful of your hand."

"I have forgotten it," she said. And felt the hard warmth of him come upon her, and move above her, and descend to the longing between her thighs.

"It has been so long, since I felt you so. Would you forgive me, Catherine, if I can't wait? Would you—"

"Don't make me wait. Since summer—I have been waiting for you."

She found her bliss in the moment he came into her, and would not let him wait for his own.

"Next time," he whispered. "is for you."

"Next time," she said. "is already upon us."

"Hush," he whispered. "You are the one who frets about ears beyond the curtain. If they hear you, you'll hate me on the morrow."

"I think," she said, "the keep won't be so bad. Not at times like this."

"I promise you, there will be many times like this."

"William?"

"Yes?"

"Don't make me wait."

Eleven

The snows came then and the people of Lundale, soldiers and villagers as well, ceased to fear danger outside the bounds of the settlement. In the perfect, untrodden surfaces of the common fields they could see, each morning, that no thieves had approached in the night. Only the delicate tracks of foxes and the deep, narrow tracks of deer marred the broad fields to the west. To the east, the sheep were in the folds and the few that wandered did not go far; beyond the well-trampled snow surrounding the sheep pens, no sign of trouble marked the white land. And beyond it all, at the edge of the great forest, not even wolves had come far past the shadows of the great trees.

From the top of the keep, Catherine could see those fields, and the paths of the village folk where they walked to their byres, and to the sheepfolds beyond. All those paths, worn dark by burden and passage, led at some point to the palisade gates; the great hall was the center of the vast white world, surrounded by fields, edged by the river, bounded in turn by the vast forest.

Each morning, Catherine took Alflega up the

steps from the new sleeping chamber to the sentry's walk on the roof of the keep. Wrapped in two cloaks and clutched safe against her mother's body, young Alflega had begun to learn the look of the land. She seemed to understand the words, though she could not speak them clearly, with which Catherine pointed out the village, the fields, and the shining river that curved about the southern bounds of her world.

Catherine had strained to see the manor stockade from this vantage point, but could not see its place beyond the dark mass of the forest. One morning she thought she saw the smoke of the hearth fire at the manor house, but the smudge of pale grey had soon disappeared into the lowering winter clouds.

For a reason she dared not admit to herself, Catherine's gaze turned always first and last to the river. As the winter came on, the water changed from blue depths and white rapids to an untidy patchwork of grey, then to glittering traceries of ice. As Yuletide approached, and the sun was most sparing of its warmth, the river began to shine brilliant silver in the low light of each cold dawn.

A burden lifted and vanished on the first freezing morning. Before the ice had come to slicken and cover the secret fording place, Catherine had struggled with the temptation to go back to the forest to see, once and for all, whether the woman she had seen walking beneath the oaks had stayed on in the forest, in the household of William's small, secret army.

For all the intimacy she shared with her husband each night in the tall keep, Catherine knew that he would not relent in the matter of the strange household in the forest. He turned aside her questions with humor or reproach. Sometimes both. And never revealed anything beyond what he had told her in the first week of his homecoming: forty of the king's guard and a few women had taken the manor, and wouldn't leave before spring. Anything beyond that was guesswork William would not indulge with answers.

Now that the fording place was obscured by the cold and would not show itself again until spring, Catherine could put temptation behind her; for the time being, the mystery William had brought north from Henry Plantagenet's court would remain unknown and isolated in its own frozen world.

On this particular morning, the sentries were impatient for their fellows to appear to end their cold pre-dawn watch. They turned from their posts to look beyond Catherine, to the place where the narrow stairs descended to the three round chambers of the keep.

William emerged from the well of stairs, wrapped in his great heavy cloak, tousled from sleep and cold bathing water. He smiled across the windy space at Catherine, and cocked his head to amuse Alflega. He called to the sentries. "All quiet?"

The younger sentry, the homesick one whom Catherine pitied for his youth, cupped his hands about his mouth and shouted back. "We saw no one save the king's men."

"Where?"

"—fording place, where they always turn back."

William reached them at the highest step of the sentry walk. "There were two?"

"Three, this morning. They made no signal, and rode back where they came from."

"Good."

William descended the wooden platform and joined Catherine at the battlements. "Are you reconciled to waking each morning in this place? You must admit it's a fine thing to awaken and go up to see so much of the world."

"Aye, there is that one good thing." Catherine took a last look at the ice-bound river and turned back to let William take the child into his arms. "You are waiting for a signal at the fording place?"

He folded the child within his arms, sheltering her from the wind. "We agreed, Catherine, not to speak of the king's men. It does no good for us."

"One day, when you are an old man, I'll trick you into telling me every last thing you did for King Henry."

"One day, when the times are better and King Henry is at peace, I'll tell you all you want to know. I swear it."

"Then you'll have to take care to live that long. To keep your promise."

Alflega had curled into the crook of her father's arm. "She's cold," said William. He took Catherine's arm and carried Alflega with them to the stairs. "I will keep another promise today," he said. "Your Osbert is fitting a door on the chamber. The sentries won't wake us tonight when they pass by."

He led the way down the tight spiral of stone and entered the high chamber that took up most of the keep's narrow width. Daylight sliced into the space through six arrow slits within the grey walls. From the east, it streamed across the chamber to cast pale columns of light upon the inner curve of the stones.

"If we move the bed," said Catherine, "we'll have the light of dawn in our faces each morning."

William frowned. "It would be better to leave it where we can see the door."

Osbert's voice rose from the stairs below. With much heaving and thudding, a worn oaken door hove into view.

"That was fast."

Osbert wiped his brow and nodded in obeisance to William. "Didn't build it for you. Took it from the granary and sawed it smaller."

Catherine ran her hand down the heavy, scarred wood. "And what will you use for the granary?"

"The old door from the byre. It's good enough to keep the creatures out of the store hut; we took it out of the old wood waiting for the bonfire." Osbert called down to Radulf and heaved the door into position. "This one," he said, "won't be for the bonfire, not in our time. It was all that was left of the chapel. I used it for shelter myself, that first winter after the trouble. Used it as a wall."

"Where? In the forest?"

"No," said Osbert. "That first winter, we were

afraid the king's men would come into the forest to look for us, and charge us with killing the king's deer. The king's new deer—before the trouble, they were the old lord's deer and ours too."

"Where, then?"

"The sheepfolds, and this door. Set them up over there at the edge of the meadow where the dead are sleeping. Thought the graves would keep the Plantagenet's soldiers away. It worked, for here I am. And here's Radulf too."

Osbert looked behind him and growled in approval. "Good. The bar brackets are still in place. Thought they'd be gone, or broken off. The bar must have broken first."

The significance of Osbert's words struck Catherine an instant later. She sat down on the unmade bed and willed her mind not to return to the reason why the door of this chamber was missing.

William shifted Alflega to his left arm and helped Osbert steady the door against the wall. "Come back after noon to set it in place," he said.

"My lord, I have leather for hinges right here. I'll do it now, if you—"

"No. Come back later."

Osbert glanced at Catherine, then shrugged. "As you will."

"Thank you," said William. And turned back to Catherine. "I'm sorry," he said. "I didn't think to ask why there was no door, when the ironwork was here already. It was—"

"Yes. It must have come down on the day they died." She looked about the chamber with renewed dread, half expecting to see traces of old blood-stains on the walls. "I wasn't here, you see. I was in the forest, and didn't see how it—"

"I'm sorry."

She looked up. "You weren't here. You couldn't have been."

"I should have thought of the door before I brought you here. It has made it worse for you."

William set Alflega down upon the clean rushes Hadwen had spread on the floor. The child sat where she was, looking from Catherine's face to William's.

For her daughter's sake, Catherine managed to smile. "It was a long time ago."

"Catherine, if you need to go back to the hall, we'll manage somehow. I'll double the sentries outside the walls."

"In winter? No." She looked again at her daughter. "If you're certain she's safer here, then we'll all stay. If there are ghosts about, they will understand."

"Aye. Of all souls, they would understand."

He set his hand upon the near bracket and frowned. "Is Hadwen in the hall?"

"I think so."

"I'll take you to the abbey tomorrow, if it pleases you. I'll ask Hadwen if she would watch Alflega the whole day tomorrow. We shouldn't take the child abroad on the road, not before springtime."

"She'll be happy with Hadwen." Catherine reached for her daughter. "Wouldn't you, sweet one? Do you want to see Hadwen?"

William lifted the child from her arms. "It will be a cold ride. Can you find boots?"

"Mine should be dry again. If not, I'll borrow boots."

"Find the best ones you can, and wear your scarlet cloak. I swore to your lady abbess that I would keep you well; if she finds your boots shabby, she may not let me take you home again."

"Not if you give her the gold piece."

"Aye. She'd take it, and then scold me for a miserly husband, and only then take you back."

"She's not so fierce, once you know her."

"Catherine, I lack the courage to know her well. It took all my valor to talk her into allowing an immediate marriage for us, and to send you with me on that first day. The threats she made in case I thought to mistreat you would have frozen the blood of the king himself."

"They must have. The abbey wasn't sacked after the rebellion."

"Then she's the one you must consult, if you want to steal me away from the king's wars."

Catherine looked at him with no humor in her eyes. "I intend to, William. Believe me, husband, I will do just that. Dame Alflega will know what to do."

Twelve

She woke in the hour before dawn, and watched William as he moved about the chamber. In the faint amber glow of the low brazier, he broke the skin of ice upon the water bucket and set it beside the iron grate. The ashes glowed red, then flared bright yellow as William stirred the fire to life, and set new wood above it to catch the rising flames.

He knelt beside the bucket and splashed water upon his face, and rubbed it dry before plunging the cloth into the bucket to wash his body. Deep beneath her coverlets, Catherine shuddered at the sound of the ice shards stirring against the bucket sides; each time the frigid washing cloth rasped upon William's body, she felt the cold as if it had touched her own flesh. But still she did not look away.

As the new wood blazed, the light of it flared crimson upon William as he bathed, catching the lines of his long, muscled limbs, leaving in shadow the many scars that Catherine had seen upon them. In that half light, even the worst of the scars—the mark of the arrow that had come so close to killing him—was not obvious. Catherine saw his face as it had been before the fighting at Chinon, as it must have been when he had first taken up his sword in the Plantagenet's service.

John had spoken, one late spring night, of how quickly the fortunes of William's people had changed following their troubles with the Capet king in Paris. The fighting skill of William's father and older brothers had bought shelter for them all in the household of Geoffrey of Anjou, and had led to the chance for young William to win his spurs fighting for the Anjou heir, Henry Plantagenet.

John had hastened to say that William had been too young to join the Plantagenet when he had crossed to England a decade ago to assert his control over the barons loyal to the dying King Stephen—too young to join in the violence that the Plantagenet had brought to Nottingham and then to Lundale.

If William had been but a year or two older, if he had been in the company of Henry Plantagenet on that evil day when Lundale had lost everything, would the villagers have accepted him now as their lord?

Catherine burrowed deeper in the warmth of the bed, and thought back to the early days of her return to Lundale. Osbert and Hadwen and all the others who had survived the destruction of Lundale had made their lives in the forest, and had come back from loyalty to her, and in the hope that their old way of life might be restored. If Osbert and the others had disliked William of Macon or mistrusted him, they would have vanished back into the greenwood within the first season of Lundale's resettlement.

Now that William had returned for the winter and begun to shape Lundale into the well-defended fief he envisioned, the villagers and the shepherds seemed pleased enough with their new lord. No one had left, and there had been talk of a few more families willing to return.

Catherine sighed. She, too, was pleased enough with William of Macon and trusted him so far that she had put aside her suspicions of his part in the events unfolding at the forest house. Her people had decided to put their trust in William of Macon. She would give him her trust as well.

For now.

She watched William pull on his chausses and tunic, and draw his heavy black surcoat over his head. He picked up his boots and moved to the door, moving in silence past the bed and the cradle, and into the darkness beyond. Catherine closed her eyes and slept again.

Across the chamber, at the edge of the firelight, Alflega still slept in her high-sided cradle.

Catherine sat up. William put a finger to his lips, and crossed the floor to look upon the child's face and smile back at Catherine. "She's fine. Let her sleep until Hadwen comes," he whispered.

Through the narrow embrasures around the chamber, the last of the slow night wind drifted to the brazier fire, sending the flames high with each small gust. As it curled past, the draft was cold and smelled of snow and forest.

William had returned, his hair damp from his early bathing, with a ewer of steaming hot water in his hands.

Catherine smiled. "I saw you washing in ice water before dawn," she said. "I wasn't eager to do the same."

"It wasn't easy. Too cold. I couldn't stand to have you do that." He set the ewer beside the fire. "There is bread and cheese down there, and Hadwen is waiting to come up for Alflega."

"A moment."

A cheery babble rose from the cradle. William turned and began to speak to Alflega, telling her, as if she understood each word, that Hadwen would take her down the stairs and to the hall and feed her barley porridge and milk.

Catherine listened to his words as she scrubbed her face in the luxury of cloth-wrapped herbs and hot water. She glanced across the chamber and saw that William had wrapped Alflega in her warm bundle of blankets and was carrying her about the chamber, mumbling a soldier's song that Catherine would one day need to encourage her little daughter to forget.

Catherine washed and stood close to the brazier as she pulled on her warm green kirtle. William brought Alflega to watch as Catherine opened the clothing chest and began to rummage through the contents. He set the child down upon the bed and opened the chamber door to catch up Catherine's boots, dried and brushed clean. "Hadwen said she had to dry them once again over the fire. She said something about a soaking they got not long ago."

"That was many days ago," said Catherine. "That time I stumbled into the river. That was all."

Catherine took the boots from his hands and sat down to pull them on. William knelt before her and pushed aside her bandaged hand. "Don't hurt your fingers," he said, and held one boot open for her foot.

Beside them, Alflega frowned down at her mother's feet and began to examine her own small toes.

"It was a little out of season to wade in the river," said William. "Did you fall?"

"A misstep. Nothing more."

William held the second boot and pushed it onto Catherine's foot. "Even when your hand heals and you're riding again, maybe you shouldn't ride alone at the river. It's dangerous. Osbert says someone drowns in it, once each generation."

"That's an old story. No one dies in the river. And I'm not the sort to drown," she said. "I'm not often so clumsy."

"No. Of course not."

"But if you want to carry me about the countryside on your saddle, I'll be agreeable to that."

"Once your hand is whole again, I'll have to steal your boots to keep you from going about alone. I'm worried it's not safe."

"The raiders have gone. You said there was no sign of them."

He frowned. "In Nottingham I should have learned something about the brigands who stopped the abbey folk. It troubles me that none of the king's men saw anyone on the road that day. It's the season for such trouble, but we haven't had so much as a sheep stolen. To my mind, that's more troubling than having the usual thieves about."

"We had no problems with raiders last year. Word must have spread that you had left a garrison here at Lundale."

"Then the cattle thieves' spies did us a service last year. If I catch one, I'll remember that."

"Will you continue looking for thieves? In the forest?" Catherine raised her gaze to William's face and chose her words with care. "There are people still living in the forest. They watch what we do, and come out to trade with the shepherd lads from time to time. They have nothing to do with raiders."

"Who are they?"

"Those who still won't return to the village. Kinfolk—some cousins of Lundale people. They have built shelters among the trees, and live in the wildwood. The villagers barter bread and grain and cloth for the venison and furs the forest people bring to the far meadows."

"They are killing the king's deer."

"The forest is full of game. The king never comes here, and won't miss what they take." Catherine leaned forward and placed her hands upon William's shoulders. "They have seen the king's men living at the manor house, and have abandoned that part of the forest. I pray the soldiers will be content and won't pursue them."

William raised his brows. "You seem well informed of their movements and intentions," he said. "Is it Osbert who brings messages?"

"No. No one in particular."

"Of course. Pray tell this to—no one in particular—that I must know if strangers appear among them. I will pay well for anything I hear."

This should have been the moment to ask him why a woman in a costly cloak walked in the forest with armed men to protect her. Or guard her. Or keep her kinfolk from her.

No, the woman in the forest was not the stranger he was seeking. She would be no stranger to William—

Catherine turned her mind back to William's own question "Can your soldiers not defend themselves, William? Forty of the king's men will not need warning if a few hungry raiders try to steal their bread. There must be something more that troubles you."

William blinked first. "My purpose is to avoid bloodshed. It was not my choice to bring the king's men here for the winter, but we must do this for the king or fall out of grace, and into danger. Will you not help me in this?"

"Will you not trust me in this?"

He looked away to the eastern embrasure and shook his head. "The sun is up, and we should be on our way." Alflega lifted her arms and smiled as William carried her out of the chamber.

Catherine picked up her cloak and followed. She had lost something in that exchange; for now, she had no way to know exactly what it was that she had missed.

Five men of the garrison rode with them, two well ahead and three far behind William's black palfrey. Perched upon William's lap with a blanket to cushion her from the saddlebow, Catherine watched the forest as they rode beneath the dark, spreading branches of the ancient trees. Though she had traveled this road south through the greenwood many times, she had never, since childhood, had the luxury of ignoring the road and peering deep into the dense, living tangle of holly and ivy upon oak.

They passed the turning place where the smaller track to the manor house began. The outriders did not turn to look down that narrow road as they passed, nor did William speak of it. Nor did he seem surprised when riders appeared a short distance beyond the crossroads.

So these were the king's men. Catherine stared at the three hard-faced men who emerged from the forest on their tall, rangy mounts to challenge their passing. On the day of William's return, the four who had stopped her from following the manor road had looked just as stern as these riders.

Forty such men would frighten away even the boldest thieves. No wonder that local brigands had given up the land so far that even Lundale's distant flocks were safe.

At a small gesture from William, the riders turned and disappeared into the forest. A moment later, the land was silent. Catherine shivered; she might have imagined them, ghosts in the morning mist.

William nudged the palfrey forward.

Catherine pointed in the direction in which the riders had disappeared. "Do the garrison men know who they are?"

William glanced down. "The garrison?" His tone told Catherine that his mind had been elsewhere.

"Yes. The garrison and Lundale and the king's men. How do you keep them from attacking each other on the road?"

"Oh. They know to stay clear of each other. And," said William, "they are content to know that alone."

"Unlike your wife."

"Aye. Unlike my curious wife."

As they rode south, the forest opened. Here, the low sunlight poured free past the trunks of great trees, into the snow-carpeted spaces between them. In this part of the greenwood, a rider might stray from the road with no harm done; a horse and rider, or a small wagon could pass between the great oaks in any direction.

"I mislike this part of the forest," said William.

"I don't," Catherine said. "The light is strong, and you can see a rider coming from a distance."

"The brigands stopped the abbess not far from

here." He looked behind him, and rode on. "It's too quiet."

"Blame your soldiers then. Ten of your sour-faced king's men would silence the crows."

He laughed; the sound of it rang among the bare trees. "If the ravens are silent, it's because the abbess has long since frightened them away."

Thirteen

At the turning place, where a tall cairn of moss-shadowed stones marked the road to the abbey, William called the outriders back to him, and went before them to lead the way on the narrow road to the abbey.

"The first time I came here," said William, "the rain was so heavy that my horse almost walked into the cairn. John and I turned down the road in search of shelter, and there was the abbey." His voice went lower still. "And there you were. One day, I should discover who built the cairn and give a gold piece to his descendants."

"Will you not wait to see whether you're happy with the wife that you found waiting for you?"

William hesitated. "Aye, I should wait. In twenty years, Catherine, remind me to decide whether it shall be a gold piece or a feast of crows."

Twenty years. The words had seemed to come easily to him—

"Look—here she is," said William.

At first, Catherine thought it was a child's figure before them, waiting beside the road a scarce half-mile before the abbey gates. She had forgotten, in

the months of her marriage and her new life at
Lundale, how very small was the abbess, the Dame
Alflega, and how delicate her birdlike features.

"So. You have managed to get this far. It is cold
and I have been waiting the whole morning
through, wondering whether you people had decided to turn back and forget us here."

Yes. Catherine had forgotten much in the past
months. Thin, exquisite features. A voice both lilting and indelicate. And certitude. Always, in all
things, certitude.

"You knew we were coming?"

Dame Alflega's gaze swiveled up to focus upon
William. "Do you think I must go without tidings,
just because I'm so far from the center of things? I
have some few ways to know what goes on. Now
come along. It's cold."

A small, unworthy corner of her mind echoed in
silent laughter as Catherine heard William's un-
necessary but swift apology.

The abbess waved away an outrider's proffered
hand. "I'm too old to ride such a beast," she said.
And cackled in amusement at the man's shocked
face. "The horse, sir. I spoke of the horse. How can
you think such a thing? William of Macon, I am insulted by your man. Now come along."

The abbess turned and began to walk down the
road.

William called after her. "My lady abbess, will you
take your place in the saddle with Catherine?"

She turned and made a gesture of impatience. "I

have become old in the past fortnight. I no longer sit a saddle."

"But you have a fine saddle and that gentle white mule," said Catherine.

"No more. Gone. The beast and the saddle. Both gone."

"Did the brigands steal them?"

"Do you think I would allow such a thing to happen?"

"No," said William. "of course not. But such things befall us—"

"Only upon the careless," said the abbess. "I suppose I must tell you. I gave the mule to the priest Adelbertus and sent him south to find the king."

"Ah," said William. And fell silent.

"Do you not wish to know why?"

"Yes," said William. Catherine had never heard him speak with such meekness.

"I had some few things to tell Henry Plantagenet concerning his behavior towards his bishops. There will be trouble for him if he continues to interfere in the business of his priests."

"Aye," said William. "There is trouble coming."

The abbess lifted an elegant finger. "Trouble doesn't come to kings, young man. They make their own trouble and when it's ripe they send it out across the land to plague us all."

"Ah," said William.

Catherine smothered a smile.

"If Henry Plantagenet continues to quarrel with that archbishop he chose—chose himself, you know—for Canterbury, we will have more trouble than he can imagine."

The abbess pushed the hood from her head. A fine halo of white and gold stood about her face, wispy as a young bird's down. "So I put Adelbertus on the mule and sent him off to deliver my advice. The king will listen, or he will not. If he will not, there is nothing more I can do for him. I'm old now and it is too large a burden for me, to be troubled with such things." She gathered her cloak about her and sighed. "And I am much too old to be standing about in the winter air. I must get back to the abbey."

With a small flourish of her cloak, the abbess turned away.

William pointed to the small figure marching down the road. "We cannot let her walk while we ride."

"She wants us to dismount and lead the horses. Please," said Catherine. "She loves to have her way."

"Is that so?" William sighed. "Come then. Onto my knee, and I'll set you down."

"Not on your leg. It's—"

"—recovered." William placed his hands upon her waist. "Even if it were not, you and I would have to dismount somehow, and walk with your little abbess. Come," he said. "She has stopped. She's waiting."

He lifted her from the saddle to his knee, and then lowered her to the ground. William signaled the outriders to stay mounted, and climbed down from his saddle; leading the palfrey, Catherine and

William walked into the range of Dame Alflega's frown.

"There are matters to discuss, William de Macon. I had expected you here long before this day."

"My lady, there were some distractions. I trust the king's guards have been useful in protecting the abbey?"

"Yes. I thank you. They have been most diligent and courteous, and have amused me with their tales of wars and intrigue."

Catherine marveled that William's smile did not falter at those words. "I will commend them," he said. "and ask them to tell me which stories most amused you."

"Hmph." The abbess took his proffered arm and began to march toward the abbey gates. "There's more trouble beyond bishops, I hear, for that foolish Plantagenet boy. He's turning his back on the trouble with his bishops and planning to invade Wales. Yes, Wales. But I expect you know all about that."

William cleared his throat. "I do not know the king's mind. He has put down rebellions in Normandy and Brittany already this year—"

"Henry Plantagenet spent the entire summer sulking. No one knew where he was. It's a wonder the barons remember his name."

"Madam, that's not true. The king has shown great interest in England. All last year, and most of this—"

"As I said, he shirked his duties the whole summer long. He should spend more time where the

barons can find him, and not riding about the
country as if his people were huntsmen and Henry
Plantagenet the quarry."

Catherine watched with sympathy as William attempted to treat the abbess with respect while
ignoring her flirtation with treason. "You know
much about the king's habits," she heard William
say. "Have you friends among his courtiers?"

"I know none of them, aside from those who
rode through these lands—including Lundale—a
decade ago. Our meetings were not cordial."

Catherine stepped forward and took the abbess's
other arm. "William knows all about the sack of
Lundale, Dame Alflega."

They had reached the gates of the abbey.
William raised a hand in greeting to five men gathered about a campfire outside the high walls, and
called out a promise to join them.

"My men must have spent a cold night," said
William.

"Some of them came to the refectory to eat last
night," said Dame Alflega. "Though invited, they
wouldn't stay beyond the hour."

Catherine saw a subtle twitching at the corner of
William's mouth.

William escorted the abbess to the doors of the
abbey hall, and bowed in farewell. Dame Alflega extended a delicate claw to grasp the sleeve of his
surcoat, and held it between thumb and first finger.
"We will speak now, William de Macon."

He nodded towards the palfrey. "Later, if it
please you. I must—"

"Leave the horse with your men and come along." She turned back to Catherine and made a vague gesture. "Go and see Alice. She has your old chamber now. And Sister Birgetta is in the refectory. You may come to join us in the garden, in an hour or so."

Catherine was left on the porch of the abbey, watching her warrior husband hustled across the stable yard in the abbess's tiny grasp.

The five outriders stared after them. "Don't worry," said Catherine. "Your lord will be perfectly safe."

Catherine walked to the far side of the great hall, where a narrow door led to the sleeping chambers of the abbey nuns and the orphans who had arrived in increasing numbers in the past decade.

She followed the cloistered walkway on the south side of the abbey and listened to the familiar sounds of children, sheep, and poultry.

Within the walls, little had changed. Catherine made her way to the small chamber where she had slept in all her years at the abbey. She found Alice, youngest of the orphans who had come into Dame Alflega's protection in the killing times a decade ago, sitting on the narrow pallet bed. Beneath her freckles, Alice was as pale as a dove's wing.

More comfortable in the kitchen garden than the chapel, Alice had never, in the years Catherine had known her, spent a willing hour indoors. From the look of her, Alice had forsaken her old habits of late.

"Alice, are you ill?"

"Oh, Catherine!"

Catherine sat down and placed an arm about Alice's shoulders. "Alice, I have never seen you so dispirited. Is there some trouble for you?"

"No. Not now. But I dare not go into the garden, not until your husband's soldiers chase the strangers from the roads."

"Ah. It was you with Dame Alflega that day." Catherine hugged Alice and whispered words of reassurance. "They have already run away, most likely. The men-at-arms have been searching the roads in all directions these past days, and found nothing."

Catherine drew back and looked into Alice's eyes. "Did they harm you in some way? I heard that they held you only a few moments, and then rode away. Is it true?"

"Dame Alflega frightened them."

"I can't think how."

Alice's giggles became laughter, then moved on to tears. "It was terrible, Catherine. You can't imagine." Alice raised her head and sniffed. "Or maybe you can, now that you're married."

Catherine's heart turned over. "Alice, did the man ravish you?"

Another giggle, then a sob. "No. But he pulled my cloak from me and thrust his hand right down upon my belly, as if I were one of Sister Birgetta's dogs wanting a scratch."

Catherine expelled a sigh of relief. "That was what

he wanted? A hand upon your belly, in plain sight of the abbess? He must have been a madman."

"No, not a madman. He was a foreigner. Took his hand away and babbled something to his fellows, then rode away. The priest, too."

"They told me there was a priest. Did the priest do nothing to stop the one who touched you?"

"No. Once the babbling began, he turned away. Never even looked at Dame Alflega, though she was calling upon him to honor his vows and protect the innocent."

"Alice, you can't spend the rest of your life in this chamber. Isn't it safe to go out now, and walk in the garden, within the walls?"

"Dame Alflega says not. She thinks they were looking for a girl who looks like me, and fears that they might see me from a distance and commit other outrages. Oh Catherine," she cried. "I am so frightened. At night, I hear them out in the forest, just outside the abbey walls."

"Hush, Alice. Dame Alflega is speaking to my husband right now. If the abbey isn't safe, he will send more soldiers."

"I think it's the beginning of war, Catherine. Your husband has brought a small army he keeps nearby. There must be a reason. Oh Catherine, must we go through all that again? Will we lose the little we have left?"

In the end, Catherine did not wait the necessary hour before she followed Dame Alflega and

William into the abbey garden. At first she did not see them where they sat upon a wooden bench close by the high stone wall that kept the winter winds and creatures of the forest from Dame Alflega's tender herbs.

"There is nothing else you need to know," William was saying.

"Young lord, whatever you're doing for the king, you shouldn't have started it without speaking to me."

Catherine was reassured. Even the fierce Dame Alflega was finding William a hard man to interrogate. She drew back and waited out of sight, standing upon the mulched path between the rosemary hedge and a bed of brown stalks. She wondered who cared for the lilies, now that she was gone.

"I can guess what you're doing up there in the manor house, and it's a risky thing. I know. I have done such things myself, but only with good reason."

"There is a good reason—one that you cannot know—for all that I am doing."

"I already know enough to tell you that you must think of your daughter before you take on any more tasks for Henry Plantagenet."

"I am mindful of my daughter. How can you doubt that?"

"You vowed to protect Catherine. You are all she has in the world, you and that hot-head cousin of hers."

"I am set on my course, and cannot change now.

It's settled for the next few months. In the spring-time, I'll think again and make a plan."

"I am not pleased. You should have come to me and told me everything. I gave Catherine into your keeping."

"And I have sworn to keep her safe. I will. Catherine and our child will want for nothing."

Dame Alflega looked up and craned her head around the rosemary hedge. "Ah. Catherine. Come here then, and sit with us."

She advanced down the path, dreading to hear the abbess's next words. William was silent at her side, frowning at his boots. He had been speaking of providing for her. Had he plans to leave England, never to return? Would she and young Alflega return to the abbey to spend the rest of their days here, abandoned by William at the urging of the king?

"You have a sour look to your face, Catherine. Did you not find Sister Birgetta?"

"I saw Alice. She's near sick with fear."

The abbess made a gesture of dismissal. "She's a flighty one."

Catherine gathered her courage. There was no better place, and no better company, in which to watch William's reaction to her next words. "Alice told me what happened. She said the men were speaking in a foreign tongue, and a priest among them was watching as one of the brigands treated Alice with discourtesy. She must have feared they would ravish her."

In that moment, Dame Alflega's face seemed old and burdened with care. "So did I, child. So did I."

Catherine drew a long breath. "I believe it was no such thing. The men were looking for a woman carrying a child."

William looked up.

"The man who accosted Alice took away her cloak, and pressed his hand to her belly. Then he let her go without another glance. I believe he was looking for a pregnant woman."

"It is possible."

William turned to Dame Alflega. "Did you understand what they said? Which language were they speaking?"

"Not French, nor Flemish. No words I have ever heard in the common tongue. Not Latin—"

William grinned. "There are damned few brigands who conduct their business in Latin, Dame Alflega."

"You will not blaspheme in my presence."

William's smile broadened. "I will remember."

"As for the language of the thieves," said Dame Alflega, "I took it to be Scots. Or Welsh. Impossible to tell the difference."

William's smile faltered. Catherine looked away, afraid that William would see that she had noticed his dismay. That she had understood the link with him.

He had been fighting in Wales, though the king's war had not yet begun. In the wild country beyond Hereford, he had taken deep wounds in a brief skirmish. And then, with his wounds not healed, he had dragged a small army and—Catherine feared—a pregnant noblewoman to the forest house.

It was impossible that William had taken a woman hostage, and that her kin had brought armed men to scour the roads near Lundale to find their missing daughter. Their very pregnant missing daughter.

No. Though William was in some ways yet a stranger to her, Catherine would not believe that he would take a woman hostage.

If he had indeed brought a hostage north, William must have done it at King Henry's behest. If so, out of shame, he would not tell his wife.

Catherine's thoughts went to young Alflega, back at Lundale with only five men-at-arms to protect her. How many brigands had been waiting in the forest as their fellows had accosted the abbess? How large a party would ride out of the forest to search Lundale one day?

Above the cold earth, the rosemary hedge was fragrant in the noonday sun. Catherine had missed that familiar scent and the shelter of the abbey walls. Now, she must pray that she would not need to return here to live once again near this garden she had loved so well.

Soon, before she went mad with dread, she must confront William with her knowledge of the pregnant noblewoman in the forest.

William stood and took the abbess's arm. "It grows colder," he said.

"Yes," said Dame Alflega. "Come inside, both of

you, and we will speak of other things." She led them into the shadowed porch and through the stout door of the abbey hall. At the end of the long refectory, not far from the hearth, Dame Alflega pushed open the narrow door to her own chamber. "Wait here," she said.

Three of the abbey's orphan girls sat at their looms, not far from the fire. The sounds of whispers and muffled merriment floated down the long chamber. William smiled in their direction and bowed his head. The giggles ceased.

"Do you miss them?" He addressed her with easy courtesy, as if he had no secrets from her. As if he cared for her.

"I do," said Catherine. "There wasn't time for farewells, that day when you came to find me."

The abbess returned, and beckoned them into her room. Beneath the barred and shuttered window, her writing table had been cleared of its clutter. On the smooth surface of the wood rested a leather sack.

"Your inheritance," said Dame Alflega. "It took me many years, but I got it back, at last, from the goldsmiths of Nottingham. I told them you had wed a knight high in the king's regard, and that it was a shameful thing to send you to him with no dowry." She paused. "And I may have said something about the king's justiciars."

William opened the bag and raised his brows. "There's silver here, and some gold pieces. It isn't often that a man weds a dowerless girl and then finds himself richer for it."

Catherine raised her head. "Dowerless? Lundale was my dowry."

William turned to her, confusion in his eyes. He looked to the abbess, then back again to Catherine. "Lundale would have been worthless to me without you. Your help was dower enough."

"I don't understand—"

The abbess cast a nervous glance towards Catherine. "Now don't look to the past for trouble. It was all for the best."

"But you told me—"

"You're wed, and home again, and happy, and the rest doesn't matter. And I have forced those thieves in Nottingham to return your father's money. Where's the harm in that?"

She hefted the bag and dropped it. She smiled at the sound. "Fifteen marks, and two smaller gold pieces. In the end, the goldsmiths proved honest."

Catherine closed her eyes. "The money is most welcome. But last year—the land—was I not part of the charter for the land?"

William sat down beside Catherine and put an arm about her shoulders. "Dame Alflega. What did you tell Catherine when you suggested that she wed me?"

The abbess glanced at the door. "You have been wed for months. You have a child. Surely you have spoken of the charter, and come to an understanding, and—"

"What did you tell her on the day we wed?" William's voice was without expression, his words spoken with dull precision.

"That the king had given you Lundale, and you needed to wed Catherine to keep it."

"That was the truth," he said. His arm tightened about Catherine. "Without you, the land would have been nothing to me. The tenants would never have returned for a stranger."

Catherine shook off his arm. "My lady, will you tell me in clear words? Are you saying that the king did not give William the land on the condition that he wed me?"

The abbess made a vague gesture. "I didn't see the king's charter."

"William? Did you tell her that the king had sent you to wed me?"

His surprise could not have been feigned. "No. I thought you understood—"

"Enough!" Dame Alflega closed the door upon the curious faces of the girls at the hearth. "Do you two never speak to each other? Catherine, your husband didn't know you existed when he came to my door last year. He was traveling north to find his lands, and stopped at the abbey to ask which road led to Lundale. The king's men at Nottingham had read the charter and told William where the lands lay, but it was early spring and the roads were bad. William and his old squire came here to ask the way. What was I to do?"

There was no answer to her question.

"I might have sent a stable lad to take him to the crossroads. Instead, I—" The small, precise voice trailed off.

"Instead, you wed me to a stranger." Catherine

brought her hand down upon the bed in annoyance. In her passion, she had used the wrong hand.

"Catherine, have a care for your hand—"

She held the throbbing fingers to her bosom. "It doesn't hurt."

The abbess had retreated to the far side of the table. "He was a decent stranger, Catherine, and had a charter from the king. And I made sure he was unwed—"

"How?"

She made an impatient gesture. "I asked him. And the old man—John—as well."

William raised his head from his hands. "Catherine, I didn't deceive you. I thought the abbess had told you. I thought you understood."

The abbess raised her chin and attempted to look down upon them. "You see? It doesn't matter to you. If it did, you would have spoken together of whose land it was, and how you came to wed. There was no harm done. And much good. You have a child, and the people have returned to Lundale."

Catherine dropped her head to her hands. How many times, in the months of her marriage, had she overruled William in the small decisions she had made, certain that she had the right, telling him that she knew best what must be done to restore Lundale to wealth? He had never spoken of the king's outright gift of the lands, nor said that she had returned by William's choice, not by her own right. "You were too courteous," she said. "You never reproached me when I spoke of the land as mine."

"Catherine, the land was yours, before the last wars. And it was worthless to me, until you brought the tenants back out of the forest to farm it. This was truth, not courtesy."

He moved to the table and brought the sack of coins to her side. "And now you are a wealthy heiress as well. You might have done better than wed me."

Dame Alflega moved between them and raised Catherine's chin. "You were always too fast in your thinking, too swift to act. I never lied to you. Had you asked the needful questions, I would have told you what I knew. It is unlike you, Catherine, to dwell upon what can't be changed."

Catherine looked from Dame Alflega's flushed, imperious features to William's watchful eyes. Was it pity that she saw in his gaze? If she had known to look for it when they wed, would she have seen pity in his eyes even then?

Pity for an orphaned girl whose family had chosen the wrong faction in an old war and crossed from prosperity into death and disgrace?

Robert had sensed that something was wrong. Robert had noted that William kept her far from the king's notice. Far from sight of the court. . . . She had had nothing to offer him but the labor of her own hands and the good will of his tenants.

"Catherine. Speak to me."

"Do you have another wife?"

"Do you think me a faithless knave?"

"It seems," said Catherine, "that I must remember to ask the obvious. In all things."

"No. I had no wife, and wed you in good faith. And will keep my vows to you."

The image of the woman in the forest came to Catherine's mind and would not depart. In her cloak, the lady had appeared rich. In her bearing, she had seemed noble. And William had hidden her close to Lundale. Close to him.

"Have you ever wished for another wife?"

"By the Rood, Catherine—"

"You will not blaspheme," said the abbess.

"I have never wished for another wife. One is enough." William snatched up the money pouch and placed it in Catherine's good hand. "Come. It's long past time we started home."

Fourteen

William sent the outriders before and behind him at greater distances than before; if Catherine wished to speak with him, she would be well out of earshot of everyone but her husband.

She did not.

Instead, she sat straight before him on the saddle, her spine rigid and her inheritance upon her lap. She had forgotten the single glove she had worn to the abbey, and the woolen cloth she had wrapped about her bandaged hand was missing as well. The fingers of her good hand were clutched about the money pouch, and her knuckles had begun to turn blue from the cold.

"I could hang the pouch from the saddlebow," he said.

She shrugged and placed the sack in his hand. "It's yours, William. Put it where you wish."

Ominous words. William tied the drawstring about his swordbelt and placed a hand upon Catherine's back. "Put your hands inside your cloak to warm them," he said. "I won't let you fall."

"Thank you," she said. "You are kind and I am grateful."

Her speech, cold and formal, was more frightening than the previous two miles of silence.

"Catherine—"

"Would you please," she said, "tell me what happened on the day we wed?"

He sighed. "I never meant to deceive you. I had no way to know you were deceived."

"I understand. Please tell me what happened when you met Dame Alflega."

"If that meddling old woman had kept silent, we would both be happier today."

"I see." Beneath his hand, her spine was as hard as a new lance.

"I meant she should have been silent today. Catherine, if you continue so, you'll find fault in each word I speak. I'll speak if you'll listen to me without anger."

"I am not angry. Not at you."

"Then don't be angry with the old woman. She did as she thought best, and I'm happy for it. I don't regret wedding you. How could I? What say you, Catherine?"

She turned her face from him. "I'm angry with myself."

"For wedding me?"

"For neglecting to make certain of the truth."

"And if you had known the king hadn't sent me to wed you, would you have considered marriage with me?"

She glanced back, then faced the road again. "I might have. And I would have been—"

"What?"

"Humble. Grateful." She wrapped the cloak more tightly about her. "What you will."

"Ah." His wife's spirit was diminishing with each passing moment. He searched for words to give her strength. "What would I want with a humble wife?"

"Peace. Comfort. Obedience."

"Any one of them would be good. Especially obedience."

"You will have it."

This was worst of all. As a child in Normandy, he had heard tales of those who returned from the dead to take their places at the hearth, watching but never speaking. Never objecting when the living moved past them without courtesy. Catherine was well on her way to such a state. How long would she remain so cold and silent? "You wanted to hear what happened when I first saw you," he said.

"I would like that, if you are willing."

"Aye. I'll tell you. It was springtime. You remember."

"Yes."

"And it was raining. John and I had presented the king's charter to the warden of the castle at Nottingham, and asked for a guide to show us the way to Lundale. We spent the night."

William closed his eyes and remembered. It had been a damned good thing he had stopped at Nottingham. The warden's wife had crept into his pallet at midnight, and they had shared the dark hours in sweet sport. He had taken such pleasure in her that he had been drained of such hungers for days to come, and was therefore able to show restraint with Catherine.

What would have become of them both if he had taken Catherine that first night in immoderate passion?

"You spent the night," Catherine prompted.

There was something in her voice that made him fear she had read his mind. He cleared his throat. "Aye. And the next morning we found the guide had left without us." The fellow had no doubt been offered a better fee by an early riser. After that night of memorable excesses, William had slept well past dawn.

"There was no other to be found," said William. Not at that hour.

"So you set off alone, you and John."

"Aye. The rains continued all that day, and we slept in an alehouse beside the road. In the morning, the mud was deep and the road hard to follow. We made it as far as the abbey crossroad, and smelled woodsmoke to the east. So we took the abbey road and the abbess met us at the door. She gave us hot pottage and said she would find a stable boy to lead us north to Lundale.

"She went away, and then returned without the lad. Then she took me aside, and told me that Lundale was deserted, its people afraid to return to the fields. She said they feared that King Henry would send a tax collector. Or worse."

"They had seen worse, when the king's army came."

"So the abbess said. She told me the Lundale

people and their children were living in the forest, and there would be no one to plant a crop for me, or take care that the hall and the keep stayed upright. Each autumn, she said, raiders would use the keep when thieving in the area. She said it would be foul after seasons of brigands and rats had used it."

"That was true enough."

He paused, searching for the right words.

"Go on," said Catherine.

"Well, the abbess said all that, twice over. She had John in a temper; he urged me to leave the place to the vermin and give the charter back to the king. Then the abbess told me that the old lord's daughter was under her roof. Said you were orphaned during Henry Plantagenet's expedition to put down his enemies in Nottingham and places north, in the last year of King Stephen's reign."

Catherine cried out in anger. "The barons were right to fight the Plantagenet's army! King Stephen had sworn to allow the Plantagenet to take the crown when he died, putting aside his own kin by that oath. His pledge was meant to end the wars. Yet Henry Plantagenet would not wait for the old king to die; when he brought his army to Nottingham he was an invader. Nothing more."

William's temples began to pain him. He had heard such arguments over guardhouse ale since he was a stripling squire. "The barons had no intention of honoring King Stephen's oath. That's why—" William broke off his words and turned back to the matter of his marriage. "If we fight that war again in words, we'll not have peace in our house. I'll not speak of it again."

"Nor I." Catherine sighed. "Will you continue? You were at the abbey, and Dame Alflega told you I was living there."

"That's what she told me. I asked her if you would ride with me to speak to the old tenants and draw them back to the village, and to the fields. I had no way to know who they were and where to find them, and no hope that they would hear me out. And she said—"

"What?"

"She said she wouldn't trust a gently bred young maid with me. I swore to her that I would treat you with all honor and bring you back as pure as you were, but the old woman would have none of my promises."

"Not surprising."

"What do you mean?"

"You were a stranger with a scrap of vellum showing the king's seal. You might have been a thief who had taken it from its rightful owner. Why should she have trusted you?" Catherine paused. "That's exactly what she did. She trusted you," she said. "And so did I."

"You speak as if you had been wrong to take me at my word."

She looked away. "No, William. Never that. You have never lied to me. Not yet."

The pain in his head subsided at her words. William squared his shoulders and pulled his wife closer to his chest. After a brief hesitation, she sank

back against him. This late wooing of his despon-
dent wife might succeed, if he made his way with
care. "Where was I?"

"Dame Alflega didn't trust you."

"Ah. Yes. She bade me wait and brought a priest
to look at the king's charter, and questioned us—
both John and me—about my past."

"About your parents' trouble?"

"Yes. I told her all she asked—everything. My father's rebellion against King Louis in France, his
defeat, our flight to Normandy, and the new lands
my father won there. And I told her how the king
had come to grant me the land at Lundale."

"She told me King Henry had rewarded you for
valor."

"Those were the words he used. By the time your
lady abbess had described my new land and its
filthy keep, I had begun to understand why King
Henry hadn't given it away sooner."

Catherine shifted towards the saddlebow. A small
voice in William's mind chided him for blundering
so, straying so near to insulting his wife. He vowed
to choose his words with greater care.

"Of course she had not seen Lundale in many
years," he said, "and had forgotten how well placed
were its fields, and how fertile. And she didn't know
how well the keep had weathered the years."

It was impossible to tell, by the set of Catherine's
mouth, whether she was mollified. "You said the
abbey priest had read your charter," she said to
prompt him.

"Aye, he read it. And said he thought it written

by a royal clerk, with the king's own seal upon it. And he read my name from it, and said it was unlikely that a thief would have been able to read that same name upon the page, and the direction of the lands. I had grown tired of their questions and took back the charter and told them that John and I would find the place ourselves, and then she said it—"

"That we should wed?"

"No. She said to follow her to the garden. Just me. The rain had stopped and you were there, digging among the herbs and the first lilies. You didn't see us, and I didn't speak, for the abbess had cautioned me to be silent. She took me back into the refectory and asked me if I would wed you and take you to Lundale as my wife. If I wanted the tenants to return, she said, that was what I must do." William was silent for the space of a breath, willing his next words to have the grace he needed. "I wasn't thinking of tenants and crops when I said I would take you to wife, if you were willing."

He heaved a sigh. "I waited where she left me, right there at the nuns' table in the refectory, for half the afternoon. John found me there and I told him what I would do, and we sat there longer still, until at last John said that the abbess must be having a hard time persuading you to speak to me."

"I was covered in mud from the lily bed. Alice and Dame Alflega were scrubbing the soil from my fingernails and heating water for me to bathe, and deciding which kirtle I should wear, and whether I should veil my hair. And through it all, the abbess spoke of you, and of marriage. I agreed to look at you, and speak with you."

William smiled. "I remember."

"I peeked through the door before we went in, and thought you looked a fine man. And you spoke me fair. I don't remember a word the abbess said to us both."

"Nor I. I looked at you, close enough to smell the flowers in your hair, and waited for you to speak. And when you said you would have me, I was so stupid with joy that I hadn't the words to answer you."

Catherine nodded. "I remember that. You looked so shocked that I began to fear that you had changed your mind." She closed her eyes and began to frown. "I see how it happened. Dame Alflega could have told us that a blue dragon had taken up residence in the keep and we wouldn't have heeded her. Not that day."

William pulled her closer still. "Never doubt, Catherine, that I was happy to wed you. Trust me in that."

She looked up at him and touched his face.

He should have seen it coming. He should have kept the reins well in hand and his palfrey—his cursed palfrey—on the road to Lundale. Instead, the beast swung his uncurbed head east at the crossroad, and turned down the narrow track that led into the forest, and to the manor house.

Fifteen

Catherine's hand dropped as if burned by the touch of him. "You had better turn the horse," she said, "or I may catch sight of your secret army."

Though they were within sight of the crossroads, the wide-trunked oaks were close about, and the outriders had lost sight of William. He hauled his mount around to return to the road, and nudged it forward to the sounds of his escort shouting his name. He put an arm about Catherine's waist as he kept the palfrey from shying at the sound of approaching hoof beats and raised voices.

From the forest behind them came more shouts, and the sound of approaching horsemen.

Catherine craned her neck to look past his shoulder. "What is this? How many sentries do you have between here and the forest house?"

"Enough." William stroked the palfrey's neck to calm the beast as he called back to his men.

"And if one of my people—even Robert—came this way by mischance, how many men would come out of the forest to stop him?"

"Enough. Enough to stop him."

Catherine listened in silence as he called into the

forest to order his men back to their posts, then waved to his outriders to proceed.

"Damn this beast," he muttered.

"It's not the fault of the beast," said Catherine. "It knows you turn towards the forest house whenever you pass this way."

"Catherine—"

"I am not angry," she said. "I am speaking the truth, much as I loathe it." She reached forward and began to play with the palfrey's mane. "You must have thought it odd, each time I would complain that the king had neglected to return my mother's dower house with the rest of the land. You knew I had no right to any of it."

"Catherine, I never thought that."

She hesitated, and turned her face back to him. "Does the king know that you took a Lundale orphan to wife?"

"Of course. I told him when I went back to fight in Normandy."

"And was he angry?"

"Why should he be angry?"

She shrugged. "An odd question. Of course he was angry to see you wed into a family who had opposed him when he took the throne."

"Catherine, he wasn't angry. If the king held grudges against all the children of his old enemies, there would be no peace in England."

"Yet he sent forty soldiers here for the winter. The king remembers what happened at Lundale. Oh, William—the king must be suspicious of us still, and you have entangled yourself with us by marriage. If you had asked the king's leave to marry me, he would have refused it."

"Catherine, I'm a soldier, not a man of great property or influence. The king didn't expect me to beg his leave to marry."

She settled back against him, so quiet that he began to think she had fallen into sleep. Then down the road, just beyond the fording place that marked the beginning of Lundale's lands, Catherine straightened in the saddle and demanded to be set down.

"I want to walk," she said.

"It's cold, and you have been out on the road much of the day. Won't you stay here, where you are?"

"I want to walk. Please set me down."

William obliged, then climbed down to join her on the deeply rutted track. "Then we'll walk together."

"I need to think."

"Then I'll be silent, right beside you." He led his horse behind them as Catherine walked north towards the far corner of Lundale's recovered land.

The sun had begun to melt the snow from the black earth of Lundale. William wished that the sunlight might thaw the ice in Catherine's demeanor.

At the edge of the forest she turned to face him. "Don't tell Robert that you wed me without the king's leave."

"Would it matter to him?"

Catherine reached down to free her cloak from

a clump of dead nettles. "I will have to trust you not to speak of what I must tell you."

"I can keep a secret."

Her lips curved in a slight smile. "So I have learned. William, there is trouble with Robert," she said. "He is worried about me. About Alflega's future."

"Ah. He fears she'll never wed with that name to burden her."

"William, I'm serious. Robert mistrusts you and fears that you will put me aside one day to wed—"

He did not dare to touch her. "To wed another? Is that what Robert has said?"

"Perhaps."

"You believe I would annul the marriage and take another wife? Why should I do that?"

She stepped away.

"Tell me, Catherine. What reason did Robert give?"

"This is what he said. You haven't taken me to the king's court, not even when the king and his courtiers were in the north, not far from here."

"Catherine, I was fighting in Normandy until recent times. I wasn't able—"

"I know. But Robert worries about it. And he wonders why you hadn't tried to bring him into the king's presence to show the Plantagenet that we are now resolved to be his loyal subjects. Robert believes this is more evidence that you are not serious about bringing us back into the king's good graces."

She drew a short breath. "I know now why you

didn't do as Robert had hoped. This marriage wasn't part of Henry Plantagenet's plan for you and you might have provoked the king's anger had you brought me to his court."

Catherine scuffed her boot across a dead branch on the ground. "And most of all, Robert fears that one day you'll leave me here and wed another woman. A wealthy one, from a family well regarded by the king, to give you influence and to make you rich."

"He's wrong. We'll be rich enough, if the next year goes well. Even without that bag of coin the old woman gave you today, we would have been rich enough."

"Rich or not, you will have no influence with the king if he doesn't trust your wife's family."

"Influence is a dangerous thing. Turns on you and bites if you don't manage it carefully. If the king overlooks me, it may save me much grief."

"Robert believes you must want these things— riches and the king's regard."

"And that makes Robert dangerous to me. Is that what worries you?"

"I don't believe he would strike at you. Not so long as he believes you are resolved to care for me and for Alflega."

The throbbing had returned to his temples. With sickly prescience, he realized where Catherine's words were leading. "And what has alarmed Robert, to make him think that I am not devoted to you?"

Catherine raised her injured hand and shook

the crimson folds of her cloak from the arm. And pointed to the forest through which they had passed. "Your army," she said. "Robert doubts that King Henry needs his men wintered so far from him. When he was in the south, Robert heard talk of all the king's troubles—with the Welsh, with the Normans, and with his own English bishops."

William shook his head. "What is your cousin suggesting? That the king's men would be better sent south, to threaten a clutch of stubborn bishops?" He smiled. "Though you think little of our King Henry, you should recognize that he's a little more subtle than your cousin Robert."

Catherine was not provoked to laughter. She stood straight before him, her face oddly pale beneath her shining raven hair. "What will you do, William, when Robert discovers the woman in the forest?"

She knew. Somehow, she had discovered the lady Mathilde. If you had wanted a comfortable wife, said the small voice in his mind, you would not have chosen this one. The abbess said it as well, when she had first spoken of Catherine. But he had been besotted at the sight of her, and thought it a fine thing that she had a mind of her own.

"It is only a matter of time," she continued. "Winter has just begun, and I have seen her. Robert will discover her too."

The knot in his chest became a pain as sharp as any knife. "There is nothing to discover. I told you there are some women living up there."

"Cooks and camp-followers, you said."

"Aye."

Catherine's eyes darkened to a deep, bitter green, the color of a leaf in the last days before the frost. The last color before the killing cold. "I have seen her," she said. "William, I have seen her in the forest."

"Catherine—"

"She is no servant, William. No common woman. And she carries a child."

There was nothing in her voice to betray her intent.

"Go on," said William.

"If Robert hears of her, there will be trouble. If he sees her, Robert won't be content with rumors. He will demand to know what you intend to do. With Lundale, and with me."

"How long ago?"

She looked at him in puzzlement.

"How long ago did you see her?"

"Near the time of solstice. She is far gone with child, William. Whoever she is, she shouldn't be kept so far from comfort. Whatever you are planning, keep that first in your mind."

His wife had not ceased to astonish him. She had done as much as accuse him of bringing a pregnant mistress to take her place, then in the next breath upbraided him for failing to care for the woman.

His mind clamored with answers. Defenses. Fears. He set his hand upon the pommel stone of his sword and looked straight into his wife's eyes.

"You have left me no choice, Catherine. There is but a single way out of this trouble." He unsheathed his sword and raised it, hilt uppermost, blade pointed down to the black earth between them.

Her eyes widened.

"I shall have to trust you," he said. "I will swear upon this sword, and upon my hope of salvation, that all I will tell you is the truth. Will you swear, Catherine, to keep secret what you will hear, and to keep faith with me, with what I have sworn to do?"

She placed her good hand upon the pommel stone. "Saving my honor, I won't speak of it. Yes, I swear."

He looked beyond her. "Damnation," he said. "Your cousin Robert comes. Catherine, remember—"

"I have sworn," she said. And placed both hands over his to force the sword down into the ground in the moment Robert reached them.

She looked up into her cousin's eyes and frowned. "Damnation," she repeated. "The serpent has escaped."

Robert looked from William to the grey palfrey standing near behind them, the reins dragging upon the earth. "Escaped?"

Catherine relinquished her grip on the sword and pulled her cloak close against the cold. "A snake," she said. "A serpent lying cold upon the field. I set William to kill it, but it woke before we struck. It escaped us."

"A snake out on the ground in winter? That's bad luck," said Robert. He pointed to the palfrey. "You have a steady mount. Didn't run at the sight of a serpent."

William managed to shrug. "He's a good beast," he said. "Doesn't look beyond his own nose for trouble." He sheathed his sword, and turned from Robert's thoughtful gaze. He left them, then, and went back to fetch the horse.

Sixteen

Catherine watched her husband cross the melting furrows to pick up the reins of his palfrey. At her side, Robert calmed his restive horse, then stood in the stirrups to look about them. "Your snake has hidden himself well." He went back into his saddle and watched William's approach. "Or perhaps you imagined it."

She glanced down the field and back again, attempting to appear worried that a serpent might return. A quick glance at Robert revealed that he had believed her tale; he, too, continued to watch the ground just beyond his horse's hooves.

In that moment, Catherine began to feel a sly pleasure in her success. She had deceived Robert for William's sake. Not a large deception. Not a lie that would do harm. If she could turn her cousin's attention from the truth so easily, there might be some hope that she could keep him from discovering William's larger secrets.

It was a skill she had not thought to learn. Dame Alflega had taught her never to lie.

Dame Alflega, said a small voice in Catherine's

mind, had proved to be a skillful, well-meaning liar herself.

"I think it's gone," said Robert. "But stay near me just in case."

Catherine had never lied to Robert before, not even in those terrible days when they had been child fugitives from the Plantagenet's wrath. Not even when they had been taken into Dame Alflega's care, and Robert had begun to grow restless within the abbey's walls. They had disagreed often, and Catherine had relied upon honest arguments to keep Robert from folly. Now, the folly was more likely to be her own.

William led his horse to where they waited, and looked from Robert to Catherine.

William met her distracted glance with a wink. He unhooked the money pouch from his belt and held it out to her. "Look at this, Robert. It seems I have a rich wife and you a wealthy cousin."

Robert stepped forward and hefted the sack of coins. "Where did you find it?"

"At the abbey. Dame Alflega gave it to Catherine. Said she had been to Nottingham to deal with the goldsmith who had kept Catherine's father's wealth."

Robert handed the bag back to Catherine. "I didn't think there had been that much."

William laughed. "Maybe not. Maybe your Dame Alflega frightened the smith so badly he emptied his coffers in the hope that she would spare him."

Robert dismounted and led his horse beside them as they walked back to Lundale. Ahead, in the distance, columns of woodsmoke rose from the round huts outside the palisade walls. "It wouldn't be the first time the abbess had done such a thing for us," said Robert. "But I doubt she was so successful in the past. Those first years—they were hard times."

Catherine took William's arm and stepped past an ice-crusted puddle. "When Osbert took Robert and me to the abbey for shelter, Dame Alflega waited until the Plantagenet's soldiers had left Nottingham, and traveled there to speak to the goldsmiths. The town had been sacked as badly as—everywhere else." She felt William's hand upon hers, and turned to look at him. "Even so, she managed to find the smith who had kept my father's gold; the man told her that he had managed to hide some of it before the soldiers reached his house. It was buried, she said, beneath the door stoop. She made him dig it up before her eyes and give her all he could. She believed, though, that the rest of it was elsewhere, buried in a churchyard. After all these years, she must have forced him to get it."

"I doubt he did it willingly."

Robert laughed. "You begin to understand how well Catherine and I were protected in those years. No dragon would have kept us safer."

"She brought back enough to pay for my keep and for Robert's. And she made us understand, though we were but children, how much of it she would need to use for the abbey itself. Each year she would write down the sum and show us where it was written in the abbey's book."

"Had the abbey been sacked in the rebellions?"

"No. One way or another, Dame Alflega had shamed the Plantagenet into sparing the place. No, the abbey was unharmed and its lands never lost a crop. Dame Alflega needed the money to feed and clothe other children who had been orphaned. A few of us were from noble families, many more were children of tenants from miles around—infants too young to live through that first winter in the forest."

Robert shook his head. "It was crowded with children, in those years. At times, we sounded like a flock of geese. Fear of Dame Alflega was the only thing that kept us all from running wild."

"But some did," said William.

"Aye," said Robert. "Some of us managed."

They reached the village before the sun went down. From the kitchen shed beside the great hall came the smell of roasting meat and bread; in the hall itself, the women had moved their looms to the walls to make way for trestle tables.

On the dais, perched in the lord's chair, young Alflega was tangling a length of woolen thread over her fingers. Hadwen looked up from a bench beside the child. "Your daughter didn't miss you at all," she said. "But we will need to make three new shuttles in place of the ones she cast into the fire."

William picked up his daughter and set her upon his right arm. "How did we come to have such a costly child?"

Catherine set the money pouch upon the table. "This will help."

He raised his brows and wiggled them for Alflega's amusement. "Aye, it will help, if our girl doesn't decide to send the coins after the shuttles, into the fire." Alflega's giggles became louder.

"Hush, William. She understands what you're saying."

"Do you think so?" He set her down and frowned. "We'll have to be careful, won't we?"

"Yes. Tonight, William. We'll be sure she's sleeping, and you will tell me everything."

He touched her hand. "As I swore. Everything."

Alflega's small fist came down to rest upon her parents' hands.

"Aye. We'll need to be careful."

It was not to happen as she had wished.

The sentries' horns sounded twice, then twice again over the sounds of speech and singing in the hall. William picked up his sword and ran with Robert out into the bailey yard, leaving a sudden hush in his wake. Catherine picked up Alflega and rushed at Hadwen's side to the doors and saw the men of the garrison milling about the byre, calling to each other as they led their mounts from shelter. Beyond the palisade walls came the sound of sheep and confusion.

Hadwen thrust the money pouch into Catherine's view. "Were you going to leave it for the raiders?"

"Into the keep," William called to them. "Go into the chamber, and bar the door."

He led his destrier from the byre and climbed into the saddle. Unlike the gentle palfrey William had used to carry Catherine to the abbey, William's warhorse was restive, impatient to be out of the yard. In the bobbing light of the riders' torches, Catherine saw Radulf emerge from the byre with a polished spear in his hand.

"Not you," she called.

William turned and caught sight of the lad. "Into the keep with you and your spear. Stay beside the door and protect your lady."

"I'm coming—"

Hadwen caught him just as he reached the gates, and sent him off balance with a swing of the money pouch. She led him by his ear to the tower. "You heard your lord. You're to stay and watch over our lady."

Radulf's face was contorted in disappointment. "I heard him. But can't make out a word he speaks. Let go!"

They ran upstairs into the guardroom, and climbed again to the third level, to the sleeping chamber. Catherine pulled Hadwen into the room and thrust Alflega into the woman's arms. "Wait here. I'm going up to see where they're heading."

"Your husband said—"

"Aye," added Radulf. "You're to stay here in the chamber with Hadwen and the child and I'm to keep guard outside the door."

"So you heard our lord William right," said Hadwen. "No more of your nonsense about that. Catherine—"

"Later," said Catherine from the stairs. "I'll be down later."

She shouted ahead to the lone sentry on the parapets, and made her way up to the highest point of the walkway. In the loom of the single torch, Catherine saw that the long cow horn was back in its place, hanging by a leather strap from the timber railing.

"What did you see?"

"Nothing. The man at the gates sounded his horn, and I blew this one to carry the alarm. The sheep are loose from the folds, but that watchman at the gate wouldn't sound the alarm for that."

Far below them, four torches flared in the dark fields. Two moved east to skirt the palisade walls, and two set out across the dark fields to the west.

By those wind-blown flames Catherine saw that there were six riders in all—four torchbearers and two men who rode unencumbered within the loom of the burning brands. William, Robert and four men were abroad in the night. Six of the garrison and ancient John were left to defend Lundale. Two sentries and five men at the gates.

Catherine shivered beneath the cold night sky. The darkness was vast above her and beyond the receding light of the torches, and yielded no hint of the danger that had called William forth. Her people were gathered within the bailey yard, safe behind the gates, trusting seven armed men to keep them from harm.

"What's that?"

The sentry turned to follow a faint sound behind

them, far to the east. "The sheep," he said. Catherine strained to see movement within the darkness. The three riders searching that direction swerved from their path and stopped. The yellow firelight shone upon the plump, pale backs of Lundale's sheep. A shout rose from the scene, and the riders moved on.

"Look there."

The sentry had turned back to watch the western fields. The riders had reached the edge of the forest and turned south. "The fording place," said Catherine.

"They won't go beyond," said the watchman. "From there on, the king's men patrol the road. Night and day, they take it in turns."

How much did the men of the garrison know about the winter settlement at the manor house?

"Why?" said Catherine.

"Wouldn't do for the king's guard to lose their fine horses to thieves," said the sentry. "Who would pay them to fight if they couldn't keep their own camp free of raiders?"

The torches reached the fording place and shone bright yellow upon the glittering surface of the river. The two flickering fires traced a slow circle about the shallows, then moved together, and back to the east. "They're on their way back," said the sentry.

"Is Lord William with them?"

"Hard to tell."

Catherine watched their slow progress toward the walls. The riders swept past the gates and headed west; for a long moment the flames illuminated the empty sheep folds, then moved on.

"They'll be hours chasing the sheep," said the watchman. "Cold work."

"If you see trouble, after you blow the horn, please call down the stairs to Radulf and tell him what you have seen." Catherine made her way down the dark spiral of stairs.

"Who goes there?" Radulf's voice was as young as a girl's in the darkness.

"Only me."

In the final turn of stair before the chamber door, Catherine saw Radulf's pale face in the light of a single taper. "I took it from the guardroom," said Radulf. "It's too dark up here."

"That was wise," said Catherine. "We would need it to get down the stairs carrying the baby."

"Right. That's why I brought it."

"Of course."

Radulf's face relaxed. "Then I'll stay here all night," he said in a deeper voice. "and keep the taper burning. In case. Did you see Lord William out there?"

"I saw the men ride out. Go up, if you like, and tell the sentry you want to look."

"No." His voice had descended almost to man's timbre. "I promised my lord that I'd watch over you. He rapped on the chamber door. "Open up, Hadwen. The lady Catherine's back."

Catherine pushed at the door and found, as she had expected, that it wasn't barred. Alflega was in her cradle, and the brazier blazed bright against the far wall, below an arrowslit that drew the smoke. Hadwen was asleep in the bed. "Would you like to sleep beside the fire?" Catherine whispered.

"No," said Radulf. "I have my duty." He pulled the door shut.

As she climbed into bed, the bolster rolled aside to reveal the money pouch Hadwen had secured there. If silver and gold could buy shelter from the kind of danger she now faced, Catherine would have sent the coins uncounted, without regret, to Henry Plantagenet to buy William's freedom from the king's wars, and from his schemes. But the world didn't work that way.

Catherine placed the feather pillow over her inheritance and drifted into sleep.

Seventeen

He smelled of saddle and sheep, and should have slept in the guardroom. William rounded the last turn of the stair to find the young lad Radulf asleep on his feet, propped against the door of the sleeping chamber. At his feet, a taper had burned down to a puddle of tallow upon the flagstone at the chamber threshold. It was a good thing the boy had remained at his post so long; without him, William might have missed the sight of the tallow on the stair, and fallen on his bad knee.

He hesitated before waking the lad, but the aching in his knee was worse than before, and would make a descent of the stairs an ordeal.

It had been foolishness to keep half the garrison out to scour the fields by torchlight. The sheep would not be gathered by men on horseback, and the beasts had wandered the night through, causing confusion and very likely masking the escape of the raiders who had pulled down an entire side of the wicker pens that had held the ewes.

He had been worse than foolish. In the end, it had been Catherine's impulsive cousin Robert who had pointed out, after William had collided with another rider in the dark, that it would be prudent to return to the keep and put off further searches until dawn.

William rubbed his knee and frowned. He was getting old. Of his twenty-five years, ten had been spent in Henry Plantagenet's service. In the first years of that decade William's injuries had healed quickly, and he had not missed a single campaign or skirmish of importance. This last wound had been slow to cure, and William had been hard pressed to find a way of padding the leg for the long trip north. He had managed with the help of a Shrewsbury apothecary and paid the man well for his skill, for this journey was one that Henry Plantagenet would not allow William to delay.

It could be that the little Welsh urchin who had struck him had tainted the blade of his knife, and had left William's leg poisoned as well as slashed. Or it might be that William was indeed getting too old to climb out of a sickbed and ride two hundred miles in early winter for the king. For anyone.

Radulf awoke with a shriek that frightened them both. William gestured him aside and pushed the door open. Catherine had been careless to leave it unbarred.

"Go down and find yourself a piece of floor in the guardroom," he said to Radulf. "You did well to keep watch."

He pulled the door shut behind him and looked about the chamber. Young Alflega was in her cradle, and there was a bulky form rolled in the coverlet beside Catherine. He didn't bother to prod the larger form; it must be Hadwen.

He didn't bar the door. His guardroom was crowded with enough sleeping soldiers to trip an intruder, and the wetnurse was sure to appear in a few hours to feed Alflega.

There was just enough room beside Catherine to rest his weary body for a moment before removing his clothes. Not all of them, for Hadwen might awaken to find him there.

William yawned and pulled Catherine's sleeping form closer to him. If he removed his chausses, Hadwen would be upset and Catherine would see that he had damaged the damned knee once again. Better to leave it covered. For he had no wish to see the bruises in the light of dawn. He had no wish to see another bruise on his body for a long time. For a week or more, if he was lucky.

He awoke long after dawn to find the chamber quiet and the coverlets pulled across his shoulders. William closed his eyes again and imagined what he should be doing, and decided that all of it could be put off. All of it save speaking to Catherine.

William pulled the blanket over his head and frowned inside that dark haven. He had promised Catherine an explanation of the task King Henry had set him, and she had promised to honor her oath of secrecy. Today, if his cousin-by-marriage allowed him a little privacy with Catherine, William must deliver on that risky promise.

He shifted his weight slowly, fearing that the movement would bring back the pain in his knee. By some miracle, his leg didn't begin to ache. William smiled and reached down to his knee; there were bandages there, and a wet poultice swathed in soft wool.

William pulled down the coverlet and opened his eyes. Catherine was across the room, sitting in the narrow stream of sunlight coming through the eastern arrow slot, her hair a mass of black and burnished copper in the morning sun. "Good morning," she said. "Does your leg pain you?"

He raised it from the mattress and caught the scent of herbs and evergreen sap. "What did you use on it?"

"Something from the forest," she said, "and herbs from the abbey garden." Catherine rose and walked to the door. "I'll bring hot water to bathe it," she said.

"Have a lad bring a bucket or two, and I'll manage it myself."

He fell back against the mattress and closed his eyes for a moment. Then Catherine was back with Radulf and two steaming buckets. "Leave them," she said. "And let him sleep again."

William reached and caught her hand. "Stay," he said. "And we will talk."

She nodded to Radulf and waited for him to shut the door. "I'll deal with your leg, and you speak." Catherine glanced about the chamber. "This is as private as we are likely to be, for the next fortnight."

"No. What cruelty do you intend?"

"It's nearly Christmas. We will have people in the hall feasting in greater numbers, I hope."

William groaned. "You hope? It's a beehive as it is."

"There are rumors that our tenants will ask their kin to come out of the forest and share our board at Yuletide. If they decide to stay, we'll be able to clear the rest of the old fields after the winter, and plant twice as much next spring. This is our chance, William, to bring Lundale back to what it was. And the people in the village will be happier with all their kin restored to them."

"It would be good to clear the forest of all but the king's people in the cold months. It's lucky that their hunting hasn't brought about conflict. If one of the people living in the wild brings down a deer and catches the attention of the soldiers at the forest house, it will take all my small influence and your good wit to keep them from the assizes at Nottingham."

Catherine unwrapped the poultice covers and frowned down at William's knee. "Husband, it is time you stopped ruining your leg so regularly. If you would give it a year away from the wars, it would heal well and give you no more pain." She sighed. "Can you not tell Henry Plantagenet that you will miss the next war or two?"

He caught up her good hand. "If you would vow to stop rushing into danger without thinking first. And never again place yourself between men with swords drawn. And stay away from the river."

"Well then. I'll promise. You have my vow. No more riding into the way of men with swords drawn. Now what will you promise?"

"I cannot promise to stay home from the wars. Henry Plantagenet's mind is not a chronicle book; he most remembers the last thing you did for him. A man could fight in his army for years, and then neglect some trifling matter of taxes or of law. The king will remember the latter, and forget the years of fighting. "If I give up the king's service and stay here for the rest of my days, the king will either forget me or become annoyed that I'm not there when he needs me. Either way, he might decide to give this land away to another."

William pointed to the money pouch beside the cradle. "When Henry Plantagenet is irritated, not even the gold in that sack will change his mind. He would accept it, and make it part of his royal treasury, but remain just as angry as before. Believe me. I have seen it happen."

"And if your leg festers next time, and you lose it? Will Henry Plantagenet permit you to stay home then?"

"Come, Catherine. I will do what I must do."

She made a small sound of dismay and turned to busy herself at the clothing chest. William looked away from the sight, from the grace in the line of her arms, from the way she swept her hair from that slim neck before she looked down into the coffer. These were the small memories that would one day bring him to grief.

He had not expected to become infatuated with

his wife. Yet the first day he had parted from her, the day he rode south to find men for his small garrison, he had been consumed with thoughts of her. On the road through the great forest, he had become careless and failed to notice the approach of brigands from the wildwood. John had heard them and warned him in time; together they had sent the ragged fellows to flight.

Barely a month later, after the fortnight in which he had made Catherine his wife in truth, William had left John in charge of the new garrison and had set out alone to rejoin Henry Plantagenet's army in Normandy. John had chided him for the loss of his uncanny instinct for danger, and told him to turn his mind from Catherine as soon as Lundale was behind him, lost to sight. In the weeks he had traveled to Normandy, William had managed to do this; only in the nights, in alehouses and in thickets beside the long roads and in the sodden discomfort of a ship's bow, had he allowed himself to think of Catherine.

His days had offered scarce time for such thoughts. William had lost all joy in a battle well fought, in a skirmish won with skill. And he ceased to care how many villages he had added to the lists of King Henry's possessions.

John had sent word that Catherine was with child. And when the rebel archer had come so close to putting an arrow through William's skull, William had known a new fear—that he would never again see Catherine, never know whether she had survived her travail, never see the face of his child—.

He turned to the sound of Catherine's voice.

"William, will you not answer?"

"Forgive me," he said. "I didn't hear you."

She returned to the side of the bed, and placed a hand upon his forehead. "I said that your leg will fail you if you go back to fight for the king before it's strong again. And I asked whether Henry Plantagenet deserves to have you back at all."

"He is my king. When he goes to war, I'll follow him."

Catherine's mouth set into a grim line. "Follow him. Aye, you should follow him. But take care he doesn't send you before him, into danger he won't face."

William caught her hand. "What is this you say? You don't know him. He's no coward, Catherine. He's a fair lord, even generous at times. He gave me this land. If not for him, we would never have met. Never wed."

Her gaze did not falter. "Of late, he has been sending you into greater danger. This is clear to me, though I haven't seen a battle or stirred from this place. When I first saw you, there was one single scar upon your brow. One scar. And now—"

William reached up and tugged a strand of her hair. "Now Catherine, if you had taken a good look below my—brow—you would have seen more than a single scar."

She flushed then, and shook her hair free. "You know what I am trying to say. Since you took these lands and went back to fight for the king, you have nearly died twice over. Each time I see you there are more scars, badly mended wounds."

William closed his eyes and sighed. How could he tell her—he would never tell her—that his desire for her and a kind of homesickness had taken the edge from his skills?

As a young, unfettered man who had taken little care to remember the names of the women who had shown him kindness in their beds, William had possessed all the cold, passionless control he had needed to fight with intelligence. Then, last year, in his first skirmish after a sleepless night spent thinking of Catherine, William had discovered how dangerous such devotion might be.

And in the moment when the arrow had sliced past his jaw last summer in Normandy, William's crowded thoughts had been of Catherine and the child she might bear as a widow; if his squire had not pushed him to the ground, the next shaft that flew in that ambush would have drilled straight through his heart.

No, he would never tell Catherine the true reason why the dangers had increased.

"In the spring, William, send word to the king that you cannot fight for him. There are forty men up there in the forest house to take the message." She paused. "Or are they headed somewhere else, when spring comes? Perhaps some of them are clever and realize that there are better ways to live than at Henry Plantagenet's whim."

He touched her lips. "You must mind what you say. You may say these things to me, if you must, but never to anyone else. Not even to Hadwen. Not to Robert." William grimaced. "Especially not to Robert."

Catherine sat back and began to plait her hair. "I have already sworn not to speak of the king's business. If I ever learn it, I'll be sure to keep my word."

"Ah. The matter of the forest."

"Yes," she said. "The people in the forest."

In the moment he took to find the words, her face lost its color. "Tell me all," she said. "Both good and bad. Tell me everything."

"Bar the door, and come back here. I'll not speak this above a whisper."

Her eyes grew wide. Catherine walked past the brazier without a care that the fire was low; she found the bar in the shadows beside the door, and set it into the brackets. "There," she said, and came to kneel upon the rushes beside the bed, her arms upon the mattress.

He drew a breath and began with the worst of it. "The king has insulted the Baron Pandulf. Insulted the man who must supply shelter and all other things for the army King Henry will take into Wales."

Catherine drew closer still. "Good," she whispered. "Then he won't have his war, will he?"

"Hush. It doesn't work that way. There still may be war, whatever happens this winter."

"Go on."

"The baron Pandulf doesn't know, and with luck he may never know, how the king has injured him.

It is my task to be sure that all things unfold in that way."

"You are hiding the king's bad deed?"

"I am giving shelter to the king's pregnant mistress. A young kinswoman of Ivo Pandulf."

"Royal adultery?" Catherine raised her brows. "Even here, so far from the king's councils, we hear of such things. It is not uncommon for a king to seduce the wives of his courtiers. Why must this particular one hide from the world?"

"This one," said William, "was no wife of an ambitious vassal. She was the untouched maiden daughter of Ivo Pandulf. This was something beyond what may be allowed. It was a mistake."

"Well beyond what is allowed." Catherine closed her eyes. "She is the woman I saw in the forest?"

"Aye."

"Why did she ride so far in her condition? Why is she not hidden somewhere in a convent? Such arrangements are made. Dame Alflega once had a guest we never saw—"

William groaned. "I don't doubt that. Your Dame Alflega would manage it."

"Then why not send the girl where she may disappear among other women for a time? She has left her father's house in any case. Why is she here?"

"It isn't that simple."

Catherine sighed. "There is more?"

"Much more. The girl is a bastard daughter, but held in high regard by her father. She is half Welsh, through her mother. Has hundreds of kinfolk all up and down the Marches. Somehow, through servants' talk or her own indiscretion, the girl's plight reached the ears of the Welsh lords."

Catherine's eyes narrowed. "The girl's indiscretion? The king is a grown man, wiser in the ways of the world than any soul in Christendom. It's his fault—"

William frowned. "Do you want to hear this?"

She frowned back. "Everything. Tell me everything."

"The Welsh lords heard that King Henry had taken a noble maid to his bed, and sent spies to hear more of it. Through some mischance, they learned that she was pregnant. And they learned where they might find her."

William sighed. "In the beginning, when the girl told Henry she was pregnant, he told her to send a message to her father and tell him she would go to the convent where her mother had died. She was to send word to Pandulf that she wished to pass the winter praying for her mother's soul and learning tapestry work from the nuns."

"That would have been sensible. Did the baron not allow his daughter to go to the convent?"

"Pandulf sent word that he would allow her to go, and gave the messenger gold to pay for her keep. I was in the party sworn to deliver her there in secrecy. There was trouble along the way, and we learned from a Welsh prisoner taken after a skirmish that he and his fellows were searching for a noblewoman with child. He was to bring a priest who knew the woman, show him that the girl was pregnant, and the priest was then to tell Pandulf."

"And Pandulf would turn against the king."

"Yes. And the invasion of Wales might never happen."

"And you wouldn't need to go to war this spring."

William smiled. "It always comes back to that, with you."

Catherine brought her hair before her shoulder and began again to plait the dark, shining mass. "I'd ride south and find this baron Pandulf myself—"

"Catherine!"

"—if I hadn't sworn to keep this secret. Much good might come of telling him."

"And much trouble. If the Welsh manage to get a priest to swear the girl is pregnant, and name the king as father, word will reach Queen Eleanor. If she becomes angry enough to renounce King Henry, he will lose his lands in Anjou and Aquitaine as well. And I'll need to go over there with him to win them back."

Catherine shook her head. "The queen can't just walk away from her husband, and take back her lands."

William laughed. "She did exactly that to Louis of France. Divorced him and wed Henry Plantagenet. Took her lands from Louis and brought them to Henry. No," he said, "Queen Eleanor is the greatest danger of all, in this affair. She tolerates the king's infidelities with servant girls and unfaithful wives. A noble maid from a rich family is another matter."

Catherine sighed. "So the king gave the trouble of all this to you."

"He did. Said that no one, not even the Welsh, would imagine the people hereabouts would hide the girl to help Henry Plantagenet. A place with your history—death and devastation at Henry Plantagenet's hand—is the last place on earth where the Welsh would look."

"So the king told you to bind up your ruined leg and ride north with that girl, and leave her in a deserted stockade in the forest with a small army to keep the Welsh from finding her. And you did as he said. Despite the stupidity of that plan, you did as the king said."

Her words were edging towards rebellion. Treason. Her parents had lost everything by such thoughts. His own parents, speaking of a different king in a different land, had lost nearly as much. Yet her anger was balm to his soul.

There had been few souls, in these past weeks, in whom he could confide. The forty men who had sworn to see, hear, and speak of nothing surrounding the king's mistress had been told very little of the girl's background. William had told John a little more than that; the old warrior had greeted the news with a grunt of displeasure and nothing more.

Now Catherine knew the truth of it. She alone, hearing of his task, had echoed his own hidden anger.

"It was a stupid plan," she said.

"It was," he answered. "But there was nothing else to do. Had I turned from the matter and stayed at court, the king would have blamed me if it went wrong in another's hands. And he would have wondered, if rumors began, if I had spoken of it. Believe me, Catherine, I did what I thought best. I am no creature of the court; this went beyond a fighting man's ken."

"It goes beyond anything the king should ask of you."

"I have tried, as best I could, to keep this trouble away from you and your people and the child. If it goes badly, no one at Lundale will be drawn into the consequences. We must keep it that way."

He saw her blink away the unshed tears in her eyes. "Well, husband," she said, "That is more trouble than I had imagined. And I forgive you all—I say there is nothing to forgive, save your foolish secrecy. Why did you not come to me on that first day and tell me what you had done?"

"Robert. Your cousin Robert. I nearly told you, that day in the fields, just before he came. To me, Robert looked and sounded like trouble in the brewing."

He reached to place a finger upon Catherine's lips. "I know he's a good man, careful of his honor. But he hates Henry Plantagenet even more than you do. You'll have to keep this from him, Catherine. It's your burden now, as well as mine."

She nodded. "I know. I won't fail you. And I'll help with the other—what is her name?"

He frowned. "Mathilde. Her name is Mathilde. You are not to go near her. Remember, it may go wrong. There are so many ways this may go wrong. And you mustn't be involved."

"Yes, William. You needn't say it each time you open your mouth. But I'll ask you if you and your good King Henry thought to send a midwife along with the poor child."

The image of the splendid traveling litter, pack-horses bred as well as any royal palfrey, and two silken-clad serving women came to William's mind. "I'm sure he did."

"Well, make certain you are right. When I saw the girl in the forest she had a great belly before her. If she doesn't have a midwife, we'll have to send Hadwen, and be damned to the king's secrets. Or take her to the abbey."

"Ah. The abbey." William dropped his head to his hands and groaned. "I have to do something about the rumors at the abbey."

He heard Catherine's low laughter. "Rumors are the lifeblood of the abbey. You can't change that."

"Lifeblood or not, I have to stop one source of them." William heaved a great sigh. "Dame Alflega already knew there was a pregnant noblewoman at the forest house," he said. "Yesterday, even before you came into the abbey garden and spoke of the matter, Dame Alflega had told me that she had heard rumors of such a woman. She was trying to get the truth from me."

Catherine smiled. "For that, I do pity you. In all the years I spent at the abbey, there was never a rumor or bit of mischief that Dame Alflega left undiscovered."

William turned away to find his boots. "I had better take a new lot of guards to the abbey. The oldest of them with the worst tempers should be the best. And I'll warn them first that they're not to speak to the old woman. Not a word."

"You know you're already too late," said Catherine.

William sighed. "It was my mistake to choose the ten most agreeable of the king's men to protect the abbey. If I leave them there a day longer, Dame Alflega will have them working under her orders, taking messages down to Winchester for her. Spying for her—"

Catherine laughed. "I think you're right."

"I'll ride out now, and be back by nightfall."

"There are clean leggings," said Catherine. "And more bandages for your leg, with sheep's wool to cushion it. It's the least you can do, if you're determined to ride today."

He accepted the clothing from her outstretched arms and stood quiet as she bound up his damaged knee.

"You will have to tell the king's men about the foreigners and the priest. And ask Mathilde's serving women if either of them knows how to help her when the child comes. Don't forget."

"I won't forget."

He had been right to tell Catherine of the task he faced. Though he had risked much in telling her, a rebel's child, of the king's secret trouble, William felt his spirit unburdened for the first time since he had left Winchester.

It was not a bad thing to have Catherine's opinions ringing in his ears.

A midwife. Had Mathilde and her velvet-clad ladies up in the forest done something about a midwife?

Eighteen

The looms were down, their work folded away and frames stacked in the store huts, not to be used again until the days of Christmas had passed. Young Alflega was displeased to see them gone and announced her opinion in a voice that drowned out all but the most valiant attempts of others to speak.

"She likes to cling to them as she learns to walk," said Hadwen. "That's why she's missing them."

"Aye. I saw her use them," said William. "I was too late to stop her when she picked up the sticks with the wool on them and tossed them into the fire."

"I'll carve them more of those sticks," said John. "Just put one of the looms back—just one of them might do—and Alflega will stop crying. Poor little girl. Her little voice must hurt when she screams so."

"Well, these big ears feel worse." William scooped up his red-faced daughter and held her at arm's length as he addressed her. "Come, Alflega. Give us a rest from that temper, or I'll bring Big Alflega to tell you so."

The child hiccoughed and peered into his face. A lilting stream of word chatter followed. "Aye," said William. "That's better. We were lucky, this time, that I didn't need to call the lady. Big Alflega—Dame Alflega—is a fierce lady with big black eyes and claws as big as a dragon's teeth. And when she comes near—"

John cried out in dismay. "Don't tell her such tales. You'll frighten the lass, and she won't want to visit the abbey. She knows what you say. Every word of it."

"She's a bold little soul. Not afraid to face the abbess, are you?" Young Alflega giggled and began to examine her father's chin.

Straw and herbs of the fields, gathered in late summer and dried in the byre loft against this day, lay weightless and fragrant at the door of the great hall. Beyond them, in the light rain falling upon the bailey yard, the old rushes formed a sodden path between the kitchen shed and the storehouse. The women of Lundale had kept their pattens from the mud as they stepped upon the rushes to pass from the granary to the storehouse, and back to the hall.

It was the eve of Christmas. An abbey priest had come the day before to say mass for the villagers and their lord, and returned that same day to the safety of the abbey walls. In that brief visit, William had stood with Catherine and her people in the morning mist within the low foundations of the ruined chapel at the edge of the village, unable to recognize more than the outline of the old church in those sadly overgrown ledges of stone. And when the priest had left, Catherine and her people had walked north from the village to a clearing within the forest, a small meadow where the dead slept in unmarked rows.

There, the people of Lundale had set holly and evergreen upon the mounds they had not yet forgotten. And from the forest surrounding that place, they cut holly and green boughs to bring back for the hall.

William had carried his daughter in his arms to the ruined chapel and on to the place where her forebears slept, following the villagers as they moved from one great oak to the next, taking holly from the overgrown trunks, leaving the largest of the ancient trees more lightly burdened as they cut. This was work best done by those who belonged to these lands; rather than by setting his clumsy hands to the massive trees, William was content to watch, his daughter safe and warm within his cloak.

Then the men had bade him follow deeper into the forest to find a great log to burn in the length of the great hearth in the hall. William had set the child in Catherine's arms and gone into the darker, older woods beyond the meadow and searched for a fallen tree large enough to burn for days, small enough to drag home across the leaf-covered ground.

William had discovered, in that search for a yule log, that he knew less of the common tongue than he had believed. Working beside his tenants and taking his turn at the leather rope with which they dragged the chosen log, William saw the confusion he caused when he spoke the words he had learned with difficulty from his English comrades in Normandy. That awkwardness had vanished in the next few hours: William had not needed words as he lent a shoulder to the work at hand.

Now, on the day of Christmas Eve, the old hall and the kitchen shed were the busy center of preparations. The men of the garrison had been pressed into service in the rafters of the hall to wind garlands of holly about the ancient, blackened beams. William, forbidden by Catherine to risk his knee by climbing after them, retreated to the timber walls, walking the bounds with Alflega in his arms, listening to her babble, imagining that he had begun to hear the odd word in the drift of it.

Alflega caught sight of a pannier heaped with honeycakes in her mother's arms and launched herself after it. William caught her before she fell, and distracted her with the prospect of rolling about in the newly spread rushes.

There hadn't been such a Christmas for him, before this year. William tried to remember when he had last watched the pleasant confusion of a feast day. Long ago in Macon there had been such feasts in a place where he had scant childhood memories. Then, after the long and frightening flight to Normandy, there had been Yule feasts at garrison tables in the company of the mercenary soldiers his father had led for one Norman lord after another. And then he had come of age and offered his own sword to Henry Plantagenet. William had followed that restless lord, protecting him from treachery at Christmas courts from one end of his empire to another; in those years, Yule feasts had been but a few hours' respite from the rigors of winter travel and sentry duty.

William caught Alflega as she disappeared into the mass of sweet summer hay and dried thyme, and began to pluck the straw and twigs from her hair. He could be happy here, with this life. If he never left this place again, he would miss nothing of the excitement of the Plantagenet's court or the armies, and the temptations that swarmed about both.

Alflega ceased her explorations and stared with her mother's large green eyes into William's face. Her small hand rose to touch the scar across his cheek.

"Never fear," he murmured to his daughter. "One day, I'll be home for good, and you and your mother will have me with you to watch over you for all time."

Alflega smiled.

William smiled back. His own words sounded odd to his ears. Now that he had spoken them, he closed his eyes and considered the thought. One day, one day soon, he would manage it.

They had begun to feast an hour past noon, and had continued at board well past nightfall.

The great yule log, dragged by many willing backs through the woods and across the fields to the hall, had smoked and hissed as the ice steamed from its bark all afternoon, and then burned hot and clear by nightfall.

The doors of Lundale's great hall stood open to the night, for the yule fire had warmed the long chamber to be as hot as a summer day. Those who had gathered and cooked the feast and eaten their fill sat at their trestle tables drinking mead seethed with precious spices, glancing from time to time at the darkness beyond the doors.

On this night, even the gates of the palisade were unbarred and propped open, and the men of the garrison took turns to watch the place where the dark bailey yard met the greater darkness beyond the wall.

William had told his men to keep watch against armed raiders and to turn a blind eye to poor folk who might slip through the gates on this night. Prompted by Catherine, he had told his sentries that they should not question those who looked as if they had been living rough in the forest, or stop the villagers from slipping outside with panniers laden with hot food for those who had come hungry to Lundale's feast but did not dare to come within.

William had seen new faces among the feasting crowd, faces that resembled those of his tenants. Catherine had recognized a cousin of Osbert and Hadwen's younger sister; both had lived in the forest in the decade since Lundale's fall. On Catherine's advice, William had not tried to approach the newcomers, but had raised his cup to them from where he sat on the dais. If these folk decided to give up their shelters in the forest and return to the village, Catherine had explained, they would send word through Hadwen or Osbert, who would come to him and ask whether another hut might be repaired. That was the way it should be done.

It was a strange thing for a warrior, a man who had earned his bread by going out to confront a problem with sword in hand, to sit and wait for Lundale's remaining fugitives to end their long exiles in the forest. Without Catherine to guide him, he might have gone into the greenwood to find the exiles' hovels and bring the half-starved folk, willing or not, back to the village. Catherine had been right, of course, to forbid him to do so, for those who didn't trust him would have gone back into the forest and found even more remote places to shelter.

With luck, if all went well, at the next Christmas feasts there would be more families in the village and more souls at the Christmas tables, among them the wariest of the people in the forest. When that came to pass, William would feel that he had brought the settlement back to what it should be. He wanted that, for Catherine's sake.

"What will they do tonight, the soldiers in the forest house, and the women?"

William frowned. Looking across the ancient chamber with its warmth and light and feasting, he, too, had wondered how the small party of strangers were faring in the isolation of the forest house. "The women wanted a priest, so I sent some of the men to bring one from Nottingham yesterday. I went up there and found that they had chosen an old one with dim eyes and deaf ears. He won't hear all they say in confession, nor will he remember their faces. But he will eat well—they all will. They had to build another storage hut to hold all the supplies we brought from Nottingham in the past weeks."

"It's a lonely place for the women there."

William took her hand. "It's lonely for the men as well. The winters are worst, when a soldier is far from home."

Catherine sighed. "I wish we could bring them here—Mathilde, her women, and the men-at-arms—just for this night."

"You know we can't."

"Aye. I know." Catherine looked down the well-laden board, and to the happy folk crowded about the trestle tables lining the great hearth pit. "Still, they come to mind tonight."

William placed his arm across her shoulders. "There were hard times for you, I vow, in some winters past."

"Last year was the hardest. I knew you were in Normandy but could not know how you fared, or whether you lived. We kept Christmas in this hall, but it was a sad time for me, wondering whether you would come home to see the child I carried."

He looked down the table to where John held Alflega on his lap, feeding her bits of honeycake.

"With luck, I may be home for the Yule nights next winter."

Catherine raised her drinking cup and sipped the sweet mead within. "I pray that you will. And I pray that all will go well, up in the forest house."

"Speaking of the forest, the strangers at the hearth have left. Have your fugitives decided not to stay?"

"They know there are twelve days of feasting. They may come again tomorrow, and the next nights. Some don't have far to walk—they have shelter not far from the meadow where the dead are buried."

"We found the yule log near there."

Catherine smiled. "Then the forest people may have been watching you."

Osbert rose from his bench and raised his cup in the direction of the dais. He began to speak in the English tongue, his voice raised in loud and fulsome phrases which William strained to understand; he ended with a flourish and a great draught of mead.

"He has praised you," said Catherine. "Now you must speak as well."

"You told me they don't understand when I speak their words. I have come to believe you."

She laughed. "This night, of all nights, it doesn't matter. The mead makes all words fair."

Beyond her, Robert leaned forward and filled his cup. "Go ahead, William. Speak back to him in fair words, as best you can, and if you blunder I'll rise and speak for you."

William rose and raised his drinking cup. The mead had robbed him of the English words he had learned to speak. The upturned faces of the villagers and the hush that rippled down the hall made it impossible for him to remain silent.

He drew a long breath and spoke a verse of a song he had learned from his mother, from the bards who had sung in the old hall in Macon. Catherine's people listened to the foreign words with courtesy and some interest. As he ended, there were shouts of approval—for his verse, or for the fresh jugs of mead Hadwen had brought to set upon the boards.

He turned to Robert. "How was it?"

"You didn't offend."

"Catherine?"

"They were pleased, William."

"For all you know," said Robert. "They may have thought you were promising them a gold piece each."

Then Osbert stood again and walked to the end of the hearth pit. His voice rose in one short word that stopped the renewed chatter at the tables. Catherine's people filled their cups and shifted upon the benches. All faces turned to where Osbert stood in the firelight.

William turn to Catherine. "Trouble?"

"No," she whispered.

Osbert began to recite in guttural tones, the force of his words rising and falling and rising again in cadences that pleased William's uncomprehending ear.

"A Christmas tale?" he asked.

"Not for Christmas," said Catherine. "It's the story of a king beset by monsters, and the brave foreign knight who traveled to that land to fight the creatures."

William raised his brows. "An odd tale," he whispered back, "for a Yule night's feast. They tell such stories in Normandy to frighten the children at Samhain."

"He tells the same one at Samhain," said Catherine. "It's the only one he knows, but it's very long and he chooses the parts he likes best for each season. Now hush, or Osbert will fret."

"Which part is he speaking tonight?"

"The journey north, and the knight's offer of help to the king beset by troubles."

"Ah. Henry Plantagenet would like it. What happens?"

"At the end? The knight kills the worst of the creatures, the one who spawns all the others, and the knight dies. And he has a hero's funeral, far from home." Catherine was silent for a moment, her gaze upon Osbert. "I never liked the end," she said.

William covered her hand with his own. "Next year, I'll find a bard for the Christmas feast, and he'll bring us another song."

Nineteen

Near midnight, William climbed the stairs to the sentry post upon the roof of the keep, and gave the watchman a cup of hot mead to warm him. Catherine followed, bearing bread and meat and honeycakes. "When you finish the watch," she told the sentry, "there will be more for you in the hall."

William looked up at the vast, glittering stars and snugged Catherine into the warmth of his cloak. He had never seen the heavens above Lundale so brilliant, so clear. A deep, windless cold had descended upon the land, banishing the winter mists from sky, river, and earth.

On this crystalline night, William could see far across the dark lands, and count the faint, covert fires of those who had kept to their secret shelters within the forest. "There are so many of them out there, that kept to their hovels tonight," he said. "I thought the cold would bring more of them here to us."

"They have had many hard winters out there, since they gave up the village," said Catherine. "This year, the ones who came to our board may give the others a good account of you." She reached outside the cloak to touch his hand. "They will learn to trust you."

He glanced across the walkway to the sentry, and beckoned him near. "It's close to midnight," he said. "Leave the mead and the food for the next man and go over to the hall. There's a great vat of Yule wine beside the fire. I'll take the rest of your watch."

Then they were alone, with the firmament above them and the sounds of mortal merriment below. Beyond the keep, across the bailey yard, song and voices and the sound of a harp rose into the darkness. Firelight spilled from the open door, and along the low roof of the ancient hall, smoke holes shone crimson bright from the Yule fire, and the scent of burning herbs and spices drifted together with the sounds of revelry through the chill night. From the shadows of the palisade walls came softer voices and distant laughter.

Catherine looked to the south. "I think I can see the light of the manor's fire. Do you see it—larger than the others?"

Far in the distance, rising from the black horizon, a thread of smoke from the forest house wove it way upwards, a faint line of grey and crimson amid the stars.

"Aye, I see it," said William. "Yesterday the men-at-arms said something about a bonfire."

"It must be a strange season for that poor girl, to pass Christmas far from home, with only strangers to protect her, and only serving women to comfort her."

"She was well and happy enough," said William. "when I saw her yesterday."

"And is there a midwife with her?"

He smiled and drew her closer. "Yes, she has a midwife as well. One of the serving women says that she has the skill. The woman will send word if it's going wrong; I'll have to ask someone here to help if that happens."

"Hadwen knows more than most. But she won't keep a secret."

"It's a risk we'll have to take."

Catherine pushed the hood of her cloak back from her hair and turned to watch the southern horizon. "What will happen to the girl and her women, once the child is born and winter is past?"

"I'm to send word to the king when the child is here. Before spring, the girl should travel back towards Shrewsbury, where she's supposed to be passing the season in prayer."

"There must be a wet nurse, then, for the child."

"It will be fostered out young, most likely."

"The king didn't tell you where?"

William shrugged. "There wasn't much time for that. After the skirmish in the borders, King Henry rode out to where we had taken shelter; the Welsh patrols had increased, and we feared that there would be no safe place for Mathilde in the whole of the Marches."

"No safe place for the king's shabby honor," said Catherine.

"Aye. For now, the king's honor and Mathilde's safety are the same matter."

"King Henry saw you after the skirmish?"

"He came to us. He spoke with Mathilde, then

asked me to take her party north with all possible speed and hide her at Lundale, for his enemies would never think to look here. I told him I'd take her north, but not to Lundale. Said that I would find a better place."

"You refused to take her where the king ordered?" Catherine shivered.

"What was I to do, bring them here, where so many would see them, and wait for the rumors to go abroad? The Welsh lords' spies would have followed the tales to their source, and found Mathilde with little effort. The king's enemies, both Welsh and rebel English, would have been swarming around us within a fortnight."

"He must have understood that."

"The abbey would have been a bad choice for the same reason. Then I thought of the day that first summer when you and I rode to the old manor house."

"I remember," said Catherine.

William drew her back into his embrace. In that magic fortnight of the last year's summer, he and Catherine had spent a day at her family's ancient dower house, rejoicing in the shadowed solitude of the abandoned hall, far from the curious eyes of Lundale's tenants. In that day, he had promised her to ask the king to restore the manor to them, to add it once again to the lands her family had once held. And he had sealed the vow with more than words. . . .

Catherine sighed. "If we speak of that day, we'll forget all else. Tell me first what happened in your journey home. You remembered the forest house—"

He cleared his throat. "Aye, I remembered the place had been abandoned but was still sound. Outside Nottingham, I sent some men ahead to be sure it was still empty and they found no one there but your work party. You know the rest."

Catherine sighed. "That girl must have thought she had come to the end of the earth."

"She doesn't complain. There were enough fine things in the packsaddles to make her comfortable and there was gold from the king for all else. I sent some of the men down to Nottingham to buy hangings for the walls, a feather bed and the like."

"Still, it's a lonely place."

"She has her women for company, and the men camped beyond the stockade to protect her. It was the best I could do."

William looked out across the dark lands. "If you go up there next summer, you'll find the shelters the men built outside the walls. They were too many for the house."

"Does the king know where you settled them?"

"Not yet. No one knows. Only you." He drew her closer still. "You're trembling."

"It's not the cold," said Catherine. "It's the future. So much could go wrong. That poor girl up there could die in childbed."

"She's young," said William, "and seems strong. She made the trip by litter. No harm was done."

"You did all you could," said Catherine. "But so

many things cannot be helped. A hard childbirth. The king's whims."

"The king's whims have already had their day. Now we are dealing with the aftermath."

Catherine shook her head. "When the child is born, if it's a son, the king will want him to have his place in the world. If the girl were married, the child would have a name, for the husband wouldn't dare to disinherit the king's child."

"Then he'll find her a noble husband and for the sake of her child the girl will agree. By springtime, the king will have someone in mind."

"And if her father objects? He might begin to suspect the king's motives. And if her father discovers that the girl wasn't at the convent this winter, he might disown her. After all, she's a bastard child herself. Close enough to the baron to touch his honor, but easy to renounce if the baron is angry."

William hesitated. "I believe they would tell him that the man chosen to be her husband bedded the girl last summer, when he first desired her for a wife."

"Would the Baron Pandulf believe that tale? He must be a man of the world."

" He may decide it's the easiest course, to accept the story as it's given to him. Such things have happened before, but never to a man as powerful as the Baron Pandulf." William sighed. "I pray Henry Plantagenet has seen, this time, that he has gone too far. He should turn to widows and daughters of servants when his lusts move him to folly. Mathilde must be the last of his risky conquests."

"I pray you won't tell him so. Leave that to his confessor."

William drew her closer and kissed the end of her nose. "Look about you, Catherine. The stars are brighter now than I have seen them in many nights."

In the faint light of the stars, Catherine's eyes seemed huge, darker than the night itself. "Come," said William. "It is Christmas, and there are better things to think upon than the king and his schemes. In a few weeks, Mathilde's child will be born and by springtime our own part in this trouble will be ended."

Her hand closed over his wrist. "Listen to me," she said. "It may not end when spring comes."

He smiled. "One way or the other, it must."

"Have you ever wondered why he chose you to deal with this matter of the girl and her child?"

Often, if the truth be told. In that slow journey home, there had been too many nights to lie awake with the pain of his ruined leg, wondering how the brilliant mind of Henry Plantagenet had failed to see that the journey would be too difficult, and that William was the wrong man to deal with Mathilde's dilemma.

William shook his head. "We both know that a place in the king's guard isn't always a boon. When trouble comes, Henry Plantagenet looks about him and points his finger at the nearest man he believes he can trust. In this case, I happened to be there and the task fell to me."

"Was it that simple?"

"Most things, Catherine, are that simple for a king who has decided to pass a problem of his own making onto another's shoulders."

She did not laugh. He imagined that he heard a whispered oath in the darkness. "What are you saying?"

"Is it possible that there is something more to the king's decision? You say you resemble Henry Plantagenet, from a distance. If the skirmish in Wales had gone wrong and Mathilde had been discovered, would the king have taken responsibility?"

"No. Of course not."

Catherine stepped out of William's embrace and turned to face him. "I believe that if the ambush had gone in favor of the Welsh lords, if you had been killed and Pandulf's daughter captured, the king might have pointed to your body and said that you were the man who had dishonored Mathilde. Witnesses would say that they had seen you, not the king, riding out to tryst with her. Some might say it for the king's sake, others might believe they had seen you, not the king, from a distance. And William," she said, "a child of the king's might resemble you."

William expelled a long breath. "It's possible. All of it is possible."

"Then you agree that the king might have intended to use you so."

"Aye. Such things happen." He had known, from the day Henry Plantagenet had told him the nature of the task before him, that danger had already closed about him. "I knew the risks I would face, but understood that I would have found a greater danger in refusing to take on the task. The king had told me how the Welsh lords could stop his invasion of Wales. The king wouldn't have allowed me to walk away from the remedy, knowing what I did."

Catherine turned away from him and began to pace along the sentry walk.

William had learned, in the past weeks, that when Catherine began to pace back and forth as she was doing now, it could only mean that dire thoughts were hatching in her mind.

He followed her and caught her arm as she turned to pace back again. "There's nothing to be done. Believe me, Catherine, I turned it over and over in my mind and there's nothing I can do but keep the girl safe and hope that she doesn't die in childbed."

"You don't see it, do you?"

"What?"

"The real trouble ahead." Catherine glanced down the sentry walk, as if worried that another would hear her words. "You are the man Henry Plantagenet trusted to see Mathilde through this winter. And if the child is a son, you are the man he will trust to raise it."

William considered her words. "Would you mind," he said at last, "if we had to do that?"

"We might not do it together, William."

His heart stilled at her words. "What nonsense is this?"

Catherine pulled her cloak about her. Above her

shoulder, a star pulsed bright, then traced a path of silver in the sky as it fell. "The king is too clever to take the chance that Mathilde's father will discover her missing from the convent. William, if Pandulf discovers that Mathilde is gone, it will be on your head. On the way north, any number of people saw you with her. And if the child is discovered, it will have the look of the king. As do you. You will be named as the father. You will have two choices: to fight Pandulf, or wed Mathilde."

"It won't happen. There was another girl sent to the convent in Mathilde's name."

"But if it does happen? If Mathilde's father goes there and sees that she's missing?"

William sighed. "Then I'll have to fight Pandulf."

"And the king would punish you for it. He would have to, William. Don't you see? The king has given you more than the care of Mathilde for the winter. He has passed the burden of his mistake—and all that will come from it—onto your shoulders. And you will have no choice in the way you must resolve it."

"Nonsense—"

"You would have to put me aside and wed Mathilde."

"Catherine, no. Stop and think. We are wed and we have a child. God willing, there may be another next year. I will not put you aside."

"For the king, if he demands it—"

He took her by the arms and pulled her to him. "You are my wife, Catherine, and I will not let you go. Not for Henry Plantagenet. Not even for his honor. There are limits, Catherine, to what a king may ask his subjects to do."

She shook her head and murmured something against his chest.

"What, Catherine?"

"My father thought there were limits to what the Plantagenet should ask a man to do. And he suffered for it. Please, William—If it comes to such a choice, set me aside and wed the girl."

"Catherine—"

"She may not want to live here—with you. But if she does—" Catherine took an audible, gulping breath. "I'll go back to the abbey. With the child. I won't be so far away—"

"Hush, Catherine. The king wouldn't ask such a thing. He's not a monster."

"He is. Ask anyone here."

"Listen to me. I won't be parted from you. We are wed, Catherine, and no man—no king—will change that." He felt the warmth of tears upon her face. "These are odd thoughts, wife. Odd humors in your mind." William forced his voice to lighten. "Maybe you are already breeding, and imagine disasters, as women do at such times."

She nodded against his breast, then stepped away and pulled the hood of her cloak to cover her head. "Well," she said in a new, stronger voice, "in the time we have been imagining what the king might do, a hundred Welsh lords might have advanced and surrounded the walls. I wouldn't have noticed."

"Nor I."

William looked behind him, to the north. "Your forest people have become careless in their lairs. A half-blind man could see those campfires far to the north."

She shook her head. "Osbert says there are two families living north of the fields, not far from the meadow; all the others shelter to the east and west. They are very careful." She turned to the north and rubbed her eyes. "Those fires are very bright."

William rubbed his arms against the cold. "Maybe they're no longer afraid of discovery. Maybe they have decided to trust me."

A delicate sheen of ice had formed upon the stone battlements; his own breath was visible in the light of the stars. "That sentry is damned slow. I'll watch alone, if you want to go back."

"They move," said Catherine. "The fires to the north are moving."

As he watched, the distant points of light seemed fixed. Then two of them shifted, and disappeared, the blinked again before merging with the others. "Some must be torches," said William.

They stood in silence and watched the far distant fires. "They don't move now," said Catherine. She had spoken with effort, as if slowed by the cold.

"It was nothing," said William. "And you are half frozen. We'll go down together and I'll find the sentry."

"He should watch the north, just in case."

"He will," said William. "I'll make sure he does. Now come."

At the top of the stairs, just as she stepped down

into the narrow spiral, Catherine hesitated. She looked up again at the sky. "It's a rare thing to have a night so clear," she said. "I don't like to leave the stars behind."

He pulled her close and kissed the chill sweetness of her lips. "I'll bring them back for us," he said. "In our chamber, they will return and dance for you. I promise this, Catherine. Tonight. Any night of your choosing, they will dance for you."

"Tonight," she said. "Tonight and forever."

She turned once again to the first stair and gasped. "William. Do you see—?"

He raised his head and knew, in that moment, that the stars would not dance for Catherine this night.

The fires—distant points of flame—were moving once again. Far to the north, a river of torches flowed from the east and from the west, moving toward the campfires beyond the forest, to the place where the forest met the open land.

Massing at the road that would lead them to Lundale.

Twenty

It was loyalty that had brought him to these lands two years ago. Henry Plantagenet's reward for his loyalty had given William the right to Lundale and had led him to Catherine. And now, in the end, it was an act of disloyalty to Henry Plantagenet that would make bearable this last parting.

If he had kept to the narrow path, to blind obedience—if he had kept secret the king's foolish sin, he would never have seen steady determination in Catherine's gaze as she watched him prepare to ride out into danger. On this day that might well be his last.

Instead, he had broken his vow of silence and had told her everything; and he blessed the hour that he had dared to tell her.

How could he have left her here at the bailey gates, knowing that he might not return, knowing that she might never understand the task that Henry Plantagenet had placed upon him? Catherine might have spent a widow's years never knowing why he had brought secrets to these lands, why he had risked the very conflict that would soon be upon them.

Catherine, daughter of a slain rebel, had shared her obstinate spirit with him. Though he would keep his vows of loyalty to the Plantagenet, Catherine's gift, rebellion of the soul, would be William's strength on this terrible day.

His wife's smile was steady. She pointed to the young lad Radulf, hanging back in the crush of armed men and their restive mounts. The boy stood straight, eyes upon William, mended spear in his hand. "I'll send the sentry down from his post," said Catherine. "Radulf has offered to take his place. He's a good lad, and knows the land well. He'll keep a careful watch."

"I must leave enough able men to defend the gates," said William.

"Radulf tells me he knows what to do with a spear, if it comes to that," said Catherine. "Radulf is eager to fight. Too eager, I think. If you leave him behind without a task, he'll follow you on foot, and be of no use to anyone."

Her voice was low, as calm as if she were discussing the disposition of next spring's seed barley.

"All right."

William beckoned Radulf forward and spoke to him in the common tongue. "Will you stay atop the keep all day, lad, if you're given the sentry's post?"

Radulf nodded.

"Then repeat what I said, my lad."

Radulf nodded again.

William looked back to Catherine. "He doesn't understand, does he?"

Catherine placed a hand upon Radulf's shoulder

and spoke to him in accents William had heard, but never really understood, in the fields of Lundale. The boy's face brightened, and he replied. A moment later, Radulf nodded with such force that William feared for his skinny neck.

Catherine raised her head. "Radulf swears most readily that he will watch for trouble, and he won't desert his post. And he says he knows how to sound the horn."

"Well then, have Radulf go up to the watch post, and send the sentry down to me. He'll ride out with the rest of us." William could use every sword he could muster. He had counted almost one hundred torches last night in the hours before dawn, and feared that more riders might join the host by daylight. He wouldn't know the final extent of the intruders' force until he had reached their camp.

William brought his thoughts back to the defense of Lundale's walls. He nodded to Catherine "I'll trust Radulf to watch. But the men at the gate itself must remain."

She nodded. "They will remain."

"The sentry will take the last horse in the byre, save your palfrey. Best not try to ride away if the day goes against us. But the horse is there. You can judge."

Catherine nodded again. "I don't expect to need it."

"Bring the villagers inside the palisade."

"Aye. And their cattle. Osbert is gathering them."

"And you will be in the keep, with the women

and children. If you can't parlay a truce when they first come, if it comes to—"

"If the gates come down?"

"Yes. If the gates come down, stay in the keep. Even if they try to burn you out. There are buckets on each level to keep the floor timbers wet. Even if they heap wood outside the keep and set it alight, they won't do much harm beyond the smoke. In this cold, it will be hard for them to fire the door of the keep. John sluiced it down just now; no matter how much kindling they might bring to the door, there will be ice to slow the flames."

"All right."

"If it goes that far, and the door begins to burn, you must parlay with them in earnest. John will help you with that. Go and shout down to them from the roof of the keep. They will listen. Demand safe passage for all. Surrender in any case, and let them carry away what they will. Alflega—"

"I'll keep her safe."

"Keep Alflega among the other children. Unremarked. If they see she's your child, they'll take her for ransom."

Catherine met his gaze, her eyes clear, without a hint of tears. "It won't go that far."

"Of course not. But it's good to have a plan."

"Yes. To see you come home at the end of the day to look after such things yourself. That's my plan."

From the far side of the byre, Robert led his mount to join the company. The old war hammer from Lundale's rafters was slung by a leather line from his saddle; at his side, the pommel stone of his sword gleamed blue in the light of dawn. "I'll ride with you," he said. "If you'll have me."

"Aye. Right gladly." William looked up at the sky. The clouds had not returned; it was as bright and clear as midnight last. Even without their campfires to draw the eye, it might be possible to see something of the intruders' number and position.

"Robert," he said. "You know the lay of the land. Go up to the sentry post and take one more look about. When last I saw it, there were three camps visible to the north. Hard to tell how many men. Take a last look and see whether they have moved."

"I will." Robert dismounted and thrust the reins into William's hands; he set off across the yard.

William watched him run through the door. "Your cousin has a strong arm. I pray he won't see friends among the intruders."

"He'll stand fast with you," she said.

He glanced again at the cold, unmarred sky. "The sun is higher. It's time to ride out."

He looked into Catherine's face and he saw all he had ever desired from her.

Passion. That he might have seen before this fortnight past. Before there had been trust, they had passion. Of all things in their marriage, desire had come most easily to them.

And now there was trust as well.

It was because of her trust in him, her understanding of the burden he had carried, that his wife now showed resolve. If Catherine had tears, she was keeping them for the morrow.

"Come," he said. "Give me a good kiss, one to last me the whole day long."

"Aye," she said. "If you'll bring it back to me before the sun sets."

She must know how unlikely it was that he would return. It was Catherine who had fretted over his ruined leg and told him that he must not try it in battle before it healed. Many months must pass before it would be sound again. Catherine knew, as well as he did, that if the fighting went badly and he had to give up the saddle, he would be less than helpless in combat on the ground. On this day only the most skillful among his small party would survive the day, if it came to a fight.

He might not be among them.

Once again, William gave thanks that he had broken trust with the king and told Catherine what he must do for Henry Plantagenet. If he fell, and if she chose, Catherine herself might deal with his burden in her own way. Alone.

"Have the king's men gone ahead?"

"Yes. They should be gathered north of here, along the road through the forest. Twenty of them."

"Ten of them are with the women in the forest?"

"Yes, ten. And ten at the abbey."

He removed a gauntlet and ran his fingers through his hair. Ten of the king's men were at the abbey, camped outside the walls to protect it. Before dawn, he had sent a rider to warn those ten men that they must be ready to defend the forest house instead, if it should be attacked. If that came to pass, the abbey itself would have to depend upon Dame Alflega's wits and lethal tongue to see them safe. She had done it a decade ago, during the rebellions, and she might manage it again.

Ten more men would remain at the forest house, to keep watch and to patrol the road.

The others, twenty of them, would join the Lundale garrison to ride out to meet the enemy. It would be the worst odds he had faced in all his years of warfare.

Had he blundered by sending too many of the king's men away to defend the lady Mathilde from a distance? Had he sent too few?

Catherine moved closer and pitched her voice low. "Would the girl and her serving women not be safer here? Would we not all be safer together?"

"No. Those men beyond the forest must be there to take Mathilde. I don't want you involved. They haven't gone near the forest house, may not know it exists, as far as we can tell. If they break through, they'll look here first."

Catherine reached up and caught his hand. "William, I will remember what you said about parlaying for a search. If we get that truce, we may suffer nothing more than one or two ruffians emptying the granary, looking for the girl."

"And if the men patrolling the road see intruders here, they will move Mathilde away if they can. It's a gamble either way, but this plan is the best I can do."

In that moment, he felt his own resolve begin to falter. "Catherine," he said. "If there had been a way to keep this danger from you—from the child—I would have done—"

"William, there was no other way to meet this day. You have done all you could do to turn danger from us, and now we're in God's hands. Both of us, and Alflega. In God's hands."

Catherine touched his heavily bandaged leg, and smoothed the padding wrapped about the knee. Then she reached to adjust his cloak as he leaned down to brush her lips with a kiss. A fine, swift kiss of the sort a woman gave her man when the eyes of her people were upon her, a brief embrace that made it clear she didn't doubt his safe return. A brave kiss.

"Ride well, William, and come back home. Come home to me before sunset."

"And have you a word for your cousin?" Robert took the reins from William's hand and swung up into his saddle.

"See that you look after your cousin-by-marriage. I want both of you home this night."

Robert laughed. "Don't worry, Catherine. I'll not let him lead us to the Nottingham stews after the fighting. We'll come right home."

He turned to William. "From the sentry post, I saw nothing changed. Camps to the north, a party of your king's men waiting for us on the road. No one in the forest save the manor's sentries, just beyond the fording place."

William gave a last tug to his swordbelt and drew the chainmail helm forward about his head. He raised his hand in farewell to John, then turned to

Robert. "Let's not keep the king's men waiting." He led his men through the palisade gates. Though he felt Catherine's gaze upon him as he led them across Lundale's frost-laden fields, he did not look.

He did not dare look back.

The waiting had begun.

The road north would allow only slow passage this time of the year—deep ruts from autumn travel, pools of melting snow and rainwater covered by thin skins of ice. Trees fallen in the high winds of autumn, branches driven into the earth by their weight, frozen into the deepest mud of the roads. William and his men would not reach the intruders' camp before noon.

In the morning hours, there had been much to distract Catherine from thinking of William. The villagers, all of them groggy from a night of revelry, a few beginning to rue the effects of their spiced mead, had at first greeted the news of intruders with disbelief. As the morning wore on, Osbert and John had persuaded the villagers to drive their cows and the best of the sheep into the bailey yard and bar the palisade gates against attack.

By noon, the village was deserted and the bailey yard about Lundale's hall was a confusion of cattle, prized swine, and panniers of wool dragged from village hearths. Catherine had brought buckets from the hall to add to the ones resting full on each level of the keep, and set others beside the well in the foundations of the tower.

The women of the village climbed from one floor to the next, choosing places where they and their infants would bed down if they were besieged this night. By early afternoon, the novelty of the keep and its stark chambers had faded, and the villagers, men and women both, had returned to the heart of Lundale's great hall to await news. There, John had taken charge of all the women with children, counting heads, cautioning them to be ready to run back into the keep.

Catherine brought out the salted meat and venison set aside for the second Christmas feast and sent her women into the kitchen shed to cook it. There was no need, she told them, to go hungry on Christmas day, even in the threat of danger.

Alflega, delighted by the noisy confusion at the hearth, staggered from one knee to the next, peering into faces, giggling at children in their mothers' arms, drawing John in her wake as she traversed the vast, crowded chamber.

"She'll not remember this day," said Hadwen, "for anything but the sight of so many people in one place."

"I pray so," said Catherine. "William said that if— if there's any trouble—"

"He spoke to me," said Hadwen. "Wants your Alflega among the children. Not kept aside, unless it's desperate. He's a wise man, your husband. He'll not let that pack of thieves come near."

Pack of thieves. That was how the villagers spoke of the armed camps on the edge of the forest, of the raiders who waited beyond the trees, with open land at their backs. Catherine prayed that the people of Lundale would never have reason to learn that the outsiders were no ordinary thieves.

In the afternoon, the excitement had subsided and Catherine's people began to fret at idleness. Osbert's wife remembered that she had left a sack of precious flax seed hanging from the roof tree of her hut, and demanded to have the great bar lifted from the gates so that she might return to fetch the small treasure. Osbert himself accompanied her and returned much later in her wake, dragging a stray goat on a tether.

A milch cow began to bawl and there was confusion about the milk buckets. A search of the keep did not yield that particular bucket, and the gates were once again unbarred to allow three villagers to go back and fetch forgotten things.

A rider galloped from the northern road along the edge of the forest and splashed across the fording place. The villagers hurried back inside the palisade and dropped the great bar in place across the gates once again.

The rider did not reappear. From the fields and the forest, there was only silence. In the meadows to the west, sheep wandered, then flocked together, then wandered again. Within the palisade, the rams tethered outside the byre bleated in unceasing distress.

Catherine climbed up to Radulf's sentry post and found that the lad had taken to his task with some energy and much pride. "Our lord William is at the edge of the forest," he said. "But the raiders moved back away from him. See their campfires? They left them and moved north. Afraid of our lord William, they are."

"Can you see how many there are?"

"A lot. More than thirty. That's all our lord William has. But he scared them back anyway. As soon as he reached them, they just moved back." Radulf drew a great breath. "I wish I had gone with them."

Catherine strained to see how many horses there were in the dark mass of soldiers beyond the forest. A wind had come up from the north, moving the banners of the encampments in slow fluttering grace. At that great distance, it was impossible to see them clearly; even the colors of the banners were hard to make out.

"They must be Scots," said Radulf. "John told me that beyond the lands we can see, the Scots kings have their own lands."

"That's far, far beyond what we can see. Don't worry. No one has ever seen a Scot. They don't raid this far south."

Radulf sighed. "That's good. I'd rather the raiders be Englishmen."

"Are you frightened?"

"John says it's good to be frightened, some of the time."

"He's right," said Catherine. "We're all frightened at times."

"Not when your lord William is here."

"No. Not then."

"John says our lord William is never afraid, except maybe at the abbey. With Dame Alflega."

"Aye," said Catherine. "If raiders ever come from the south, they'll not get past Dame Alflega."

Radulf turned to the south. "You can't see the abbey from here. But sometimes you see smoke from the forest house."

Catherine thought back to the night, when she and William had watched the color of that smoke rise into the starlit sky. Only hours ago. A lifetime ago.

"And you can see the king's men, way out there to the west." Radulf turned. "And more of them to the east. Wonder why they aren't with my lord William."

If Osbert's sharp-eyed son didn't know that there was an elusive guest whom the king's men protected in that house, then William's secret had been well kept. "It's their own camp," said Catherine. "They can't let those raiders steal their food."

"Then why don't they guard it? They're too far away. See? They're way over there."

Catherine shaded her eyes and followed Radulf's gaze. Far away, so distant that they were barely recognizable as horsemen, figures were moving among the bare trees. Slowly, as if uncertain of the way.

She turned to the east and saw the others. Again, they were too distant for recognition. Again, their progress was slow. It might be the ice on the ground that slowed them. Or it might be their own stealth.

Once again, Catherine faced west and began to count the figures.

"There are too many," she said.

"What?"

"Too many to be the king's men. Lord William took twenty with him. Twenty were left behind—ten at the abbey, and ten at the forest house. There are many more than that in the forest."

Radulf snatched up the horn. He raised it to his lips, then cried out as it clattered to his feet. He raised it again, and blew. A slight whimpering sound rose to Catherine's ears.

"Try again."

Radulf filled his lungs and blew a deafening blast.

Below them, voices rose from the bailey yard, then stopped. Far beyond the walls, the figures in the forest ceased to move.

And then they began again to advance.

Radulf's teeth chattered in the silence. "Maybe they won't come here."

"Maybe."

"They're all south of here. Nearer the forest house. Maybe they'll steal the food there and leave."

"Hush." A glance to the north revealed that William and his men had not yet emerged from the forest into the open land. The campfires of the intruders still burned; nearby, the dark shapes of horses on a picket line were visible. There was no fighting, so far.

"Maybe they don't want to fight our lord William. They might just steal some food and go."

"Will you not hush?" Catherine placed her hands upon her face and tried to slow her panicked breath. Think. She must think. Why was it so hard to think?

The strangers to the north did not seem eager for a fight. From the east and west, others were advancing upon the forest house. Upon a small force of men and some helpless women. Upon that girl, most helpless of all.

From the east and the west, the intruders would close in about the forest house and it would be too late, even if William had heard the horn, for the Lundale men to turn back and ride that great distance soon enough to prevent disaster.

Would it be disaster?

Catherine lowered her hands and looked south to the forest house. Men might die there. And other men would die if fighting started near the distant campfires, or if William made his way south instead, in time to oppose the interlopers approaching the forest house.

If allowed to reach the forest house, the intruders would face only ten men, who might surrender when they saw so many raiders at their walls.

If they took the forest house, the king's enemies would capture the baron Pandulf's daughter and show the baron that she was with child. Tell him that she had been used by the king. William had said— What had he said? That without the good will of Pandulf and the Marchers lords, there would be no invasion of Wales.

Catherine began again to pace. A hundred fears and defenses and consequences flowed through her mind as she tried to decide what to do in the face of this new threat.

If she did nothing to prevent the stealthy riders from taking Mathilde, William and the men of Lundale would live. Mathilde would be gone, her dilemma would be revealed. Henry Plantagenet's sin would be revealed. And there would be no reason for the king to compel William to put aside his family to deal with the consequences of the king's foolish lust. Little Alflega would never know how close she had come to losing her home to the king's unacknowledged child.

Behind her, Radulf raised the horn again and sent a bleat of alarm into the silence.

"Stop it."

Once again, the horn clattered to the ground. "They didn't hear."

"You did enough. Now stop it and let me think."

There was no good reason to stop what must happen this day at the forest house. No reason to stop it, and every reason to hope they would take Mathilde from this place and put an end to William's burden to keep the king's secret. There were fifty men or more moving towards the forest house, and at least that many at the northern encampment.

If the girl were taken, the king could not fault William in this matter. And if he did, what would be the consequence? It was a better choice for

William, to face the king's displeasure rather than do battle, lamed in one leg, helpless if unhorsed.

"Lady Catherine—"

"Be quiet. I have to think."

There was nothing she could do to stop the invasion of the forest house. Nothing.

It might go badly wrong. The girl might run into the forest and be injured. She wouldn't run fast. No woman could, when far gone in pregnancy. But she might try. . . .

And Catherine would try, in days to come, to live with the knowledge that she had watched it happen, from the safe and distant sentry post of Lundale's keep. And next year, when the winter solstice came, Catherine would kneel beside the holy well in the forest, and remember the young woman who had once walked there, burdened by the past, bearing something of the future.

She turned her back upon the south, and looked upon the northern meadow where her forebears lay beneath her Yule offering of holly boughs. That sad meadow, with the gentle mounds of the dead glittering in the low winter sun, covered the earthly remains of heartache, age, and the Plantagenet's massacre. If the dead could speak, what would they say to her this day?

Catherine began to pace. It would be worse than foolish to take a risk for the sake of a reckless girl who had given herself to the king and caught a child from him.

A young, reckless girl. Catherine had not thought to ask William how old the girl was, and

what she had expected of the king, once her ordeal
was over. How young had she been, when Henry
Plantagenet had first looked upon her? And had
she been given the choice, a true choice, when
tempted to the king's bed?

"Lady Catherine, I have to blow the horn. Won't
you let me blow the horn?"

Tomorrow, if William were spared, Catherine
would look into his eyes and tell him how she had
come to watch Mathilde's capture from this tower.
He would be grateful that she had stayed, obedient
and aloof, upon this keep, within the walls that he
had repaired to protect them all. If one day he
came to wonder what had been in her mind as she
had watched the raiders advance upon the forest
house, William would be too kind, too gentle to
ask. William, who had bound up his ruined leg and
gone out to defend them all, would never ask those
questions. But Catherine would ask them of herself,
each night of her life.

"Radulf, put down the horn," said Catherine.
"I'll watch here while you go down to the byre and
saddle the grey mare. Quickly, Radulf."

She began to untie the bindings about her fingers, and to remove the narrow wooden splints that
held them immobile. Her small finger had begun
to mend, and had something of its normal color—

Radulf had not moved.

"Go on. Saddle the horse and leave her in the
byre. Tell no one. Speak to no one."

"You're going out to find my lord William, aren't
you? I'll come too."

He had taken up his mended spear and stood waiting for her answer. "No," she said. "I need you here. Watch, and blow the horn hard if danger comes close. Loud enough that Lord William will hear it. And then go down to the hall and make sure Alflega and all the children are safe. John is there, and must be in charge, but he's an old man and may not be strong enough to defend them. It may be a hero's work for you, Radulf. Will you stay and look after them for me?"

"Aye." It must have been the cold or his changing voice that lent a small quaver to the word. He bowed his head once, and turned from her to descend the stairs.

Catherine held her hand up and wondered whether she would manage to get William's old gauntlet onto it. She bit her lip and managed to flex the finger far enough to hold a bridle strap.

There would be time enough, in days to come, to set it again.

There was time to ride out through the forest and warn the girl's keepers. If she moved quickly, she need do nothing more than that. She would ride past the fording place and tell the first patrol she met.

She cast a last glance north to the meadow of graves, and stepped down into the deep well of the stairs. If the ghosts of her forebears had aught to say about her decision, they should have spoken before now. She was set on her course, and knew the risks. There would be time enough, if this day's work ended in exile to the abbey or beyond, to listen at leisure to the reproaches of the dead.

Radulf's untidy head surfaced below her on the stairs. "The mare's ready," he said. "She's the only horse they left behind."

Catherine reached to smooth Radulf's tangled hair, then thought better of it. Instead, she placed a hand on his shoulder and thanked him. "We'll tell your lord William how much I relied upon you this day; he may decide you're old enough to have that sword, after all."

Radulf bowed his head and stepped aside to let her pass. "Good luck, my lady."

Catherine continued down to the bottom of the keep, and uttered a swift prayer that this Christmas Day would not see new graves in the meadow of the dead.

Twenty-one

William had thought that trouble, if it came, would arrive from the southern road, for that was the direction from which he had traveled from the Marches of Wales. That was the direction from which a scout, or a small army might have followed rumors of a woman traveling by slow stages from the Welsh border, to disappear along the way north.

He had begun to hope, in the quiet days following the appearance of Welsh scouts near the abbey, that the spies had traveled on, passed them by. William knew that the scouts might return once they realized that the trail had gone cold. He had hoped that they would give up the chase after a few days and ride south in all haste to report back to their Welsh lords, all without giving Lundale's south forest a second look.

It was not to be. Such strokes of luck were the stuff of children's tales, not of William's own harsh world.

Now the Welsh were back with a small army and had shown themselves in strength and awaited him. Their choice of camp, though unexpected, was not a bad one. They knew, perhaps, that he could not afford to leave them there, in the open land north of his forest, poised to sweep down upon Lundale and the abbey and the forest house at their pleasure, by day or night, as they chose.

So the Welsh raiders had set their tents, made a winter camp, and spent a cold Yule eve with their bonfires burning, waiting for him to find them, and to meet them on the ground that they had chosen.

William knew that their first intention was to frighten him by their numbers alone into offering them Mathilde in exchange for peace.

At noon, William and his Lundale men emerged from the forest to a bright, windswept clearing that extended far to the north. The king's men, the twenty men-at-arms he had summoned from the forest house, had reached the place first, and waited just inside the forest's cover, well beyond bow shot of the large encampment. At William's arrival, the waiting men-at-arms began to warm their hands before the inevitable fight and to report what they had observed in their short, cold vigil at the edge of the woods.

The Welshmen knew they were watching and had seemed unconcerned. The scents of wood smoke and roasted meat had wafted from the Welsh camp to the forest, and William's men had watched the interlopers stand about the campfires, eating and taking their ease. Now that William had arrived with more men, there was activity among the tents.

Distant figures began to move among the horses on the far picket line. Half the camp mounted and began to assemble near the tents. A group of archers formed a line beyond them.

William rode a little way apart from his men and looked across the field. He had no stomach for this fight. Though he had the skill and had won much honor in battle, his will to fight was gone. It had begun to leave him on the day he had wed Catherine.

There had been some women—many women—before her, but none of them had ever come to his mind in the hour before a battle. None of them had left him this fearful of dying, so eager to live.

And now, with Catherine a scarce few miles from this field, endangered by these interlopers, William's obsession had only become worse. He would have tossed all his gold and his armor into the Welshman's campfires if it would have bought Catherine's safety for all time.

If the day went against him, would he have the courage not to barter word of Mathilde's whereabouts in exchange for a promise that the Welsh interlopers would leave Lundale unscathed?

William turned his thoughts back to the field before him and the disposition of the Welsh archers. He hadn't survived this long by allowing himself to fret before a fight. For Catherine's sake, he would not think of her again until the day was done.

Robert rode to his side. "Welsh archers. Before you came here, we never had anything but hungry thieves and the odd Plantagenet butcher. Now we have archers walking a hundred miles to kill us."

He pointed to the camp. "Comfortable knaves, aren't they? If it comes to a fight, be sure not to trample the cauldrons and spits. That's likely our mutton they ate last night, and I have a mind to eat the rest of it myself."

"Look," said William. "They must have heard you."

They watched as the Welshmen wheeled their small steeds, turning their backs on the tents to ride north a few hundred paces, and halt again well beyond their camp.

A wind rose out of the north, sending banners snapping above deserted tents. From the Welsh there was no voice of challenge, nor parlay flag among them. Their line was dense and silent, weapons at the ready but not in hand. They bore themselves as if they had all the time in the world.

William looked up at the sky and tried to see what advantage the Welshmen might expect by waiting to move. He could see no reason, no feature upon the open ground, that would benefit that silent army as the sun moved farther west.

Impatient to be done with the waiting, yet unwilling to take his men into a slaughter, William drew forth from his hauberk the white cloth he had carried to signal a parley. He waved the cloth above his head.

Robert rode forward to William's side. "Will they honor that?"

"If they're the Welshmen I believe they are, they will either ignore it or honor it. They wouldn't break a parlay truce."

A moment later, two riders moved forward from the Welsh line and halted a short distance before their fellows. There was a small flutter of white between them.

"I'll come with you," said Robert.

"No. Stay back. I'll go alone."

"Afraid I'll hear your secrets? If I'm to die today, I'd like to know what brought the trouble here. William," said Robert, "you may need help if the Welshmen expect you to dismount and stand to speak. You're worse than helpless on the ground, with your knee still mending."

Catherine's cousin had the right of it, both in the matter of William's bad leg and of the cursed secret of the king. A man should know what he fought for. "Come with me then," said William. "You have the right to hear. Tell the others to stay here together and take care not to move forward unless we signal them."

William loosed his cloak to fall back upon his shoulders, leaving his arms free to take up weapons if he were betrayed. White cloth in hand, he gestured to Robert; they walked their horses forward as far as the abandoned camp, and then a short distance beyond. There, they halted and waited for the approach of the two Welsh riders.

"What is it that they want of us?"

"A matter touching the king. They will not get what they came for."

"If we fight this day, Henry Plantagenet will be sending grief a second time for Catherine. First her parents, in the rebellion ten years ago. And now you."

"The day isn't yet done," said William. "Keep your eyes open and we may yet survive."

"Odd words from a one-legged man facing this lot. If they make a treacherous move, take care to stay in your saddle, William."

"Keep your sword sheathed, and don't break the truce. I promised Catherine to bring you back alive. Don't make me a liar."

Robert sighed. "Catherine could have done worse than wed you," he said. "I'm beginning to believe you mean well by her."

"Of course I do," said William. "Tell her so, if she has any doubts."

"Tell her yourself. She was after me for a promise as well—to bring you back in health. Not just alive, but in health."

The two Welshmen were closer now, near enough that William could see fine trappings on the small, powerful horses that carried them. The figures upon them were visible now—one a short, burly man and the other a boy. Each wore boiled leather as armor, and each rode bareheaded, carrying a helmet upon his saddlebow.

"Madoc," said William. "You are far from home."

"I am," said the older Welshman. "But I believe my journey is nearly done."

"Winter has already begun," said William. "Your journey is already too long."

"My son," said the Welshman, "had a mind to see Henry Plantagenet's lands. And his lady love."

Robert's hand moved to the hilt of his sword. "Do you insult the lady Catherine?"

William muttered a word of caution, then turned back to face Madoc once again. "My cousin by marriage," he said, "thinks it an outrage that you speak so of an Englishwoman. Any Englishwoman. And in particular, my own wife."

"Your wife? You know I don't speak of your wife. You know why I have come here, and what I seek."

William shrugged. "Tell me."

Madoc's face flushed dark. "We mean the girl no harm. There's a priest here to speak with her and bear witness that she's with child by Henry Plantagenet. We will take her to Nottingham, then back to the borders to her father, who will discover that he has given his loyalty to the wrong man. To a foolish king who would dishonor a baron's maiden daughter. The girl is somewhere nearby, William of Macon. I have reason to know I'll find her this day."

Robert turned to William in confusion. "What is the old man talking about?"

There was no way to tell whether Madoc was bluffing about finding the girl nearby. William shrugged. "Madoc may have made his journey for naught. There is no daughter of a baron at Lundale. He is mistaken. There's nothing for him here."

Madoc's boy spoke up in angry Welsh; at a sharp word from his father, he ended his tirade and lapsed into frowning silence. Madoc looked up at the sky and then back to William. "By the end of this day, I'll have something to bring back with me to the Marches. I won't be stopped. You know that. If it comes to a fight, so be it."

William met the Welshman's canny gaze, and looked beyond him, to the line of Welsh archers. "You are mistaken. There is nothing for you here. Leave now, ride away from my lands, and we need not fight."

Madoc smiled. "If we fight, you'll lose the day."

The Welsh boy spoke again, more slowly this time, and pointed to William's left leg. Madoc glanced aside, then raised his own hand in the direction of William's saddle. "My son says he took a knife to you in the Marches, not long ago. Slashed that leg to the bone, and scarred the saddle. Says you must have paid the witches to save that leg."

William turned his gaze upon the boy. "Ah. Your son. He has the look of the lad who did it."

Madoc uttered a sharp question. The boy lowered his head and nodded.

Madoc sighed. "So it was you that day in the borders. My son was full of pride that he had spilled the blood of an English knight, and left him crippled. One fewer man to ride with that Henry Plantagenet when he tries to invade Wales. My son acted on impulse, too far away for me to stop him. He did not see, as I did, that you gave him the flat of your sword, not the edge, in mercy."

"I saw he wasn't much," said William. "Just a child."

The lad's face colored in anger; he straightened in his saddle, as if to give himself a man's height.

"He looks much older today," William said.

Madoc brought his fist down upon his saddle-bow; the helmet hanging from the saddle jarred and toppled to the ground.

"This isn't going well," said Robert.

The lad climbed down from his saddle and retrieved Madoc's helm. The chieftain thrust it onto his head and glared at William beneath the well polished steel. "I owe you a debt," he said at last. "Damn you, Englishman. I am hamstrung by this debt."

"Then leave now."

Beneath the rim of his helm, the Welshman's eyes had narrowed. "You have a cold nerve, Englishman. My debt to you isn't that great. Not so large that I would go back to my people with empty hands, and tell them that Henry Plantagenet will be at their doors by springtime. But I'll not fight you, or your men, if you keep your weapons down this day."

The wind gusted again, still blowing from the north, much colder than before. It would be a cold day to fight, and a long cold night for the wounded. "We could wait here until our mounts freeze to the earth," said William. "Or you could ride away and end this."

Madoc's mouth broadened in a prideful smile. "I'll soon ride away. It's almost time to do just that. You see, Englishman—there are hundreds of loyal Welshmen willing to bring your king low in his barons' regard. My lot are abroad, searching for Mathilde of Pandulf. Seventy of them are here, and fifty are—" He smiled, and once again looked at the sun.

"What?"

"Escorting the girl to Nottingham. To show her to your English churchmen. To send word to her father to come and fetch his king's whore." He made a great sweeping gesture towards the south. "It was a clever thing that you did, to hide her in the stockade in the forest, but that place was hardly grand enough for the maiden daughter of Pandulf. The dishonored mistress of the king."

Madoc looked once again at the sun where it shone in the western sky. "Yes," he said. "It is a little past time. Your lady in the forest house is on her way to Nottingham by now. Beginning her journey home."

The Welsh scouts had been more accomplished than William had imagined. And Madoc more determined.

"If this were true—"

"Know it is true. Madoc does not lie."

William gave up the pretense of calm. "Madoc, you can't take her. She is with child—"

"Of course she is. That's why the priest must be witness and write a document. You led us a difficult chase, William of Macon. We were hard pressed to find her in time. Another month, and the girl would have whelped and there would be no proving that she had been with child, and no way to tell the king's brat from any other."

"If you have found her, then write your cursed

document and send it to Rome, for all I care. Leave her where she is."

Madoc touched a gauntlet to his jaw. "Rome. I hadn't thought of that. The Plantagenet has chased one of his own bishops abroad. I'll give the matter to that Thomas Becket, to add to his complaints."

"Carry Becket to Rome on your back, Madoc, but leave Pandulf's daughter where she is. You cannot drag her out on the roads."

"You dragged her here."

"She is close to her time. Leave her."

"If your king would leave Wales to her Welshmen, we'd not need to turn his barons from him." The burly Madoc shivered. "And I'd not have to be abroad in this weather."

Madoc raised his arm as a sign to the horsemen ranged far behind him.

Robert's hand closed upon the hilt of his sword. "Do you break this parlay?"

Madoc pointed to Robert's barely sheathed sword. "Look to your own honor, Englishman."

"You speak of honor? You, who are hounding a woman near to childbed? You speak of honor?"

The insult hung in the frigid silence.

"Robert. No." William brought his hand down upon Robert's shoulder; his gaze had not left Madoc's empurpled face. "The parlay," he said, "must end. Ride back. When you reach your line, the truce is over."

"I'll not fight you this time," said Madoc. "I owe you that for my boy's life. The debt is paid. Next time, I'll cleave your English head from your English shoulders. Go now, you and all your men. Go now, before I change my mind."

Robert wheeled his horse around. "Come, William. Before he thinks better of it. If you do have someone hidden in the forest house, you'll do the king no good by staying here to fight. It might not be too late—"

"But it is," said Madoc. "It is too late for you to stop my men. We know how to do these things, in Wales." He made an impatient gesture toward the empty tents, and the smoking campfires. "There is much to do here, and you delay me. Go in peace. And come the spring, don't let me find you or your soldiers in Wales. Tell your king to stay out of Wales."

Twenty-two

Radulf had left his post.

William saw Radulf's slight figure gesticulating from the middle of the fields, his words incomprehensible above the sound of the north wind.

It had been a long, difficult march through the north forest to reach Lundale's fields, and he had a long march ahead of him. Soon, darkness would be upon them and they would have to continue on to the forest house as best they could.

It would be worth the time to get torches from Lundale. He turned to Robert. "Ride over and get torches from the watchmen. And tell Catherine we may not be back this night."

Radulf had ceased his wild gestures; he had begun to run towards the horsemen.

"And tell that idiot lad that he's not to prance about, outside the gates. He's supposed to be on watch."

Night was falling fast. A north wind had been blowing all day, turning the air crystalline clear and achingly cold. This night, the stars would be brilliant once again when the lucid blue twilight had faded. Catherine would watch them once again from the top of the keep. . . .

William shivered and pulled the hood of his cloak over his helm. He wanted nothing more than to ride across these fields, through the gates, home to Catherine. Only duty kept him in the saddle. Duty, and the slight chance that Madoc's second force had not already taken over the forest house and abducted Mathilde.

There was little chance that Madoc's spies had failed to find Mathilde. Still, William would lead his men on to the forest house and do what he could to find and rescue young Mathilde.

They wouldn't make it as far as the fording place if Robert didn't hurry to get the torches. He had reached young Radulf in the field and had stopped to speak to the lad, wasting precious minutes.

Behind William, his men waited in silence, huddled against the cold. There was no complaint that Robert had stopped in the field. William caught the drift of their talk: praise for Catherine's cousin. It would be a long, dangerous night, they were saying; they would need Robert's knowledge of the forest in the hours ahead.

Catherine's cousin had proved less troublesome than William had feared. On the long, hard trek back from Madoc's encampment, William had expected Robert to demand an explanation of all that William and Madoc had said about Henry Plantagenet's woman. But Robert had kept his questions to himself in those long and dangerous hours, and had even volunteered to ride behind the others, watching their backs for signs of pursuit and treachery from Madoc's men.

If William had trusted Robert from the beginning and given both Catherine and her cousin some knowledge of the task the king had placed upon him, Mathilde might not be in the danger she faced today. And William would not have spent Christmas Day in the saddle, losing this game of wits with Madoc.

William brought his fist down upon his saddlebow and resolved to keep his mind upon the present. In days to come there would be time for regrets and to confess to Catherine that his own lack of trust had brought them all to this trouble.

Robert was still in the field, bent low over the neck of his horse to listen to Radulf, who had flung his spear aside with a wild gesture of despair. Robert cried out and turned to ride back to William.

In that moment, William's greatest fear was that Lundale had been attacked, and that Catherine—

He would not allow himself to complete the thought. There was no sign of depredation in Lundale's deserted village. The gates were shut, and the palisade walls without damage. Surely—if it pleased the saints—surely there had been no violence in this place. William spurred his horse towards the field to meet Robert halfway.

Robert brought his horse to a skidding halt and pointed south. "Catherine is gone. Left hours ago."

There were no words. No oath fierce enough to curse this moment.

His chest constricted in pain as if he had been struck an evil blow. How, when his heart had stilled at these tidings, did he yet live? William drew a painful breath and managed a single word.

"Why?"

Robert raised his hand to point to the forest, then dropped it to his side as if stricken by the vastness of the danger. "Radulf doesn't make sense of it. He said they saw riders at the far edges of the forest south of here. Catherine saw them from the roof of the keep, and rode out on her mare. Radulf watched her take the road south, and cross the river into the forest. She didn't come out."

In the nights he had lain awake, scheming to keep danger from his family, he had never imagined anything this bad. Catherine had gone straight into the worst of this day's danger; it might already be too late to save her.

"Where would she go?"

William faced Catherine's cousin and saw no rancor in his face. Robert's anger, it seemed, would be for another day. "The forest house," said William. "The girl is there."

They spurred back to William's men and led them at a reckless gallop down the darkening road to the fording place. The sentries were missing. There was no sign of conflict.

Beneath the great spreading oak at the river, the frost upon the ground was undisturbed. One narrow track of hoof prints traversed the whitened earth, led to the sentry's tree, then curved back to the road south. In vain, William looked for a sign that the rider had returned.

"It's a good sign," said Robert. "Only one set of tracks. No one came after her."

The sun shone low from the west in cold clarity, casting deep shadows across the forest road. Very soon, it would be impossible to follow Catherine's trail.

Light. They needed firelight. In his headlong rush, he had forgotten Robert's task. "Take two men and go back for torches," said William. "As many as you can carry. I'll go ahead."

Robert turned in his saddle to look east along the riverbank.

This was no time for disobedience. "Will you not do as I ask?"

"Send another," said Robert. "I think I know where she would come out of the forest, if she didn't want to be seen. Catherine knows how to cross the river upstream from here."

"It's too deep. For miles, it's too deep."

"There's one place. Hard to find."

"She never told me."

Robert shrugged. "She might have had reason."

The light of day was fading fast. William beckoned his men forward and gave his order for torches and a search of the road ahead. "Half will go back for torches," he said. "The rest will follow the trail on this road as best they can. I'll follow soon." He turned back to Robert. "Now show me where she crosses."

Robert pointed up the river. "It's a small fording place, a foot deep this time of year. Easier to cross in summer. We used it as children when forbidden to leave the fields."

Together they rode along the edge of the cultivated land, with the sharp slope of the river chasm to the south. They rode a pace away from the edge, in single file, looking down at the frost-slicked riverbanks and the black, ice-scummed water.

It was a cold form of hell to ride past that ugly stream, seeing the grey frost upon the rocks, imagining that each ripple might conceal a struggle, each shadow might be her hair, drifting just beneath the water.

Robert's face was gaunt and terrible in the dying light. "She has crossed the river many times without falling. She had every reason to be careful this day. For your child, and for you." He hesitated. "She might not have crossed the river at all."

If she thought she should cross, she would try it. A sudden thought, a fragment of memory surfaced in his mind. "Catherine came home with her boots soaking wet. Not long ago," said William.

Why had he not challenged her, pressed her for an explanation?

"Stay calm," said Robert. "If she walked across the river, if she was in the water of late, she knows how deep it is tonight. Think of that, William. Keep that in your mind."

"We are too slow. I'll ride ahead."

"You might miss her if you do. And make such noise that you'll bring any Welsh scouts out of the forest to find us all. It shouldn't be far—"

As if in answer to Robert's words, a high-pitched scream ripped through the silence.

"Ahead. Upstream."

A moment later, a man shouted in alarm, and the woman screamed again.

Catherine's grey mare lunged from the undergrowth before them, clambering up the slope from the river. The beast turned to face them, then sidled from their approach.

With relief, William saw two figures in the saddle. "Catherine," he called. "Thank God, Catherine—"

There was just enough light remaining to see, from that distance, that it was not Catherine with Mathilde. It was Ghislaine. Mathilde and Ghislaine. No imagining, no force of will, could turn the truth aside. He would have given his life to make Catherine appear before his eyes, safe upon the back of her mare.

William spurred forward, the abrupt motion of his destrier setting the grey mare into a nervous turn back to the edge of the field, above the river. Robert rode past and caught the palfrey's reins. "William. She's down there. She's on this side—already on this side."

He didn't see her, at first. Four men-at-arms from the manor stockade were on the far side of the river; one had thrown Blanche over his shoulder to wade across the water.

Then he saw. On the near side, almost visible through the undergrowth, Catherine's crimson cloak lay spread on the shore, darkened by the water that dragged at it.

To send his horse down the steep slope would endanger her. William dismounted and half-ran, half-slid through the bare-twigged bushes to reach the slope and make his way down to the water.

Catherine was there, her feet and sodden skirts pulled downstream by the darkly flowing water. She did not turn at the sound of his approach, but faced the water still, and stretched forth her hand towards the soldier carrying Blanche and rose to her feet. . . .

The water took her. Took her so quickly that she did not turn as he called her name.

He did not remember how he got past the rocks and into the water, nor how he knew where to reach for her hair within the black, cold depths that surrounded him. William never knew how long they were in the frigid, tugging grasp of the current before he felt a blow upon his shoulder, then a wrenching pain. Robert's voice called him, and came closer. Louder. Another blow fell upon his back, and the pain of it pulled them both upwards. Up from the darkness.

There were other hands, and Blanche's shrieks as he clung to Catherine's waist and reached for a handhold on the shore. Then Catherine rose from him onto the riverbank, and the same hands that had delivered her took his arms and pulled him after her.

The blessed sound of a small gasp, then wheezing breath came from Catherine's lungs.

"She lives," said Robert. "Can you walk?"

She lived!

William sank to the frozen ground beside his wife and took her in his arms.

She lived!

At the edge of his vision, deep black against the last clarity of twilight, William saw a crow fly out of the forest and glide low across the river. A sign of danger, this near to nightfall.

"Catherine, I'm going to lift you now. Do you think you can try to walk?"

Robert appeared at his side. "Let her go. I'll get her up the bank. Out of sight from the river."

Robert pulled the cloak from his back and thrust the rough wool into William's hand. Together, they wrapped it about Catherine and began to carry her past the underbrush, up the slope, out of bow shot of the far shore.

Upstream, where it had all begun, the river had already begun to close the evidence of their passage. Where Catherine had crossed, and where she had struggled in the depths, no sign remained upon the dark surface of the river.

At the near side, half submerged in the dark water, was Catherine's cloak. No longer crimson, for night had come at last. There was something in the sight of that mantle in the darkness that brought hot tears to his eyes.

"Don't leave it," he muttered. "Not there."

He felt Robert's hand on his back, then saw Catherine's cousin go back down to fetch the cloak.

There would be no sign, come morning, that they had passed this way.

From the direction of Lundale, there were voices

and bobbing flames approaching in the darkening night. He saw that Catherine's eyes had opened; she tried, through her chattering teeth, to form a word.

William drew her closer. "You're safe," he said. "And soon you'll be warm."

She tried again to speak. William looked over his shoulder. "They're all safe," he said. "Mathilde, her women, and four men-at-arms. They're all across the river, here with us. Dryer than you. And warmer."

Robert led his horse forward. "And they're all better off than you, William. Next time," he said, "remember that a coat of mail won't float. And that you'll ruin a lame leg by carrying armor and wife uphill."

Then the torches reached them, and there were many hands to lift Catherine onto the saddle of his horse, and to support him as he walked home at her side.

The milling crowd of people, both soldiers and villagers, and the burning brands they carried would reveal to anyone watching from the far side of the river that Mathilde had reached Lundale for shelter and that the king's men from the house in the forest had followed the girl here. William looked about him at the crowd of tenants and fighting men and knew that even Madoc with his small army would not overcome them.

Mathilde would be safe at Lundale. Tonight, Madoc would search the forest for her, and by dawn would break up his small army into groups to look in many directions, hoping to find Mathilde before she gave birth. Madoc would not allow himself, this late in the game, the time for a serious attack on Lundale.

Catherine reached down to take his hand in hers. They moved slowly across the field, with the warmth of the torches crowded about them, the brands casting light upon their faces.

Robert walked ahead, leading the grey palfrey, gazing up at Mathilde as if he had seen a vision above him in the night sky.

"—see?" said Catherine.

"Aye," said William.

He saw more than Catherine's young cousin, moving more slowly than William had ever seen him do, with an unfamiliar gravity in his features.

William saw trouble.

In Robert's upturned face, William saw infatuation. A disaster in the making. The girl was not for Robert. The baron Pandulf's daughter, Henry Plantagenet's mistress, would never be for Robert.

William passed a weary hand across his brow. This night would be for joy and thanksgiving. There would be time enough, tomorrow, to tell Robert why Mathilde was here, and to tell him who had claimed her first. Catherine would know how to say it.

For now, he would let Robert have his dream, his vision of an angel in the torch light. William brought Catherine's hand to his lips and kissed the cold from her fingers. It was Christmas night, and they all wished to dream.

Twenty-three

Catherine had awakened in William's arms, warm beneath a top-heavy heap of coverlets and, it seemed, the contents of her clothing chest.

Beneath her cheek she discovered the fine linen cloth she had brought from the abbey; in its hem she saw the small green stitches with which she had counted the days and nights of her marriage, when they were first wed. She gazed at the green silk lines and wondered how these scraps of memory had come to be the first sight she had of the new dawn she had nearly missed. The first of the dawns she might have lost forever.

She pushed the cloth aside and smiled into William's gaze. There would be no more green stitches; instead, she would pray that their days together would be so many that such counting would be meaningless.

William smiled back, and rose to put wood on the brazier. "Hadwen fetched Alflega at dawn, to let us sleep. Are you cold?"

Catherine moved beneath the great pile of woolen cloth, sending it toppling to the rushes beside the bed. "I am so well warmed that I'll never be cold again." She yawned. "I may need to go back to the river to cool off."

"You'll never go near the river again. Promise me that."

She shook her head. "It's beautiful there, on a summer day. We'll take a jug of mead down there on a warm afternoon and we'll sit in the shallows and let the fish nibble our feet."

William groaned. "I hate that river. Hate it."

"If you're going to be a true lord of Lundale, and watch over the barley fields and keep track of how many sheep wander into the forest, you'll see the river in a different light."

"Hmm."

"There's always deep water in the river. Lundale will survive, even in a drought."

"Even so, I'll hate that river forever. Jesu, Catherine. I saw you fall. I saw you—"

He broke off his words and drew a long breath. "We won't speak of it again. Never again."

Catherine shook her head. "I want to know. Is it true you were the one who got me out? With your shirt of mail sending you down to the bottom?"

He rose and placed another piece of wood on the brazier. "Your cousin Robert got us both out. He and the soldiers from the forest house." He paused. "If we're going to talk about this, you'll have to tell me how you overcame my guards and forced them to walk into the river."

Catherine raised her brows. "I think we should wait for a warm summer day for this tale. On that day of drought."

William moved to the eastern arrow slit and frowned at the sight of the grey sky. "Is there ever a day when rain doesn't fall on Lundale? I don't believe your talk of droughts."

"The old people tell of a dry season, long ago. Stay past the summer, William, and you'll see the skies clear."

"I'll think about it." He turned back. "I would stay past spring if I could, Catherine. You know I want to. But in the end the king will decide."

How she would love to have an hour's speech with William's King Henry on that matter! Catherine shrugged the thought away, and slipped from the bed. She began to look about for her yellow kirtle. "My clothes, William. I can't find them."

"Ah. Somewhere among the blankets. I see them—." He fetched her kirtle and surcoat from the tangled heap of cloth on the rushes. "I woke past midnight and it was cold, so I found what I could to warm you."

"William, I'm not ill."

"You were as cold as death last night."

She placed a hand on his face and drew him closer for a slow, luxuriant kiss. "With you to warm me, I could make a habit of such adventures."

He pulled her closer still and enfolded her in his arms. "If you make a habit of such things, I'll have to keep you close—at hand."

"Whatever is necessary to keep you here," she said. "For now, I'll—"

From the barred door behind them came a heavy thud.

William sighed and raised his head. "Go away," he said.

"I'm on watch," said Radulf through the door.

"Well then, go up and watch from the top. You'll see nothing from the stair."

"—we hope," said Catherine. And lifted her face to William's mouth. Outside the door, Radulf's heavy steps receded, then returned. An oath, and the clatter of a spear falling upon stone soon followed. The sound continued far down the stairwell.

"What's there?" called William.

More footsteps and another thud followed the first. "It's just me," called Radulf. "My spear fell."

"Indeed."

"I came back because I forgot there's a message," shouted Radulf. "Robert says could you send word when you're coming down. Especially Catherine because there's a baby."

"Of course there's a—" William raised his head. "What baby? Radulf, what baby?"

"Dear lord," said Catherine. And pulled her green surcoat from the tangled bedclothes. "If it's Mathilde—if she's early because of the journey—"

William caught her as she raised the bar from the door. "Remember, Catherine. Remember what you said to me. You did the best you could. Beyond that—"

"I know. I pray our luck will hold. For that poor girl's sake."

***

A glance at Robert's face told the happy tale. And a second glance at the tiny creature nestled in his arms said the rest.

"A boy," said Robert. "A fine lad with a good voice for the battlefield. You missed that part. He just fell asleep."

"And Mathilde?"

"The women say she's fine. They won't let me back in the sleeping chamber, though." He looked down at the small red face within the linen swaddling. "Hadwen thinks he's mine. Saw me bring Mathilde home through the gates and thought I had gone to fetch her from the abbey. Or wherever." Robert's smile vanished. "I didn't say she was wrong. I won't say, until we have spoken about it."

Catherine glanced at William. His expression was as worried as her own must be.

Robert looked from William to Catherine and back again. "Are you looking for Alflega? John took her out to see Osbert's cow milked."

"Good."

Robert shrugged and looked back down to the babe in his arms. "I was saying—when he was born, Hadwen brought him out and gave him to me to hold. So I took him and sat here. That's all it was."

Ghislaine emerged from the hangings across the entrance to the sleeping chamber. She pushed her hair back from her face, then caught a single tendril and placed it where it would curl down her shoulder. The maid smiled at Robert and extended her hands. "My mistress wants to see the child," she said.

Robert rose to his feet and passed the baby into her arms. "May I come see her?"

Ghislaine's eyes narrowed at his words. "Hadwen doesn't think so. But I'll be back to tell you if she changes her mind." At the curtain, she turned again and smiled. "Wait for me, right there." The hangings descended once again.

William raised his brows. "She may have more than a message in mind, Robert."

"Who—? Oh yes. Ghislaine's a friendly one." Robert looked down at his empty hands and placed them on the table.

William looked down the board. "We're alone now, so I'll speak while I can. The child is King Henry's," he said. "Mathilde came north with me to stay hidden until her child was born."

Catherine took William's hand and spoke softly to Robert. "Mathilde is the Baron Pandulf's daughter. Her father doesn't know of the child. Or of the king's—interest in her."

"I know," said Robert. "She told me."

William and Catherine looked at each other in surprise.

Catherine turned back to her cousin. "When? When did she tell you all this?"

"Late last night, when her pains started in earnest. Hadwen said that I should walk with Mathilde, up and down the sleeping chamber, until her time came close."

"Hadwen woke you to do that?"

Robert shrugged. "I was with Mathilde when it started. She couldn't sleep, and had come out to warm herself by the hearth. We spoke of small things, but when her pains came on and I was walking her back and forth last night she told me her dilemma. All of it."

William drew a long breath. "When spring comes, the king will send his orders. Mathilde will go back to the convent where her father had left her, or she will wed."

"Is—is there a betrothal?"

"There wasn't one when we left on the journey north. By now there may be."

Catherine's heart stilled at the words. She knew what that betrothal would be. That threat—the possibility that the king would want William to put her aside and wed Mathilde—would bring the end of her happiness, for all time. And might bring heartbreak to Robert as well.

"Robert," she said. "This is a matter the king may decide for Mathilde. And if he does send word to us in the spring, we must all abide by it."

Robert's face darkened in anger. "Aye. We know what happens when you cross the Plantagenet's will."

William raised his head. "We don't have to make it easy for him."

Robert looked up. "What do you mean?"

William placed his arm about Catherine's shoulders, and set his hand upon Robert's fist. "We'll begin by vowing, the three of us, to trust one another in this matter of the king. And in the matter of the Welsh spies. I should have spoken of it—all of it—to you both when I first brought Mathilde north. I regret that I didn't."

Robert shrugged. "You didn't know me. And hardly knew Catherine, though you had wed her. You had to be careful."

Catherine smiled. "Careful. An odd word from you, Robert."

Her cousin met her gaze. "There are times when prudence is necessary. This is one of them."

William took his arm from Catherine's shoulders and placed his hands on the table. "This is what I think. Mathilde and her child will be safe here if she—she and her women—live among us as if they were from the village. They will dress as the village women do and the child will be cared for as one of our own. If you agree, Robert, we'll let Hadwen and the others continue to regard the child as your own and Mathilde as your lady."

"Mathilde and her two women must use the sleeping chamber," Catherine said.

Robert smiled. "I understand."

"The king's men will continue to use the forest house, but half will come here, to make the garrison strong. Today I'll send them to get the women's clothing chests from the manor house and we'll store them here, as if they were Catherine's. I'll tell the men to break up the litter and frame, and burn them. The packhorses will be brought here. If the Welsh want to spy upon us, here and at the forest house, they will see nothing to lead them to Mathilde, or to prove that a noblewoman traveled here."

Catherine leaned forward. "Yes. It would be easier for Mathilde to return to the convent, if she wishes, if there are no rumors of her in Nottingham. We can't allow tales of a well-born bastard anywhere near her. We'll keep the child here, raise him with our own, and if there are questions, we'll say he's the child of a villager."

"It will work," said Robert, "if the king forgets the child."

William looked from Catherine to Robert. "What do you think?"

Catherine frowned. "I don't like the part about the chair. I saw the litter chair. It's beautiful, and it's wasteful to burn it."

William shook his head. "It's dangerous to have it here. Mathilde no longer needs it."

Catherine sat back. "I know why you'd like it to disappear. Stealing from Queen Eleanor was almost as dangerous as undertaking to hide Mathilde."

William's color darkened to a deep crimson. "It was necessary to find a way to carry Mathilde. She was already very large with child."

Catherine raised a brow. "Of course. I understand. But it is a beautiful chair. Dame Alflega is getting old, you know. Too old to ride that mule much longer. And she does love to go down to Nottingham."

"It's a rich thing. Attracts suspicion. If I could have found a plainer one I would have—"

Robert laughed. "Dame Alflega has an eye for finery. Why shouldn't she have the queen's litter chair—and the fine packhorses trained to carry it?"

William's frown deepened. "The abbess will want to know how it came here. We can't afford to have rumors of Mathilde get as far as the abbey."

Robert shrugged. "If she doesn't know already—and she'd never tell you, if she did know—Dame Alflega isn't likely to ask questions. The abbey receives many such gifts. Always without questions."

Catherine saw a flicker of humor in Robert's eyes. "Have you reason to know this, Robert?"

Her cousin shrugged.

William smiled. "All right. When the king's men return to the forest, you'll go with them, Robert. Pick two of the men and take the litter chair with you to the abbey. The chair and the horses. Keep an ear open for word of Welsh scouts."

Robert cast a wistful glance at the sleeping chamber.

Catherine touched his hand. "It's better, Robert, if you leave us for a day or so. You'll see Mathilde and her child when you return."

She paused and looked in the direction of the chamber. "Did anyone ask Mathilde what she will do about christening the child?"

Robert shook his head. "She doesn't know what to call him. If it would please her, I'll bring a priest back with me. When Alflega was born," he said, "the abbey priest said he wouldn't come here where we had nothing but ruins for a chapel. So we went to the abbey and Catherine had a fit of weeping and named your child Alflega after the abbess, in memory of her days there."

A sly smile crossed Robert's face. "Beware,

William. There are two Wolnuthas and a priest they call Ergesboldus still there. You may have a dozen children and never learn to speak any of their names."

"I can see we'll need to rebuild the chapel," said William. "This spring, if Catherine wishes to spend some of her gold for that."

"It had best be before the late harvest next year," said Catherine, "lest we find ourselves with a Wolnutha after all."

Twenty-four

Early March, 1165

On the last day of Christmas, the winter had turned mild. The rains had begun, and the sheaves of ice that had flowed upon the river had disappeared in the new year. The waterways brimmed high from days of melting sleet. That rain and half-thawed mud upon the roads had kept travelers from Lundale in the first fortnight following the feast of Epiphany.

And then the sentries began to see riders pass by in the distance. At first, only a few horsemen came into sight; days later, a stream of travelers, weather-bound no more, began to ride north and south upon the road that skirted Lundale's fields.

Among them were a few fast riders on good mounts, couriers bearing messages from Nottingham and from York. Seldom did these mud-spattered horsemen ask for a place at the hearth; Catherine gave them food for their saddlepacks and in exchange had news of the world beyond Nottingham, word of the great conflict growing between the king and his former chancellor, the rebellious archbishop of Canterbury.

Catherine and her people had been prepared for those strangers who asked for shelter in the night. None of the outsiders, not even the sharp-eyed party of merchants who had spoken Welsh among themselves, had noticed the shy woman among Lundale's weavers who retired each night to the sleeping chamber with a few other mothers and their children. And none of the travelers thought it odd that the shy woman stayed abed each morning until the hall was empty of strangers.

The woman's child slept in a sturdy, unadorned cradle like any other, not far from his mother's loom. He was but one of several infants tended by their mothers in the warmest corner of Lundale's great hall, watched over by the burly grey warrior John, fierce and unflagging in his vigilance.

To the people of Lundale, the habits of the lord William, young Robert, and the garrison men who patrolled and hunted by day were as predictable as the hours of the day and as reliable as the sun. The women's work at the spindles and the looms and in the kitchen shed and the duties of the young shepherds were carefully set out to make certain that Mathilde would never be alone with strangers, and that nothing would inspire an outsider to look twice at the king's child.

To a traveler entering Lundale's hall for a night's shelter, the scene was one of agreeable confusion. So skillful was the artifice contrived by the lord William and his lady Catherine that a traveler would never know the truth: that beneath the surface of the spirited chatter in the great hall, some among the people of Lundale were as wary as sparrows in the shadow of a hawk.

On the day the king's messengers arrived, the rain had been blowing across the land since dawn. It was the kind of weather that sent watchmen into the lee of their posts, dulling their vision by wind-blown mud and cold.

At noon, Catherine filled an earthen bowl with the day's hot pottage of barley, herbs, and salted mutton and crossed the bailey yard. She kept to the timber walkway Osbert had set above the mud, and climbed the keep's stairs to find the sentry given duty on this uncomfortable day.

To her surprise, the watchman was out in the elements, standing against the wind's wet buffeting. "Our lord has taken a boar," he said. "I saw it from these walls—just past the river, up on the ridge. I saw the beast run onto lord William's spear." He looked down at the steaming bowl in Catherine's hands. "We'll have something more than mutton by tomorrow, I vow."

"You tire of mutton?"

The sentry pushed back the hood of his cloak and looked Catherine in the eye. "I don't mean to complain," said Radulf in his new, deep voice.

Catherine smiled. "I didn't recognize you, Radulf. Each day you're taller. Have they taken you into the garrison now?"

Radulf's thin shoulders straightened. "I'm think-ing of it."

"We need good farmers at Lundale. There's an old field below the sheepfolds that will need a good man to clear it and sow it."

Radulf picked up the ever-present spear that John had given him and held it upright before him. "I'll learn to use this first. A man should be able to defend his crops."

Catherine thrust the bowl of pottage into Radulf's other hand. "Your father will have some-thing to say of that."

Radulf lifted the bowl to his mouth and began to drink the broth that floated above the grain.

She watched a party of swift-moving horsemen ride north along the distant horizon. "How many have there been today?"

Four fingers waggled at the side of the bowl. "Four parties," Radulf said at last. "All horsemen. No wagons. The king's problems must be growing large. Lord William and Robert rode out to speak with the first lot of riders, just before they went after the boar."

The horsemen had stopped and regrouped at the place where Lundale's long fields reached the forest. Circled and then formed a line. Catherine nodded in the direction of the riders. "Where is Lord William?"

Radulf pointed south to the river. "Well, there's the boar and there's Robert riding ahead of the three bearers and—no Lord William."

Catherine frowned. "He must have taken the rest

of the men back to the hunt." The line of riders, six of them, she thought, were riding across the fields towards the gates of Lundale.

"It's the foul weather that brings them off the road this early."

She wished that William had shown the same good sense. She went down to the gate to greet the fast-moving travelers, and felt a touch of fear at the sight of their rich cloaks and their careless gallop towards Lundale's walls.

Radulf followed her down the stairs and across the yard to the gates, leaving the watch post empty. Catherine didn't chide him.

The first horseman through the gates was a sharp-eyed knight of small stature who sat his mount with weary ease. "King's messengers," he said.

"You are welcome," said Catherine.

"Six of us." The hooded eyes looked about the bailey yard, hesitated at the sight of Radulf's spear, turned back to Catherine.

"All are welcome," she said.

"William of Macon?"

"My lord husband," said Catherine. "is hunting, and will return before dark." Before then, please the saints.

The first rider wheeled his mount in a slow, exacting survey of the bailey, the walls, the keep and the byre. The narrow, nervous gaze focused upon the hall. "Shelter?"

The man spoke as if his words were arrows. Small ones. Abrupt. Deadly.

"There is food in the hall," said Catherine. "Enough for all of you."

The rider nodded and scrambled from his saddle. He left his mount with reins drooping into the mud, and splashed back to his five companions. "It's safe," he said. And held the reins of the last horse as a burly messenger dismounted.

They might have greeted her with more respect had the rain not returned at that moment. Instead, five of the men preceded her into the hall with only vague gestures of greeting as they passed. They did not offer their names. Nor did Catherine wish to ask them.

She stood inside the door, watching the rain drive the mud from the timber walkway. The last of the riders led the horses, two by two, into the byre. She looked about and saw no one to tell him where the animals should be tied; she crossed to the byre door and called her suggestions into the warm darkness. A distant grunt was her only answer.

She should have followed the others into the hall. In the moment she stepped through the door, she saw Radulf move forward, spear in hand, to stand near two tall messengers who had chosen to drink their mead in the warmest corner of the great chamber, near the weaving women's children.

One of the men had not removed his cloak. He reached an arm from beneath his wet mantle and shook the gauntlet from his hand. And stretched it towards the nearest cradle.

John rose from his bench. Radulf placed his spear between the messenger and the babe. "Careful there," said Radulf in that hoarse new voice. "That's a young one."

From within the hood of the cloak, the messenger glared at Radulf. "Then why is your spear so near the cradle?"

Radulf pointed to the heavy longsword at the messenger's side. "Better my spear than your sword."

John growled an oath and moved closer. "And I see a shortsword in your belt. You should disarm before coming so near the child. Or to my lady's board."

"An idiot whelp and an old man in his cups," said the king's man, "you would dare tell me how to wear my weapons?"

Little Alflega began to cry. Catherine darted forward and picked her up. She waved Radulf aside and moved, her daughter in her arms, between the messenger and Mathilde's baby.

Behind her, the other messengers were on the move. A spur scraped along the planked floor; a bench overturned.

"Stay," said the hooded man.

There was a scramble to right the bench, then silence.

The messenger turned his head. "Your child?" he asked.

Catherine gathered Alflega closer to her. "Yes," she said.

"And who is the mother of this baby?"

The messenger was pointing to the king's child.

Behind the sleeping chamber's hangings, Mathilde's gasp was barely audible.

"Mine," said Catherine. "They're both mine."

"William de Macon's children?"

"Yes," Catherine said.

The red-thatched hand went up to a shadowed chin. "William de Macon was in Normandy last summer."

"He was."

"Then how did he sire this child?"

Radulf lunged forward. "We don't feed discourteous knaves," he said. "Out. Get out now."

"Radulf, no." John put down his mead cup and took a step towards the cradle. "I'll deal with this."

"Send him away, or he'll suffer the consequences," said the traveler.

Catherine saw the man's hand move to the hilt of his sword. "Leave us," she said. "Radulf. John. Leave us. You need not worry. This man knows my lord William would hunt and kill by inches any man who harmed his wife, or his children. Either of his two children."

Beneath the hood, hard blue eyes stared into Catherine's face. "The babe is your husband's child, in truth?"

"I say it is my husband's child. You may ask him when he returns. However many times you ask, you will hear that the boy is William de Macon's child."

"I would speak with your William de Macon."

"By the saints—" said John.

"Sit down," said Catherine. "If you want to speak with William de Macon, take your hand from your sword and sit down on that bench and do not move until my husband returns. If you do that, you may yet live to tell the tale."

"Aye, it's a tale all right—" He sat down and pulled the cloak from his shoulders. "A false tale, if ever I heard one. So you think me an idiot, madam?"

"I do not like your manner," said Catherine. "If you threaten anyone else under this roof, you'll sleep in the byre."

He shook the rain from his dark blond hair, and used the cloak to mop his red-blond beard. "In all my days, I haven't had such greetings."

John's cup fell to the rushes, spilling the scent of spices and mead into the air. "Your grace," said John. "I didn't see—"

Mathilde stepped through the woolen curtain. "Henry," she said. "I'm here."

"Damnation," said Catherine.

"A termagant and a blasphemer as well," said Henry Plantagenet. "I had forgot that William de Macon had wed. Hadn't thought he would choose a termagant and blasphemer for the mother of his child. His only child, I take it?"

"My husband will tell you," said Catherine. She saw Mathilde hesitate a few steps from Henry Plantagenet's shoulder. The king had not yet greeted the mother of his child, but seemed eager to trade insults with Catherine. Was this the man to whom her husband believed he owed loyalty?

"You won't tell me?" He narrowed his eyes. "Then you are a termagant, blasphemer, and ungenerous with the truth. William de Macon was careless of his peace, madam, when he wed you."

Already she had angered the king beyond tolerance. There was no point in attempting to ingratiate herself. You know when to take a risk, William had said to her. This must be the time to prove him right.

"I am fond of that child," Catherine said. "Will you not foster him with us, if Mathilde agrees?"

Henry Plantagenet rose to his feet and ran both hands through his damp hair. He lowered his arms and looked beyond the cradle to the mother of his youngest babe. "Mathilde," said the king. "We must speak in private, you and I."

He glanced down at the small Plantagenet in his cradle. "You have made a fine child," he said. And walked to Mathilde's side, to follow her into the sleeping chamber. A moment later, he loosed the ties about the hangings, and the heavy wool fell into place, and the people of Lundale heard no more of Henry Plantagenet's words to the woman he had loved, for a time.

Catherine looked across the hearth and gestured towards the men who had come with their king on his secret journey. "I should have brought them here, to our board."

William drew her closer beside him on the bench. "Leave them as they are," he said. "The king chose them to be strangers on this journey. I know none of them from the past and they will try to remember nothing of the king's business here."

"What should I do?"

"Nothing. You have already done this——." William gestured to the long table and the fine-woven linen that covered it, the ewer of mead and the rounds of barley bread piled beyond, beside slabs of smoked venison. All was in readiness for the king; Catherine's fine silver cup, the gift William had carried home from Normandy, stood beside the mead, in its place for the king's use. William frowned, half tempted to the hide the cup away.

His gaze returned to Catherine, and in that moment she forgot that the cause of her past grief and the threat of future ruin was but steps away.

"Nothing," said William, "is the hardest thing to do, at times like this." He looked from Catherine to her cousin. "The abbess couldn't imagine this day. She told me that patience isn't in your blood."

Across the table, Robert toyed with an empty goblet. "We learned it from you, William. For your sake, we'll try patience. This day we'll see if it serves us better than striking before the snake turns."

William's arm tightened about Catherine. She closed her eyes and let her head rest upon his shoulder. "If the snake turns," he said, "then we will do whatever is necessary. I won't be parted from you, Catherine. Nor should Robert lose Mathilde, if she wants him."

A small smile crossed Robert's face. "A touch of rebellion from you, William?"

William raised his brows. "I learned it from you,

and from Catherine. And I have found something more important than the king's good regard."

Robert nodded once, then turned back to stare at the motionless curtain of the sleeping chamber. "How long has it been?"

Catherine raised her head. "An hour. Maybe less." For the thousandth time, she thanked the saints that Robert had not returned to the hall before Henry Plantagenet and Mathilde had disappeared into its only private chamber. Robert's new-found resolve to think before acting would not have survived the sight of Mathilde's deathly pale face as she had looked upon the king.

Robert set down the goblet with unusual care. "It has been too long. Someone must go in there and make sure Mathilde is in no distress."

William shook his head. "We would have heard, Robert. Wait. Stay here and wait. The king is a reasonable man, when it suits him. You will do Mathilde no good by angering him."

Catherine took the goblet from Robert's hand. "I thank you for keeping your temper, cousin. Pray keep it a little longer. Those who live in the shadow of a king must act with care."

William reached across the table to cover Catherine's hand, and Robert's. "We have come so far together," he said. "I swear before you and your cousin that we will not be parted. Not for anything in this world or any reward promised for the next. If this proves not possible in the shadow of a king, we must find a place where the light is clear."

Twenty-five

"The king bids you come to him."

Catherine looked up at the outsider in her hall who had the audacity to tell her when she might enter the sleeping chamber where she had been born. "As you see," she said sweetly, "there is food and drink for his grace right here. If he cares to sit here. . . ."

"No. He wants to speak with you in the small chamber. With all three of you."

Catherine kept a smile upon her face and prayed that Robert and her newly-rebellious husband would believe it pleased her to do as the king's messenger ordered. She rose, keeping her husband's hand in her own. "Robert," she said. "Will you come with us?"

Robert was off the bench and thrusting the curtain aside before she had finished speaking.

Henry Plantagenet, king of England, lord of Normandy and of Aquitaine, stood tall and displeased against the far wall, his hands set behind his back, his shoulders high, as if he made ready to spring upon the next creature who crossed him.

Mathilde sat straight-backed upon the bed, her

white hands clasped in a death grip upon her lap, her small feet barely touching the rushes. She looked up at Robert with desperate hope in her violet eyes, then looked down once again at her twisted fingers.

In Henry Plantagenet's presence, Mathilde's quiet courage seemed to have frayed; never, even on that terrible day of her flight through the forest, had the girl looked so pale. In the half-light of the chamber, Mathilde's pale golden hair had dimmed to the color of winter straw.

Mathilde turned her head to look out through the door, to the simple cradle where her son slept.

Catherine drew a quick breath. William reached for her hand and touched her palm with his thumb. He moved closer, as if to shield her from Henry Plantagenet's gaze.

Robert stood in silence, his eyes upon Mathilde.

The Plantagenet did not invite them to sit.

"I must thank you," said Henry Plantagenet, "for the care you took of the Baron Pandulf's daughter. In her dilemma." The king's leonine head turned to regard Robert with an intensity that boded ill. "The girl wishes to keep her child and be wed this spring. Her father will be displeased to hear of it." King Henry paused; a tight smile appeared above his red beard. "I will intercede on her behalf, when my invasion of Wales is complete. Until then, Mathilde must rejoin her own family in the interests of keeping peace among the barons of my border with Wales."

Mathilde continued to stare down at her hands.

Catherine saw the king's color darken in the cool silence that followed his orders.

In vain she looked for a resemblance between the stern face of the king and William's features. Those who had thought William a suitable double for the king must have aimed their deceptions at half-blind assassins, for there was nothing of the king's bull-necked coarseness in William's bearing. Indeed, it might have been wishful thinking on Henry Plantagenet's part to imagine a similarity.

"You smile, madam?"

"No, your grace. This is not a matter for joy."

"For you three it may be." The king filled his lungs in a greedy gulp, as if drinking after a drought, and glowered at Catherine. "The Baron Pandulf's daughter has told me of your kindness in her exile from her own family. You have said you wish to foster her child. I will grant that wish and leave the baby with you."

The Plantagenet spoke as if he believed that the care of his unacknowledged child was a boon beyond price. Catherine sighed. Some might see it so. The child was a handsome little babe, with all the sweetness of his mother and none of the imperious habits of his father. So far.

If Mathilde must give up her son, at least she would know where to find him.

"Your grace, I am pleased to foster Mathilde's child. You are most kind," said Catherine.

The king nodded once and turned from her to gaze upon Robert.

Was he to offer Catherine nothing more than

the task of fostering his child? If Catherine waited to ask for her heart's desire, the opportunity might vanish.

"Sire—"

The Plantagenet's gaze slid back to her. A little surprised that she had spoken again. More than a little displeased that she had done so. "Yes?"

"I thank you for leaving the child here."

"Yes, yes—"

"And vow to keep him safe. The grandson of your baron and good ally Pandulf must never be put at risk."

"Of course not."

"I would ask, therefore, that you leave my husband here with me to protect the child, and keep you informed of all that might befall him."

"I might send him home. Maybe by next summer. You'll have him back before the harvest. For now, I have a war to fight and I need my best knights. All of them." The king made a small gesture of dismissal and turned again to Robert.

"I fear," said Catherine, "that my husband is no longer one of your best knights. Some might call him useless on the battlefield."

"What is this?" The Plantagenet's eyes had narrowed in annoyance.

"William hasn't recovered from the wounds he received last fall. In your service. Dealing with Mathilde's—dilemma."

The royal head lowered farther still. In a bull, it would have been a clear sign of danger to anyone in sight. In a king, it would be more than lethal.

"Your husband killed a boar this day. I take that as evidence he has recovered." The becrimsoned head swiveled towards William. "William de Macon, do you yet speak? Or has this wife of yours taken your wits?"

William moved his arm to Catherine's shoulders. "Your grace, I'll go to fight, gladly put my sword at your service. But my wife has the truth of it—my leg was cut deep, and until I have the strength of it back, I'm useless on the ground. Had Robert not been at my side today, I wouldn't have tried to kill a boar."

"But you can sit a horse."

"I can."

It was not going well. Catherine drew a deep breath. "When that Welshman Madoc came snooping about the forest, William rode out to protect us. He lost his footing that day and fell in the river and he nearly drowned."

William looked at her in surprise. "Catherine, surely you remember it wasn't that way. It happened because—"

"Madoc? Madoc followed you here?" The king brought a heavy red fist up to strike the timbers of the wall. Beyond the curtain, the voices in the hall ceased, then began to speak again in hushed tones.

Still, Mathilde did not look up.

William tightened his arm about Catherine. "Madoc left soon after. He saw nothing," said William.

"But he tried hard enough," said Robert.

"He dared come this far into my realm? That

man has the nerve of a weasel," said Henry Plantagenet. "He spreads rumors touching my honor.
"Mathilde must be gone before Madoc returns.
William, take her back to the borders. Back to the
convent. Tomorrow."

"No!"

They looked around in surprise. The small, still
figure seated in stiff discomfort had spoken at last.

"Henry," said Baron Pandulf's daughter, "I have
said that I don't want to go back. I have told you
what I would like to do. Allow it, and you'll have no
trouble from me. Never again."

The Plantagenet's narrowed eyes shifted from
Mathilde to Robert, to William. And then to
Catherine.

"I'll think on it," he said. "I'm for York today, but
when I return I'll think on it. You," he said to
Robert, "may join the invasion in the place of your
cousin by marriage, if I deem it right. Be in readiness when I return."

"Henry—"

"Your grace—"

He halted in mid-stride and made a sweeping
gesture about the chamber. "You will all cease to tell
me what you would have me do. I'll think on it, and
you will do what I decide. As soon as I return." He
pushed through the curtain and stalked out into
the hall. He halted beside the cradle and drew a be-
jeweled gauntlet from his hauberk to set upon his
son's coverlet. And resumed his march to the door.
Behind him, his five messengers grabbed their
cloaks and ran to follow.

Catherine dashed after them. Would the king ride away without eating at their board, and drinking Lundale's mead? Had she angered him so badly that Lundale itself might suffer?

At the door, Henry Plantagenet halted and stepped back into his followers, arms outstretched.

"I am betrayed," he snarled.

Two royal messengers turned to face those still within the hall. The others slipped out the door and pounded along the walkway towards the byre.

The king raised a broad fist. "Someone among you has betrayed me, and I'll have his liver for my hounds before this day is done."

"Your grace?"

"Look," said Henry Plantagenet. "See what comes through the gates of this wretched place. See what has followed me here."

Catherine rose on her toes to catch sight of the betrayal to which the king was pointing.

The chair litter, splendid in its carved wood and leather canopy, swathed in damp woolen panels bearing broderie fit for a queen, was in the bailey yard. Suspended between two curried grey pack mares, led by two lads dressed in rich cloaks, the litter had brought its occupant through the rain in comfort.

"Speak of the girl or her child and I'll send your husband into Wales in the infantry," said Henry Plantagenet. "That is my wife. Your queen. She cannot be here, but she is. I am damned—"

He strode forward with such force that the timbers rocked in the mud. A princely smile appeared

upon his face. "Eleanor," he said. "You have surprised me—"

The curtain parted.

Henry Plantagenet drew back.

"This is Dame Alflega," said Catherine. "The
abbess from the house near the road to Nottingham. Dame Alflega, our—king—has come to see
William."

The abbess pushed the chair hangings aside and
proffered a delicate hand to Henry Plantagenet.
"You are the king? I will need help getting down
from here. My old bones won't like a fall." She accepted the king's arm and descended to stand
beside him, small as a child beside his bulk, upon
the timber walkway.

"Forgive me, your grace. I am too old to make
obeisance to you. But I will bow my head. So—"

"Never mind—" Henry Plantagenet shook his
head. "You gave me a start. The litter is much like
one of my wife's traveling chairs."

Dame Alflega's white brows rose in perfect sym-
metry. "It was the queen's chair litter," she said.
"Until Christmas, it was hers. Now it is mine." An innocent smile blossomed among the soft wrinkles of
her face.

"Ah. Do you—"

The abbess took a handful of the king's rich
sleeve and pinched it to draw his attention back to
the chair. "It would have been better to have the
frame a little lower. Your lady queen was ill-served
by her carpenters. Will you tell her so?"

The king blanched whiter still. "You know the queen?"

Dame Alflega straightened to her full, diminutive height. "It is as you see. This is the queen's chair," she said.

"I see."

"I have written the queen to thank her. A good letter, full of the small things that one hears at the abbey."

"Good woman, Dame—"

"Alflega. Not so hard to say. Alflega."

"Yes. Dame—Alflega. What news?"

She cackled and crooked her head. "I should tell her what they say of you in these parts. All that trouble with your old chancellor, the archbishop. They say he's hiding from you. The odd stories that come up in the country—." She paused. "Now I will add a postscript, to say that I have been fortunate enough to catch sight of the king right here in Lundale, dressed as a royal messenger."

Dame Alflega cocked her head again and smiled. "You see, when you were last in these lands—ten years ago?—you were fighting hereabouts and I never had a sight of you. At the time, that was lucky, was it not? Those who met you close at hand didn't live to my age."

The abbess erupted into shouts of laughter at her own jest.

"Madam, I was—"

"Never fear, your grace. God understands the need for such things." Dame Alflega glanced in Catherine's direction and winked. "Now may I ask a boon of you? Or is it too much—? To take my letter to the queen?"

Henry's face relaxed. "Ah. Yes. I'll take the letter when I return south."

Dame Alflega beamed at his words. "I have written a little request. A small request for gold to rebuild the church here at Lundale. It was leveled—as your grace may recall—ten years ago in the fighting. The queen has been so generous elsewhere that I thought I'd ask—"

Henry stepped back and gestured for silence. "There is no need for a letter. When I reach York I'll speak to the bishop and direct him to get gold from my treasury and send carpenters and a mason to build the chapel. I am pleased to do this myself. No need to write to the queen."

"But you will give her my greetings?"

"Of course."

Behind her, Catherine felt William's chest shaking in silent laughter. "Does she know the queen?" he whispered.

"I doubt it," said Catherine. And covered her mouth to hide her merriment.

"It is too cold for my old bones to stand here in the wind," said Dame Alflega.

"I'm riding out now," said Henry Plantagenet.

"Farewell, your grace," said Mathilde.

He turned back to see Mathilde upon the walkway, with Robert at her side.

The king edged away from Dame Alflega. "Fare well," he said.

"And as for you," he said to Robert, "remember

that the daughter of Baron Pandulf will require a husband of some importance. With land. If you would earn that, come to Shrewsbury in a fortnight's time and ride with my army into Wales. There will be land and gold aplenty for those who are bold enough to win them."

Catherine held her breath as Robert's hand closed into a fist upon the hilt of his sword.

"Thank you, your grace," said Robert. "I'll be there."

"All right," said William. "Now I understand. Little Rose must be called Alflega and no other name will do." He placed his hand upon Catherine's belly and began to trace the delicate lavender lines upon her white flesh. "But promise me that the next child will be Margaret or Eleanor or Johanna—Wolnutha hasn't a good sound to it."

Catherine reached up to twine her fingers in his dark golden hair. "The next one may be a son for you, William. What then? Must we name it for the king?"

He smiled in the firelight. "That would be prudent, after the fright he had. Such a gesture might be important."

"Of course I never liked the name. And few of our people would abide giving that name to anything more important than a goat." Catherine stretched and yawned. "We'll have to think on it, when we're not distracted by your touch, and your magic and your—other qualities."

William raised his head. "You wouldn't name our son Henry?"

"I'll ask Dame Alflega's advice, if you don't mind. She had a favorite confessor she used to remember in her prayers. Wilfwin was his name. And her younger brother Godelief was a man of great integrity. She has a keen memory for such things. . . ."

"You're jesting."

She smiled into his gaze. "I can't choose a name alone. It takes months of thought. Last time, you weren't here and I did the best I could. Now, this time—"

"I'll be here," said William. " For so many reasons—believe me, Catherine—I'll be here."